Scarlet's Retribution

by

Meghan Hopps

DORRANCE
PUBLISHING CO
EST. 1920
PITTSBURGH, PENNSYLVANIA 15238

Dorrance Publishing Co
585 Alpha Drive
Pittsburgh, PA 15238
Visit our website at *www.dorrancebookstore.com*

ISBN: 978-1-6393-7238-6
eISBN: 978-1-6393-7640-7

Death is predestined,
But not forgotten.
With angels we are blessed,
Who reside in heaven.

~For Susan Dean. You are missed by many.

Prologue
ALEXANDER

In a grand castle hidden deep inside Ixaemithia, a land with untold magic in the heart of Kaggaegia, many Ixaemithians roamed about without a care in the world. Outside, people happily walked alongside the luscious greens and herbs scattered about the massive lawn. Inside, hallways upon hallways led to mysterious places throughout the magnificent edifice. Jesters wearing heavy makeup and masks took to entertaining the fairest in the land with their songs and dances.

Beyond the castle lay the heart of the kingdom. There the Ixaemithians swarmed the shops, trading whatever goods they had available. Children played in the streets near their homes and horses were prepared for traveling to other villages. Nothing could go wrong in the richest village of Ixaemitha.

However, what many don't know the dark secrets deep beneath the luxurious castle. Way down in the dungeons below rows of tiny cells held scores of prisoners. In the shadows of one of these cells sat a man with chain burns on his wrists and ankles; he was covered in grime. For the past few days, a look of permanent hopelessness had been fixed to his face. He couldn't stop thinking about what was going to happen to him or to the ones for whom he cared for.

He had been kidnapped. A few days beforehand he was living peacefully with his family. The next thing he knew, he woke up here. For years he knew that someone was out to get him, but he had no clue why. Now sitting in his cell, he had reached only one conclusion. His magic. This land was made up of all sorts of weird creatures and elements. They have been disappearing by the second and now he knew why. He looked down at his hand and a small flicker of flame rose up from it, then died. He and his magic had become weak. There was nothing he could do now.

Hours had passed since his last meal they had sent into the cell, which he did not necessarily like, and then he heard a metallic clanging as the cell doors opened to reveal two hulking guards. On their chests, they wore the symbol that everyone was familiar with—the one he hated with a passion—a roaring dragon with its wings outstretched and its tail wrapped around its body. The entire thing was the color of blood but has now faded away due to extensive use. He had nothing against dragons, but this symbol hid a very dark secret.

The man tried to get away from them, but he was too weak, and they easily snatched him up into their arms. Light pierced his swollen eyes as they dragged him up from the dungeons and down a lonesome hallway inside the castle. They passed a window that overlooked a huge clearing surrounded by trees with creatures chained up and he saw something that made his blood run cold. Farther in the distance stood a huge dragon with elegant green scales and sharp horns protruding from its back and tail with its wings spanning out into a wide arc in the sky. Below the beast, a man wielding a weapon dodged the creature. Blood dripped from the beast's claws, no doubt from defending itself. The man with the weapon was indeed very skilled. Armed with his spear and only a few scratches, he ran around it and over its large tail, avoiding being knocked out. When he got the thing confused, he jabbed his weapon up towards the dragon's chest and viciously struck the creature. The man cried out, but there was no stopping the object from hitting its mark. The long spear-like weapon entered the thick hide of the dragon and pierced its heart. The dragon roared and made one last futile attempt to hit back at its attacker, but it was no use, the dragon grew weak from the wound and crumpled to the ground. The man struggled against his captors, trying desperately to escape and save the poor creature, but again he was too weak from malnourishment and couldn't get to the dragon. His dragon.

Once out of sight of the beast, the man hung his head in defeat and let the two guards drag him out of the hall. That's when something strange happened to him. He was suddenly connected to the dragon. He could feel her heartbeat slow and stop and once he knew for sure that she was dead, his magic also died. He was now a normal human-being once more.

He and the two guards entered a large furnished room with a huge throne on the back wall, little brown tables with gold engravings scattered about, and large windows on each side overlooking the kingdom below. It was a beautiful sight if it weren't the room that held his greatest enemy. His kidnapper.

They forced him to his knees, reconnected him to the chains, and left him alone in there. He didn't even try to get up. All he could do was fill with rage towards the people who captured him and had potentially just killed his dragon.

From behind him, he heard a door slam shut and he raised his head to see who had entered. A large, enrobed man slowly walked past him and made his way to the throne encased in gold. He couldn't help but sneer at the person everyone knew and respected. King George X. Also known to people as the "Dragon King." His name for the king was "Dragon Killer." And while the man seethed, George only smiled.

"You must be wondering why you are here when you could be living peacefully in your home village," the king said. The man made no noise, so he continued. "You see, Alexander, I'm sure you have studied a lot about dragons and you surely can agree with me that dragons give people power. Yes?" Alexander still did not say anything but shot daggers up at him. He merely smiled down at the broken man. "You seem like a smart man, Alex. Do you know why you are here?"

When he continued to remain quiet, George strode over to him in just three steps and slapped him. "Yes," Alex finally said, his voice filled with contempt. "If dragons give people power then you want all of it."

The king's grin broadened even more. "If people have power then they uprise. If they uprise then I would no longer be in rule. I can't risk having every dragon at my disposal, but I can… eliminate the ones that I do not own to make people powerless. Then I would be more powerful than everyone in Ixaemithia."

"Why are you telling me all of this?" Alex retorted. All he could think to do in these chains was to diminish the king's confidence and hopefully try to escape.

George did not seem bothered at all. "Why am I telling you this? You're already a broken man. What harm could you possibly do to me?"

Alex felt like saying, "If you hadn't killed my dragon, I would have already ruined you in a heartbeat," but even in his righteous indignation, he did not wish for lashings in the slightest. Instead he said, "You don't know what I'm capable of."

The king only laughed and went to sit upon his throne once again. "While you are in my care you can't do anything with my guards watching you. No one has ever escaped my prison. Not to point out that now that your dragon is dead you are useless."

"And exactly how did you find me anyway?" Alex retorted. "I was just minding my own business, but no, you just had to send your stupid *custodes domus meae*…" Alex stopped himself. Whenever he seized with anger his native language would take over his English. Focusing on talking normal, he took a deep breath and continued. "I don't think killing off every dragon is the right answer here. They are living, breathing creatures. They are innocent and beautiful. They—"

"Innocent?" the king snapped. "Dragons are fierce and dangerous creatures. Ridding them of this world would do everyone a favor."

Alex burst out laughing. "So, what then? You think you are more innocent than they are? And if you really think they are that dangerous then why not kill your own dragon? It would sure do him good than to be your servant."

Without warning, King George X stood up from his throne, walked over to Alex and backhanded him with all his might that it made his teeth rattle and left a giant welt on his cheek. Alex tried to hold it in, but a small whimper escaped his mouth, which made George smile. "Not so tough now, are you? You disobey or insult me again, you will face a worse punishment than lashings. We are done here." And with that, the king left the room. A second later the same two guards from before entered and roughly took Alex out into the hallway. He didn't say any more to anyone. His mind began to wander as he envisioned the myriad ruthless ways he could torture, and perhaps kill this horrid tyrant.

As Alex and the guards walked down the hallway, they passed the same window from before and hope clawed through his body. However, this hope evaporated instantly as he didn't see his dragon and only saw pools of blood on the ground where she had stood before. Sadness overwhelmed him as they dragged him out and into his own dingy, dark cell where he had been imprisoned for days. They threw him in, closed the door, and left him alone in the darkness for him to go insane.

1
Scarlet

On a freezing November night, a young teenage girl slipped out of her house with a bow slung on her back and a quiver of arrows on her right shoulder. She wore knee high leather boots, worn out leather clothes and her waist length bright blonde, wavy hair fell down her back. She wasn't like most girls, who wore only dresses and skirts; the thought of hunting would never occur to them. She loved to hunt. Even if she didn't, she would have anyway to support her family.

Her family was poor and couldn't afford to pay for food. That's why she hunts, but hunting makes her feel exhilarated. She didn't have a real family other than her younger sister because she had lost her parents at a young age. A friend of her dad's, also known as her Godfather, took the responsibility of providing a place for her and her sister to live. Seven years had passed, and she has yet to find the people who took her family away. She had an inkling of who it could have been, but she was young at the time and only vaguely remembered the men involved.

As she crossed her village, Drakonia, and to the nearby wooded area, she remained hidden in the shadows and out of sight of the people in the streets. Anyone who was underage could not be out past curfew. She could get into serious trouble if she was caught. Luckily, she only had one more year before she could do what she wanted.

Once through Drakonia, she entered the Forest of the Dragons. The dragons used to rule the forests and jungles, but in her time all the dragons became extinct. All she could remember were the stories that her Godfather told them when they were little and how when he was just a child, he had been up close to one. Every time she thought this, she would become saddened; she always wished to see a dragon.

She walked far enough into the forest to where deer roamed and started to search for them. As she passed under a canopy of trees, she heard a voice above her head. "Hey, Scar."

She recognized that voice and smiled. Up in the leaves of a tree poked out a head. A boy with disheveled brown hair and eyes stared back at her and smiled.

"Hey, Luke," she replied. She didn't care about being called Scar, which was his nickname for Scarlet. "I thought you were busy with your family."

Luke clambered down the tree and jumped down next to her. "Nah, had nothin' to do with me. I escaped before they could bring me into it." He smiled, showing missing teeth in the front, and walked over to a bush that sat at the foot of his tree. He took out his own bow and arrows and they took off together in search for some deer.

Scarlet knew these woods like the back of her hand. She had been hunting for an exceptionally long time now, mostly with Luke, and she knew all the best places to find prey. They headed toward a well-known hotspot for deer.

The two ventured through the thick woods and not long after, they arrived in the small meadow and spotted two stags grazing ahead of them. Luke pointed to the one on the left, then to Scarlet, saying she should get that one. Scarlet agreed and took position behind a large oak tree. She nocked an arrow, took steady aim, and let it fly. The stag had no clue what was coming next, and before it could take off, Scarlet's arrow pierced it square in the chest. Luke's deer ran in alarm, but he easily took it out as well.

After making sure there were no more deer nearby, Scarlet and Luke treaded out into the long grass to fetch the stags. They retrieved their arrows and wiped the blood off on the grass. Once they felt the weight of each deer, they knew that they couldn't carry each one by themselves. So, they made the decision to come back for the other one, hide it so no scavengers would find it, and carry the first deer to their little camp.

The camp was a clearing with rope tied to trees, a tiny tipi set up, and two log stumps: each with a knife protruding from it. When they entered the camp, they used one of the ropes to hang up the deer. Completing the task, they went to pick up the other one and bring it back. With both stags strung up, they each took the knives from the stumps and began stripping the fur off the deer. They tried to keep the fur intact so they could make something out of it, and then started to cut the meat into pieces to carry back home.

"Did you hear about tomorrow?" Scarlet asked while trying to cut through some of the tougher portions of the meat. She noticed that her knife wasn't as sharp as it used to be and wouldn't be able to do much more until she got back home.

"Yeah, but I can't go tomorrow because I have school."

"Oh, right." Scarlet forgot that he was only a little younger than her, and she didn't need to go anymore. "Well, when I'm there I'm going to go trade this stupid knife for a new one."

Luke chuckled as he saw her unsuccessfully attempt to cut through the big chunk of meat. "Here." He tossed his own knife to her. His was a lot bigger than hers and she could tell that he sharpened it every day.

"Thanks." She took the knife and, finally, cut through the troublesome hunk of meat with little struggle. She continued to cut the other pieces and put them in her satchel to carry home. She couldn't fit all the meat from the deer and knew that if she left it out it would spoil in the camp, so she threw the leftovers out away from their area and into the trees for the animals. Luke did the same and they headed back home.

"Here," she said as she handed back the knife. "Do you think I could trade this one for a new one? I believe this is beyond my abilities to repair." She held up her knife that carried dents and scratches on the blade with the edge chipped away.

"Definitely." He eyed the broken blade in her hand and took it to examine further. "There's probably a merchant who would gladly take this off you, but I'm not sure on a trade. You may have to pay for a new one."

Scarlet sighed and took back her knife. "But I don't have any coins..."

"You could try to trade, but if you can't then I'd say keep it. Maybe I can help fix it up for you."

Scarlet smiled at him, but it was fleeting. Suddenly she tripped and landed hard on the ground. Luke started laughing.

"Not funny," she said. Scarlet could feel a bruise welling up on her shin. She rubbed her leg and looked to see what she tripped over. She scrambled to her feet. "Look." She pointed to the ground and what was covered in bushy undergrowth reflected a blue and red hue. Scarlet pushed aside the branches and found what appeared to be a big rock just lying there.

Luke came over and stared at it in confusion. "What rock would be that color?"

"I don't know." Scarlet didn't care why, she could only marvel at the beauty of this rock. It was the size of a small boulder and is perfectly round. She picked it up—which took most of her strength to lift—and slowly started walking off with it.

"What are you doin'?" Luke asked, incredulous. "You're not bringin' that home, are you?"

She didn't answer and instead focused on conserving her energy by not talking. Luke only shook his head, sighed, and followed her back home.

2
Scarlet

When morning came, Scarlet jumped out of bed and peered out her window to see carriages strolling into the village. Today was the day that visitors from other settlements came to trade with them. Scarlet so badly wanted to go, but first she had work and since she worked with horses, she would have to take care of all of them. She sighed and got ready to head out the door.

As she did, she glanced over at the rock in the corner of her room. It was too heavy and there was nowhere else to put it except in that spot. Nevertheless, she still admired it from its place. Luke had been right with the colors and saying that rocks shouldn't be that way. It was odd to find it lying there in the forest.

After getting ready for the day, Scarlet walked downstairs to see her little sister awake and sitting on the floor. She played with a freshly picked flower and when she brought her hand up, she dropped the flower. It stayed perfectly in midair. Scarlet was not surprised to see this.

"Edith, you shouldn't be practicing your magic out in the open like that. What if someone was to see?"

Edith's head turned sharply, which made the flower drop from its position, and drift to the floor. Edith was only ten and she had come to Scarlet with this secret. She thought it was great, but then thought that if people were to know, they'd try to hurt her.

"Sorry," she mumbled and hung her head. Scarlet sighed and went to sit next to her. "It's okay, just remember what I told you and what gift you hold that other people don't, okay?" Edith nodded and twirled the flower in her hand. Scarlet ruffled her long, dirty-blonde hair and headed for work.

Scarlet often felt jealous over her sister's power, but she loved her sister very much and never showed jealousy towards her. Instead she would help her hide it. Scarlet figured that if she felt that way about her magic then so would other people, and when people are jealous, they tend to harm others.

When she entered the streets, there were many people bustling about and stopping at the many shops that had been set up in Drakonia for today. Scarlet stared longingly at them but continued to walk past and stopped at the village barn. The horses from the carriages were there and already needed tending to. When a man walked up to her, she knew she had to start right away.

"You know what to do," he said.

"Yessir." Scarlet hurried over to where they usually kept the brushes and brought one over to the first horse. It neighed as she came closer to it and examined its fur. This horse just needed a simple cleaning. She did what she could in grooming it and washing it down, then moved to the next horse. This one was cleaner, but the hooves needed taking care of, so she walked back to the supplies and found the picks that would remove all the dirt from the horse's hooves to make them feel more comfortable.

As she went along, she grew more certain that the traders that traveled here did not take good care of these horses. The ones she tended to were caked all over in mud and their disheveled fur was more often than not a tangled mess. She also didn't know how far they traveled, so she kept her comments to herself. The last horse that wasn't being tended to appeared to be fine and just needed grooming.

After all of those horses were fine for now, she walked over to her own assigned horse. In Drakonia, they didn't have many horses, so Scarlet took care of only one horse in the barn.

"Hey, Prince," she said. She ran her fingers through his thick, dark mane and started to groom him. He was a beautiful black stallion with white spots on his side and on his ankles. A horse like this was rare to see in many villages, which was why Scarlet liked him so much and would always take care of him for as long as she worked there. If it was up to her, she would have already bought him off and taken him as her own, but she didn't have nearly enough money to afford him. So instead she continued to take care of him.

Hours passed and through that whole time she had nothing to do but to be tempted to leave work by all the strange passersby, along with the many shops that were set up in the village. When the man came over again to tell her to take a break, she jumped up and immediately ran into town with her little pocket of coins. As she passed by the many shops, there were countless interesting things like clothes, crystals, weapons, and other merch that Scarlet had never seen before.

When she passed a blacksmith shop, she stopped and took out her broken knife. Before she could go to any other shop, she decided to stop there and trade in her knife for a new one, or at least try to do so. When she walked in, there were many different types of blades of all shapes and sizes with beautifully jeweled handles. Scarlet instantly fell in love. She walked up to a man with a face smudged with dirt and grime.

"Welcome to my shop," the man said, smiling.

Scarlet reached out and handed him her knife. "Would you be able to do a trade?"

The man examined the broken blade closely. "I could trade you, but it'll also cost you."

"But I don't have that much money," she said in disappointment.

"Well, how much do you have?" he asked. Scarlet pulled out her pouch and slid it over to him. The man poured the coins out onto the table and started counting them.

"Sixty coins," he said. "Let's make a deal. You give me half the amount of these coins, plus this knife, and I'll let you choose any blade in this room. Deal?"

Scarlet nodded and scouted the room for the right blade. All of them seemed very nice looking, but the one that really caught her eye was a sword with a long blade and a handle with curved edges. A jewel had also been placed right below the blade; a thing of beauty.

"What about this one?" she asked while picking up the sword from its perch on the wall.

"Ah, yes. This one here is the last remaining sword that belongs to this village; the Drakonian Blade. A wise decision. There are legends on this sword about anyone who owned it will inherit abilities that no one in their wildest dreams could have in their lifetime."

As Scarlet listened, she couldn't help but feel excited by the extraordinary claim this man was making.

"So, you're saying that anyone who possesses this sword would be able to obtain… magic?" she asked, thinking of Edith and her magical ability. It then made her wonder just how Edith had gotten such powers in the first place.

The man pursed his lips as if he had said something he shouldn't have, then smiled and handed her the sword. "This jewel here on the handle is supposedly an amulet that contains the magic. Of course, you shouldn't get your hopes up for this is only a legend and could not be real."

"Of course not, sir," Scarlet said, smiling. Once she had paid for the sword, the man also gave her a sheath to go with the blade that wrapped around her waist.

Before she had exited the shop, she tucked away her new sword in her shirt, not wanting to attract attention to herself, and slung the sheath over her shoulder. With the rest of her coins, she decided to go to another place and get something for Edith.

As she passed myriad shops, with everything piquing her interest, she found one that Edith would love. On display sat a necklace with the zodiac symbol "Gemini" in the color of her birthstone: emerald green. Along the chain of the necklace dotted emerald crystals, and Scarlet knew that this would be the one.

Once she had the necklace in her possession, with no more money, she headed back home to drop off her belongings, knowing that she couldn't bring her sword with her, and came back to tend to the horses again.

Later that night, everyone got ready for dinner with the deer Scarlet had killed the other night. As they sat at the table, she could see that Edith was wearing the necklace that Scarlet bought for her with a bright, happy smile on her face. Scarlet enjoyed seeing her little sister happy since nowadays she usually seemed so reserved from people, probably due to her magic.

Liam, their Godfather, came in with plates of deer meat for the three of them. He was a tall man with a small beard and short black hair. He carried a strange accent unlike that of any other Drakonian. He and Scarlet's dad had the same accent, making her think they weren't from Drakonia.

As he sat down and everyone began eating, a mischievous grin spread across his face. "Let's have a little story time. This time about your father."

Edith's and Scarlet's eyebrows creased in confusion. They hadn't had one of these nights in a long time, but they grew excited to hear another story about their dad.

"When your father and I were only teenagers, he was obsessed with dragons and would spend hours reading every book on them. One day we were out wandering in the forest and he stumbled upon a giant object that was concealed in the brush. This object was enormous and had a green shade to it that we had never seen before. When your father picked up this object, it was heavy, and before he could do anything with it, it started to crack and revealed a creature that we had never seen before. Knowing your dad, he knew immediately what it was from all the studying he had done and told me that it was a dragon hatchling."

Scarlet nearly choked on her food when she heard this. Just imagining her dad finding a dragon made her happy.

He nodded and smiled in her direction. "Yes, it is surprising. Finding a dragon egg was rare and whoever found one were considered lucky. Of course, they are also very illegal to own, but I've always believed that people had them anyways. Your father sure did; he had to hide it in the woods for safekeeping. If anyone had found out about it then he would have gotten into serious trouble."

"Is that the reason why he had been taken away…?" Edith asked sadly. Liam said nothing and lowered his head down towards his plate. Scarlet was sure that he was crying, but he then lifted his head up and offered a strained smile.

"That could be, Edith. But we will never know for sure." Liam paused, then picked up his plate and left the room.

The two girls weren't sure what to do but decided to finish their dinner and leave Liam alone for the night. Scarlet kissed her sister goodnight and headed up to her room. She glanced down at the object she had found in the woods, and briefly pondered the craziest idea ever of what it could be.

3
SCARLET

In the morning, Scarlet went through her daily routine for the day. She couldn't help but stare at the rock. The possibility of it being a dragon's egg like the one her father had found in Liam's story had filled her dreams all night. Of course, she couldn't tell anyone, but the idea excited her.

She walked downstairs to find it still dark outside and everyone sleeping. She decided to have some breakfast and then leave for work, which didn't make her feel particularly happy. Scarlet missed the halcyon days of just being a kid and hanging out with friends; not having to worry about the hardship of life.

On the counter sat a loaf of bread that she picked up and began to slice for her breakfast. Then she pulled out some goat cheese from the ice box. Since they never had much to eat, this kind of meager meal was normal for her. She sat down and started eating.

Outside the sun rose above the horizon, casting beautiful hues across the sky. Scarlet always enjoyed watching the sun rise and set every day, but lately she'd been so busy that she never had time for it. So this morning she just enjoyed the peaceful moment as she finished her breakfast.

When she got up to take care of her spot, a bright glare hit her eyes and blinded her for a second. When it subsided, she looked out the window to see Luke smiling at her with a golden watch in his hand. Scarlet sighed and opened the door for him.

"Yes?" she asked him impatiently.

Luke's smile slipped away at her tone. "Someone woke up on the wrong side of the bed this morning."

She sighed again. "Sorry, I have a lot of things on my mind right now and with you blinding me like that didn't do any good." She smiled to reassure him that she was alright. Luke looked relieved and entered her home.

"I just wanted to see if you were up to huntin' today. No school so," he said with hope in his eyes.

"Aw, man, I can't, I have work. Maybe after I get done we can head out and I can show you my new blade that I traded for yesterday."

Luke raised his eyebrow with curiosity but said nothing more and left the house with Scarlet. They parted ways just when they entered the village and she traveled her usual path to the barn. However, something seemed different now. No one walked the streets or manned their shops and as Scarlet passed the village square, she suddenly heard a person scream. She ran to the square to see a crowd of people surrounding a man who crouched on the ground and a uniformed guard standing above him with a whip in his hand. The symbol on his chest told Scarlet that this guard had come from the Ixaemithian kingdom, the capital of Ixaemithia, the land in which she lived. The symbol closely resembled a roaring dragon with its tail wrapping around itself. She had seen one of those guards before and knew what was coming next.

Before the man could get up, the guard whipped him again and grabbed him up from the ground. He tried to escape the guard's grasp, but the lashes he had received weakened him considerably and the guard had no trouble dragging him out of the square and into a carriage with the same symbol emblazoned on its side. Once they left, people dispersed with Scarlet just standing there staring at the spot where the man had just been. She felt tears streaming down her face as in her mind's eye she clearly saw her father in place of that man.

When she was ten, she had witnessed those very same guards break into her home and attack her parents. She could do nothing but watch as they had taken down her mother. Her father wasn't so easy to go out. He fought them with all his might just to get to his family, but in the end, Scarlet watched them knock him unconscious and cart him away. She had no clue whether her dad was dead or alive. The memory was very vague but after seeing what just happened to that man, everything came crashing down onto her.

After what seemed like forever, Scarlet realized that she was just standing there and needed to get to the barn. However, when she did, her boss came up to her and told her that there would be no work today. That gave her a chance to do something she would have never done before. She entered the barn, took Prince from his stable and rode out with him. She was curious to find out where those men were going. She hadn't seen anything like this happen in Drakonia in a long time.

The men had taken a route that led out of Drakonia, so she followed that path. They had not gotten that far with the prisoner before she collided with them. Scarlet didn't know why but she did not try to hide. She charged full on into them, taking them by surprise, and quickly trampling the first few guards. Prince panicked as Scarlet pushed him further until one man threw a spear at her horse. She pulled back before Prince could be harmed.

When she was far enough away, they stood face to face with each other. Scarlet pondered just what to do next when the man that had been taken peeked his head out of the carriage. Blood trickled down his cheeks from cuts across his forehead. Bruises covered his jaw, which looked to be set at an odd angle, and his eyes darted about in fear.

"Go!" Scarlet urged. "Get out of here!"

At first, he hesitated—which made the remaining guard pull out his sword and charge at him—but when Scarlet hopped off Prince to position herself between the two, the man took off running back towards Drakonia. The guard tried to follow in pursuit, but Scarlet drew her sword and jabbed it into his spine. Her mind was in a tizzy at that moment; she did not know how to fight at all.

"Don't go chasing after him," she said in a deathly quiet voice. "You do and this sword will do some harm to you."

He laughed. She couldn't see his face but knew that he was smirking. "Am I s'posed to fear a little girl like yourself? Please, the king has more guards to rid this world of your kind."

"My kind?" Scarlet didn't understand. As far as she knew they were both the same.

"Don't play stupid with me. I see that sword you hold there." He then turned around in confidence. Healed scars zig zagged across his broad face. His eyes were a dull blue filled with madness as he sneered at her. "Anyway, your attempts are futile. You can't stop what is happening."

"And what exactly is happening?"

Instead of answering he grabbed her sword with both hands and jerked it towards his stomach. Afraid, Scarlet pulled back hard on it, slicing his hands, and took a step back. He chuckled. "Don't have the guts, eh? That will be your downfall. I predict that right now we will both leave in separate directions and you will not harm me. You will ride on your little horse back to Drakonia and you will never see me again, but we will be seeing you."

That last part sent chills down her spine. The guard was right, and Scarlet let him pass unscathed. One of the horses that had been pulling the carriage had ran away in alarm. The other got stuck in its own harness and the guard was able to free it and ride it back to wherever he came from. Scarlet spent only moments there, gazing at the mess with troubled thoughts, before climbing onto Prince and riding back to the village.

That afternoon, Luke and Scarlet walked through the woods after bringing a great deal of deer meat home. They had been hunting since she had confronted those guards and freed the prisoner. She needed some time with her friend to take her mind off the events that occurred today, so they did nothing but hunt.

Luke could see that Scarlet was still distant from this morning. "You okay?"

She nodded as she stared at the ground. Scarlet didn't tell Luke of her going off after those guards. She didn't think he would appreciate her doing that. However, he did know of a person being taken at the square. Addressing his concern, she told him, "I will be, but what happened today just reminded me of a bad memory I wish to forget."

Luke only nodded and silently walked alongside her. When they almost hit their camp, they heard rustling in the brush nearby and took out their bows while crouching low to the ground. Then they saw movement. Scarlet unloaded and hit the animal square in the chest. It was a rabbit that had scurried out to get some food.

"I think we have enough food to last us for a week," Luke said, chuckling. Scarlet only smiled and started skinning the rabbit with her sword. It was hard to do since the blade was so long; she would just have to get used to it with time.

When the sun went down, Scarlet and Luke bid goodbye to each other and headed back home for the night. She couldn't wait to put her head on her pillow and just sleep away the events that occurred today. She didn't know why things like this happened. All she knew was that her life was going to change drastically.

4
SCARLET

When Scarlet returned from hunting that night, she entered the house and walked up the stairs. She heard a quiet skittering noise ahead of her and thought that maybe they had a mouse in the house. She didn't think much of it. When she arrived at her room, she couldn't believe her eyes. Glass had shattered onto the floor and clothes had been strewn about everywhere. They were covered in a sticky substance that smelled awful. She looked over to see the rock, what she thought was a rock, looked to be an egg that had cracked and now remained empty with more of that same substance inside.

"No…" she trailed off. She couldn't believe it. What she thought to be the craziest idea ever had just come true, and now she had no clue where the creature had gone. She scrambled to pick up all the clothing and blankets to see if it was hiding under any of it. There was nothing. She checked every nook and cranny of the room. No luck. The only place she did not check was underneath her bed. Scarlet lifted the covers that had draped over and immediately got a face full of smoke. She reeled back coughing as a tiny head poked out from underneath the covers, peering at her.

Once her coughing fit was under control, she saw that the creature just stared at her with big, blue eyes and had scaly blue patches all over its body. A line of tiny red horns protruded from its head and along its back and tail. A sickly sheen from the egg covered him.

"I can't believe I have a dragon," she said to herself, still reeling from everything that was happening. The dragon sniffed her, then blew out a puff of smoke with a hint of fire that grazed Scarlet's leg.

"Ow!" she exclaimed. She clutched her leg in pain. It sensed this and began licking her wound. As Scarlet watched, the smoldering burns slowly disappeared, as well as the pain, and the skin returned to normal. "Can you understand me...?" she asked the dragon, trying to know more about it.

The dragon nodded once and slipped back under the covers. Seconds later Scarlet heard footsteps and Liam opened the door to her room. His hair was disheveled, and his eyes drooped with sleep.

"What's going on in here?" he asked, eyeing all the clothes and glass that scattered the floor.

"Oh... it's nothing. Just uh... fell from my bed and knocked some things over," she lied, trying to hide the fact that there was a dragon in her room. Liam creased his eyebrows in confusion, but she could see that sleep clouded his thoughts. He said nothing else and closed the door.

"I should give you a name..." she said as the dragon popped its head out and meandered towards her. "How about... Drakon." She decided to name the dragon after her home, Drakonia. The dragon nodded again and blew out a puff of smoke.

"You can't stay in here, Drakon." Scarlet decided to bring it into the forest like her father did in Liam's story so the dragon wouldn't be at risk by staying in her house. "Will you follow me outside?" Drakon nodded once more, waddling behind Scarlet as they left the house and entered the woods. She was amazed that the young dragon understood her so well and so she brought him to her camp. Drakon seemed energized about being in the woods and tried to take flight, but his wings were too small and could not yet lift his body up from the ground. Scarlet grabbed ahold of him, which made him flail his wings to try and escape her grasp.

"No! Drakon, please stay here," she said, begging him to stay in place. The young dragon looked up at her and nodded, then sat down and folded up his wings. Scarlet sighed and knelt in front of the dragon. She was very tired yet afraid that he would leave her. They barely got to spend any time with each other. "I have to go now, but I will come back, okay? Promise me you will stay."

Drakon nodded again and laid down on the ground. Scarlet left the camp and headed back home, wondering what she should tell her friends and family.

Scarlet left the house the next day and went to grab Luke from his home. She had no work today, so she decided that Luke would be trustworthy in seeing Drakon. She wasn't sure if she should endanger the lives of her family, but she also needed someone to carry this secret with her and to be there for her, so she felt she really had no choice but to tell Luke. If not him, who else?

Luke lived in the middle of Drakonia, and his house was next to the Drakonian Tower. This tower stood in the middle of the village and meetings would take place there when deciding important rules, as well as to discuss things with the Ixaemithian kingdom's court. The court was made up of King George X's loyal subjects and his guards. Scarlet hated them with all her heart. They did awful things here.

The shops in town died down as the trading ended. All they had to do was pack up and leave on their horses. It was now easy to walk in the streets and Scarlet had no trouble reaching Luke's house. Usually, trading only takes a day or two before they pack up and leave. Scarlet never understood why since it seemed like a lot of work. They could have just stayed a week then left, but Scarlet didn't complain. She wasn't a part of it.

Luke's house was very small, and she knew that he had a hard time living there with all his brothers. Soon enough she could hear children yelling from the house as she walked up to the door and knocked. A boy taller than her answered the door and smiled.

"Hey, Scarlet," he said.

"Hey, Byron." Scarlet knew Luke's family and knew that Byron was his eldest brother out of five boys in the house. She had always envisioned this place as chaos every time she came over.

"You are lookin' for Luke," he stated, knowing why she was there. Before she could answer, Byron went back inside and brought out Luke who looked weary, yet at the sight of Scarlet, he smiled.

"What's up, Scar?" he asked.

"I have to show you something, Luke," she said excitedly. Luke gave her a curious look but didn't say anything and let her guide him out of town and into the woods.

"Remember that rock we found in the woods?" Scarlet asked.

"Yeah…" he said with suspicion.

"You won't believe what it actually is." Scarlet had a hard time containing her excitement and kept pulling on Luke's arm for him to walk faster. After a few too many pulls, Luke started to protest and tried to yank his arm away, but she wouldn't let go till they reached camp. At first, Scarlet's excitement dimmed to panic as she couldn't spot Drakon anywhere. Her panic was short lived as she saw him soar through the sky and over the trees to land on the ground in front of her. He was considerably bigger than just the night before and she realized then that dragons must grow much faster than other creatures.

"Woah…" Luke gasped. Drakon bared his teeth at Luke and blew a puff of fire in his direction. He yelped in pain and swatted at his clothes to smolder the flames.

"Drakon, no!" Scarlet hurried over to help Luke with his flaming clothes. When his clothes were no longer burning,

Scarlet turned back to Drakon. "Drakon, Luke is a friend, not an enemy."

Drakon bowed his head and growled a low growl. She wasn't sure, but Scarlet thought she heard something else come out of the dragon's growl. Almost like she heard a word, but she couldn't believe that. Dragons can't speak human.

Drakon picked his head up and cautiously walked towards Luke. He scrambled to get away, but the dragon was quick and hopped onto Luke to hold him in place. Scarlet was about to hurry over again when she saw that Drakon was doing the same thing he had done to her when she had gotten burned. He was licking Luke's wounds. At first, the boy tried to escape the dragon's grasp, but then he saw what it was doing and stared wonderingly at his healing wounds. Once finished, Drakon let go of Luke and flew back to his spot to sit down in front of Scarlet.

"That... was cool," Luke said, staring wide-eyed at Drakon.

"I know, right? I'm so happy to have a dragon. I've always wanted one."

Luke stared at the dragon, then sighed. "I wish I had a dragon of my own..."

Scarlet gave Luke a look of sympathy and went to go pick up her bow. Luke followed and they went hunting once again, but this time, Drakon would be going with them. The young dragon flew from above while Luke and Scarlet walked through the woods to their favorite hunting spot.

"Don't tell anyone about this," Scarlet warned Luke.

"Why? This is amazing!" he said with a confused look.

"Because people don't need to know about this. It's against the law to own a dragon." She also thought about her father but didn't want to tell him that. Before Luke could speak again, Scarlet cut him off and shot a look saying, "You better not tell anyone."

Luke sighed and nodded in her direction. Drakon kept up the pace with them for a while until Scarlet saw him turn his head sharply and dive headfirst through the trees. They shared a look of confusion and ran towards the spot where he had dove. Through all the trees, Scarlet could see Drakon holding a deer in his claws and was baring his teeth into its neck while it struggled to escape. They stared on in horror as Drakon mutilated the deer right in front of them and ate it raw. Scarlet and Luke decided to leave Drakon with his own things and go hunting on their own.

Having nothing else to do, the two friends scouted the entire surrounding woods and killed whatever they could. She was surprised that there were so many animals to hunt and eat, but this was also good because winter was coming and soon there would be nothing to eat.

With each prey they killed they would pile them up and after the hunt, they gathered up their kills and brought them back to camp. They then sat down and did what they usually did. They started stripping the meat. Scarlet took out her new blade and admired how well it cut through the meat. Luke glared at her in jealousy as he cut his own; Drakon just sprawled out on the ground and ate his prey raw. His new royal blue scales shimmered in the setting sun as he ate, and from time to time, he would lift his head up from his meal to scope his surroundings, then resume what he was doing. Scarlet didn't want to be there for long because it was already getting dark and she had to go home to teach Edith how to control her magic. Even though Scarlet had no magic of her own, she would still try to keep her from using it in front of people or try to at least get better at it.

With all the meat they had to strip, it took a while to finish, but when they did, it was getting darker in the woods as Scarlet and Luke said their goodbyes to Drakon, who then flew up into the trees and out of sight. They then made their way back home. Once there, Scarlet did not enter the house. She went around and into the yard. Edith sat cross-legged in the middle with her eyes closed, and all around her, flowers of different colors and sizes were blooming up from the ground. Scarlet stood there for a second to take in the beauty of what her sister could do, and the jealousy rose again. She knew that she would always feel this way, but there was nothing that she could do about it and to just support her sister all the way.

When the flowers stopped growing, Scarlet woke up from her daze, stomped out her jealousy, and made her way to Edith. Her little sister did not look up from her spot on the ground and kept her eyes closed when Scarlet came over to sit next to her.

"I'm trying to do harder magic," Edith said with closed eyes. "But it's hard… It keeps sapping my energy and I can't do anything other than make flowers grow…" Edith opened her eyes finally and stared up at Scarlet with a hint of sadness on her face.

Scarlet stared down lovingly and began to comfort her. "You know you are only little," she said, trying to make Edith happy again. "Your magic will get stronger as you grow older. For now, we can only strengthen what we can do. Okay?" Edith nodded and closed her eyes again.

In the next hour, Scarlet could see that Edith wasn't making any progress. They tried to do other magic that she could handle like making objects move and controlling water, but Scarlet found that after practicing higher levels of magic, Edith had grown tired and didn't have enough strength to keep going. She concluded that Edith should go to bed before she really messed herself up and they would continue another time.

"Next time don't try to do hard magic when I'm not there to help, okay?" Scarlet said gently as they headed back into the house and up the stairs. "I want you to have all of your strength so I may be able to help you."

Edith nodded and entered her room. Scarlet went to hers and set the Drakonian Blade down onto her bed. When she started changing, she looked over once more at her sword and gasped. The jewel on the handle glowed royal blue. Scarlet didn't know what to think, but her excitement grew. She picked it up to look at it more closely and remembered what the man in the shop said about the legend of this blade. She realized then that her life had indeed changed.

5
Scarlet

Scarlet jumped out of bed and reached for the doorknob on her two stubby legs to leave her room. Even on her tiptoes she had a hard time reaching things, but she managed and peeked her head around the corner in the hall. She heard voices from the other room as she quietly walked towards them.

Just when she was about to enter the next room, she jumped upon hearing a crash, followed by shouts from her parents. Scarlet's heart raced and she grew fearful of entering that room. She pushed her fear aside and again reached for the doorknob. The door slowly creeped open and when she peered around the door, she saw her mother lying on the floor with her long, blonde hair trailing behind her. Her father fought off strange men in uniform who were trying to take ahold of him. He was quick on his feet. There were a total of five guards in the house, and when each one came close to him, he would fend them off with either a punch or a kick that would send them smashing into one another. There would be moments when he sent them all sprawling and would quickly dart to his wife's side but was always blocked and sent back to the other side of the room.

Scarlet couldn't move or speak as she stood there fearing those strange men. Suddenly one of them raised their arm with a weapon and when her father was distracted, the guard let it fall hard onto his head. He crumpled into their arms with blood running down his face and they dragged him out of the house.

Scarlet cried and screamed at the men, but they ignored her and left the house. She fell and crawled to her mother to see what was wrong with her. She didn't respond to her prodding and Scarlet cried even more. The last thing she heard was the roar of an enormous beast that rang through her head.

Scarlet woke up in sweat and gasped for breath. She scouted her surroundings and sighed to find herself back in her room in Liam's house. She hadn't had one of those nightmares in a very long time and they always got to her. It was the time she lost her parents to the kingdom and it always made her seethe with anger.

She sat there in bed for a few minutes, trying to wrap her head around the dream, then shook it off and got ready for the day. She glanced over at the sword to see the jewel still glowing brightly and wondered if it would always glow now. She picked it up, strapped on her sheath, and left the house to go into the village. Again, she hid her sword from people so she wouldn't get in trouble, but also did not want to leave it out of her sight.

As she walked, she started to get a sense of deja vu when no one roamed the streets of Drakonia. Scarlet walked towards the village square, dreading what she would find, and saw, again, many people watching the events taking place in the square. Just like before, the men in uniform were beating up another man who was trying to defend himself. The defenseless man shouted at the top of his lungs, but Scarlet couldn't make out what was being said and he received lash after lash from the guards. With blood running down his body, the man fell unconscious and was dragged to a carriage that would lead to the kingdom. Just what happened before.

How did they get here so quickly? she wondered. She'd just dealt with a group of them herself only a couple of days ago. Now they were back and trying to take another person.

Scarlet could tell that something was wrong now because there had never been so many of these before. Her mind was racing: what could the king possibly want with them? People dispersed with Scarlet standing there once more, but as the square cleared, a family with children stayed exactly where they were and glared after the carriage that was now leaving. Scarlet couldn't see their faces, but the children were crying and trying to run after it, as if they could bring back the man that had been taken away.

Scarlet walked up to them to see everyone crying.

"D'ya know what he did?" said a woman tearfully. "One second we were wanderin' the shops an' the next thing we knew he was bein' dragged away from us."

Everyone looked to Scarlet with an eager glint in their eyes, but she only shook her head sadly. "No, I'm afraid I don't know, ma'am. I am so sorry."

The woman began sobbing again and a man next to her stepped up. "He was our brother, and these are his children. He would never do anything to put anyone in harm's way." The man's face grew beet red with anger. Scarlet was afraid that he was going to burst, but the man somehow maintained his composure.

Scarlet teared up at the idea of them losing their brother. They were in the same boat as she and it made her sad and angry at the same time.

"Why yous cryin', child?" said another man in the group. Scarlet just shook her head, bid them farewell, and left the square before she fell in tears. She wasn't going to tell anyone about what happened in her life, but she also wasn't going to let them get away with it any longer. They were going to pay for all the pain they caused.

Scarlet ran from the village, knowing she had no work to do today, and dashed into the forest. As she ran, roots and bushes seemed to get in her way, and she grew frustrated the longer it took for her to reach the camp. After pulling herself out of the last briar bush, she burst into the clearing with an idea in her head and looked for someone who could help her.

Just when she was about to search the sky for him, a huge body crashed into her that sent her skidding several feet from her spot. In a daze, Scarlet slowly stood up and locked eyes with Drakon, whose scales were ruffled up with his wings outstretched. When he realized who it was, he calmed down a bit and growled quietly.

Sorry.

Scarlet nodded and started to brush off the dirt from her clothes, then froze in place to look up at Drakon. Overnight he had grown even larger than before, but that wasn't what made her freeze. Scarlet had just heard him apologize!

"How did I…? I have so many questions, but never mind, I need you to do something for me. We can discuss this later." Drakon nodded and Scarlet told him what she needed him to do for her. He blew out a breath of fire in excitement and hurled himself into the sky.

While she waited, she sat down, took a deep breath, and contemplated what she had just done. She wasn't her usual self, but everything that happened recently drew her over the edge and she needed answers. And justice.

It felt like forever since Drakon had left and she began to worry. Either Drakon couldn't find them, or they found him and harmed him, but she sighed in relief when at last she saw a blue blur in the sky. Seconds later Drakon touched down with a squirming guard in his powerful jaws. Scarlet stood up quickly, unsheathed her sword, and walked over to him.

"If you yell or try to escape, I will order my dragon to slaughter you in a heartbeat," she sneered.

The guard glanced fearfully at Drakon, who gently dropped him and bared his teeth with his head cocked to the side, and he nodded.

"Alright then. I want answers and what you are doing to people now seems to be the right time for me to ask my questions." Scarlet glared down at the shivering guard with pity, then turned to Drakon. "Did anyone see you?"

Drakon shook his head and Scarlet saw blood shimmering from his scales along his jaw. She could tell that he had made an amazing meal out of those guards.

"First, why are you doing this?" Scarlet waited for the guard to answer, but he was frozen in place, refusing to say a word to her. She politely asked again, and still received no word from him. That's when her patience wore thin and she drew the blade up to his throat. "One more time. Why are you doing this?"

"If I tell you, the king will surely have my head," said the guard finally, his voice full of terror.

Scarlet pushed the sword even further. "I don't care. My life has been ripped apart because of you and your people. The ones I loved have been torn from me and I don't see why people are being harmed for no reason. So, you're going to tell me, or you are going to die anyways. Got it?"

The guard gulped; the sword grazed his neck. "Fine," he said in a shaking voice. "The king has requested for the heads of… certain people that could be a threat to him."

Scarlet nearly choked after hearing this but kept it in and lowered the sword from his neck. "What do you mean by 'certain' people? You are harming innocents who would never dream to overpower the king. Why does he feel so threatened?"

Again, the guard hesitated, and Scarlet had to put the sword back onto his throat. "I don't know, he has only told us one thing. The king wants the ones who carry more power than him to be immediately eliminated from this world so he can't be overthrown." The guard seemed to be struggling to contain this information, and now it all came pouring out. "During the time of the dragons, he killed all of them because he didn't want them to end up in the wrong hands. Whoever owns a dragon will receive more power than anyone can imagine. If that happened, then there would be no stopping them from reigning over this land. If I were you, I'd hide because the king's wrath will be coming down on you for owning a dragon."

Scarlet raised her eyebrows in surprise at this information and realized just how much trouble she was in. "How does the king know to find these people?"

Before he could answer, Drakon growled to get her attention.

Master, we cannot let him live. If we do, then he will tell the king about us and he will hunt us down.

"Good point," she said under her breath. "Just a little more information." She turned back to the guard and looked directly into his eyes. "How does he know?"

"I don't know, ma'am. He never tells us his secrets, only to tell us where to find these people and bring them back so they can be interrogated and perhaps executed."

Scarlet's heart skipped a beat as she heard this news. These same guards had taken her father and if this was true then her father could be dead. Her emotions took over and when she lowered her blade, the guard saw his chance to make a break for it into the trees. He didn't get far. Drakon was very keen on his movements and quickly pounced on him and slashed his claws across his throat. The guard struggled to breathe and in seconds collapsed to the ground, dead.

Scarlet could barely move but managed to sit down while Drakon came over to comfort her. She put her head on his scales and sighed, trying to keep the tears at bay.

"Drakon, how come I can understand you? How come this is all happening…?"

Drakon only growled and brushed his head against hers, knowing that his master was in distress. *You can speak the tongue of the dragons. Like the human said, when owning us you will inherit power, which also means you can communicate with us.*

"And what power is that? I don't really feel different. I can't do anything magical."

Drakon growled. *Elements*, was all he said, making Scarlet think maybe she could control magic after all, and maybe different types of magic as well.

When they both grew silent, Scarlet just sat there, letting her mind wander, until her eyes alighted on the guard once more. She realized that she couldn't just leave the body here to decompose. And the sight of it was unnerving, so with help from Drakon, they moved the body more over into the brush and started digging a hole. Drakon mostly did that job since Scarlet had nothing to dig with, and when finished, they buried the corpse.

Scarlet then went back to laying on Drakon. After the day she had, she was super stressed and tired and eventually she fell asleep on her powerful new friend.

6
Scarlet

When the sun peeked above the horizon the next morning, Drakon nudged Scarlet awake so she could go home. Instead of merely taking a nap the day before, she had fallen into a deep slumber. As tired as she was and not wanting to get up, she remembered that Liam and Edith would worry about her not showing up the night before. She stood up quickly, gave Drakon a hug, which made him purr-growl, and left for her home.

Along the way there she kept looking behind her shoulder in fear of being followed or watched. She wasn't herself today after what happened yesterday and knew that she was changing. Before today she would never have killed that man, but now she felt like something had awoken inside her. Perhaps it was revenge for what they did to her, but she knew that she would have to rein it back in or risk harming herself and others.

When Scarlet made it out of the woods and onto the road that led to her house, she ran and eventually came upon her home. When she opened the door, she ran smack into a broad-shouldered man about twice her size. On his back was the dragon symbol that every guard in the kingdom wore, and she panicked. They were after her! How did they find her? She had yet to know all their information and now it was already too late.

Liam sat at the kitchen table with his face growing pale as he spotted her and began to stroke his beard. Scarlet quietly walked past the guards—who only stared at her but didn't move—and went out the back door to see Edith once again sitting in the yard with her eyes closed. Scarlet knew then what she had to do.

"Edith…" she whispered, afraid of the guards overhearing. Edith opened her eyes and looked over at Scarlet.

"Yeah? What is going on? Who are those men?" Edith stood up, walked over to her, and tried to peek through the door. Scarlet grabbed her by the shoulders and pushed her away from the house.

"They are evil men, Edith. We need to get out of here. If we stay here any longer, they will capture us and take us away."

Edith's eyes grew in fright and she started to shake. "But what about Liam? We can't just leave him here."

"Liam will be alright. They only want us, not him," Scarlet said to try and reassure her. "Here, I will write him a note to tell him where we are, so he won't worry." Scarlet pulled a little piece of parchment from her pocket and began to write. She hadn't a clue where they were going, but anywhere would be fine right now.

Edith shook even more, and Scarlet grabbed ahold of her to comfort her as she finished writing the note. She stuck it underneath the lawn chair that Liam always loved to sit in. "There, he'll find the note and know where we are. Now let's go before they find us."

As if on cue, the guards walked outside to see Scarlet and Edith running back into the trees. They could hear shouts as they ran. Edith, hearing the guards, tripped and couldn't get back up; she was shaking too much. Scarlet saw the guards run after them and scooped up Edith, who felt light as a feather, and continued deeper into the forest. The guards were much faster than her and easily caught up to them, but Scarlet knew every inch of these surrounding woods and led the guards to the one place she herself had gotten stuck before. A row of briar bushes lined up in front of them and when she drew closer, she jumped with all her might to clear the bushes and looked down to see a gaping crack in the surface of the Earth. While exploring these woods one time when she was younger, she had come across this mini ravine and it had taken her a day to climb back out. This would hold off the guards long enough for them to escape safely.

As Scarlet landed on the other side, the guards didn't see the ravine and tripped over the briar bushes into the gaping hole. They did not tumble for a long distance, but the sides were nearly impossible to climb up. Scarlet glared down at them, laughed, and continued her journey back to camp to get Drakon.

Still holding Edith, Scarlet walked back the way they came, but avoided the house just in case, and headed in the direction of camp. Before they would get there, she knew that Edith would be afraid of Drakon.

"Edith, there is something I must show you now. We are in trouble and I need you to trust me. Will you do that?" Scarlet asked.

Edith looked up at her from her arms and nodded. "Yes."

Scarlet sighed in relief. "Okay... He may scare you at first, but he is really friendly."

Edith gave her a confused look. "Who?"

Scarlet didn't say anything, only shushed her, and set her down on the ground. She grabbed her tiny hand and led her into the camp. Drakon was there laying on the ground, asleep. Edith, eyes as wide as saucers, gasped. Drakon heard her and quickly rose to his feet, but then saw Scarlet and relaxed.

"Edith... this is Drakon... my dragon." Her eyes grew even wider, but she took a tentative step towards him. Drakon didn't move, showed no hostility at all and let her come closer to the point where she could pet his scales.

"He's beautiful..." Edith said. Drakon snorted out a breath of smoke into her face, making her laugh. Scarlet smiled at the sight of her sister no longer scared and walked up to them to pet him as well.

Drakon turned his head towards his master and gave her a nudge to see if she was alright.

"I'm fine, Drakon, but we are in big trouble and we need help."

Master? he growled.

Before Scarlet could start speaking, Edith answered for her.

"Scarlet says we are in trouble and we need to get out of here. These strange men came to our home and tried to kidnap us." Edith smiled innocently, but both Drakon and Scarlet just stared at her. When she saw their looks, she became confused, then realized why they were staring at her and shrugged sheepishly. "Sorry I didn't tell you before. I can speak to creatures. I don't know how but it just happened suddenly, and I could understand them."

Scarlet was surprised to hear this but not shocked in the slightest. If she had gained power and could talk to Drakon, then Edith could as well because of her own power. She was starting to learn more about this stuff.

Drakon still looked at Edith and Scarlet like he didn't know something. She only smiled, petted him one last time and stood up to scope their surroundings for anyone. Drakon didn't know that Edith was a sorceress.

As Scarlet searched their surroundings, she didn't notice the face in the trees until the figure landed right next to her out of nowhere. Everyone but Drakon jumped in fright until they saw who it was.

"Hey, guys. What's goin' on?" Luke said with a silly grin.

"What are you doing here? Shouldn't you be at school or something?" Scarlet asked, trying to get over the scare.

"Nah, Scar, ain't goin' today." Luke shrugged, looked at everyone's faces and frowned. "But seriously. What is goin' on here? Why is your little sis' with you? Did something bad happen at your hou-"

"Luke, we are in trouble," Scarlet interrupted. "The Ixaemithian Guards are after us and we need to get out of here. We are no longer safe."

"Why?"

"Because we hold more power than they do and now we are supposedly a 'threat' to the king."

Luke's face turned grim and set his hand on her shoulder. "Then I'm comin' with you."

"What? No! You can't! What if you get hurt? Your family will lose you!"

"C'mon, Scar. You think I'ma just leave you and worry about you getting killed? I would be stuck here and never know what would happen to my friend." Luke gave her the pout she always hated. She couldn't say no.

"Fine, but you must promise me that you won't get hurt or I will kill you," she said, smirking.

Luke smirked back and held out his hand. "And you must promise me the same exact thing."

"Deal." Scarlet took his hand, shook it and packed all the belongings she brought out here with her. It wasn't much; all she had were her bow and arrows, along with her sword, and the rope she used to hang up meat. When done she grabbed Edith, asked Drakon's permission and gently set her on his powerful back.

With Drakon following behind with Edith, Scarlet and Luke walked side by side into the direction that would lead them away from the village and away from danger.

7
LIAM

Liam sat at the table with a pen in one hand and a paper that the guards gave him in the other. He was nervous with them being there; he didn't even know the reason why they were there. A memory of his friend flashed into his mind. Liam didn't know what had happened to him, but Scarlet once told him that the guards like these ones had taken him away. If that were true, then he felt weird having them in his home now.

He read over the paper and his expression changed to confusion. It was hard for him to read it because his hand shook a lot, but apparently it was a contract. It stated that he would need to sign it to secure his allegiance to the king. Anything the king said he would have to do without a second thought. Why did he need this? Was everyone getting this same contract? What was different this time?

Liam debated whether or not to sign the very formal document. He felt uncomfortable because he didn't know if this was a trick, but the men loomed over him threateningly. One of them moved his hand to his side to reveal a sharp dagger and brought it to the table; right in front of him. Liam gulped.

Just when he was about to sign it, he heard the door open and Scarlet popped into view. She stumbled into one of the guards with a shocked expression on her face that turned to fear.

Without saying a word, she stepped around the guards—who watched her through squinted eyes—and went outside.

He noticed the looks on their faces when they glared after her, and they began whispering. Liam glanced around uneasily after their whisperings finally subsided and they both made their way outside where Scarlet had gone. Liam jumped from his seat to see Scarlet roughly grab Edith by the arm with a look of fierce determination on her face.

Before he knew it, Scarlet picked up Edith and ran into the woods with the two guards giving chase. Liam stood there hopelessly, wondering what was going on. He turned towards his lawn chair to see a piece of paper just barely visible underneath it. He picked it up, unfolded it, and read from beginning to end. It read:

Liam,

I don't have time to explain the situation I am currently in right now. All I can say is that Edith and I are in danger. The guards here at your house, they came for us. I can't tell you why, but I'll just say that we are "special," and we happen to have "special abilities." They hate that.

Edith told me to write you a note so you don't get too worried. We'll be fine. I'm just going to take her with me to a safe place so she won't be harmed. I don't know how long we will be but just don't worry about us. Stay safe.

Scarlet

By the end of it, he looked up in horror and peered out into the forest. He ran into the house, grabbed a dull knife from the kitchen and went back outside. He scanned the woods for anything: a sign of those guards, a sign of the girls, or just a sign of *somebody*, but he found nothing and decided to just sit on his lawn chair to keep watch. He had a feeling that he had not seen the last of those guards.

Deep in the woods of Drakonia, Liam and a boy his age wandered around in mischief. His friend had something to show him. They each trekked through the thick brush with their little legs, making them both stumble and kept going.

"'Xien," Liam said to his friend in Latin. "Where are we going…?"

His friend looked back with a smile. "Just follow me, 'Liel." They both liked to use their Boukasian names instead of their own. It was just the way they had grown up.

He took Liam by the hand and dragged him along deeper into the forest. Liam was always nervous entering this part of the woods. Even though dragons had been extinct, he still felt as if something was there with them, watching.

What felt like hours, they finally reached where his friend wanted to take Liam.

"Well? What do you think?" he asked.

There was a rundown little house among the trees where animals looked to have been living. Liam gaped and took a step closer to enter it. There wasn't much in there to see. What he did find were piles after piles of books. He picked one up and scanned the cover, which had a picture of a dragon on it with no title.

Liam turned towards his friend. "What is all this?"

He smiled. "I got these books from the village square. I want to learn more about dragons."

"You stole these? Why would you want to do that? And why learn more about dragons? They are just extinct." Liam was so confused and did not like that he had stolen these books.

His friend shrugged. "I don't like to read around people. They don't need to know about my plans."

"Plans?"

He took Liam by the shoulder and led him out of the little shack; towards the back. When they rounded the corner, he could see an upturned tree with a massive hole inside. Liam gasped. Two red eyes looked directly at him from the dark and he heard a low growl coming from inside. He turned towards his friend to see him smiling back.

Liam woke up in his lawn chair abruptly. His dream had been cut short by something. He looked all around, having that feeling of being watched, and before he knew it, someone from behind grabbed his arms and slid a dagger across his neck.

“Don’t move a muscle.”

8

Scarlet

Rain toppled onto the canopy of trees as they traveled on through the woods for a day now. When the rain had started, they found a little area to take a break and hid under Drakon's wings to stay dry. He didn't mind the rain and would do anything for his master.

During the day they had traveled, Luke wondered why Edith was with them and Scarlet had no choice but to tell him.

"Woah! The family of magicians… Ain't you guys lucky," he had said with a massive grin. Scarlet couldn't help but chuckle at him for his sarcasm. Edith, however, wasn't in a great mood for she was cold riding on Drakon's back, so Scarlet had to pick her up and carry her so she could warm up. It was a rough first day on their journey.

Now with the rain coming down in buckets, the days to come would be even worse and they had to find food in this weather. Drakon volunteered to go find prey, but Scarlet shook her head.

"You stay here and keep Edith warm. Luke and I will go hunt for a bit." Drakon began to protest but Scarlet shook her head again and grabbed her bow and arrows. She didn't know these parts of the woods that well, but she did learn fast and in minutes she already knew her way back. They also knew that they wouldn't find much in this rain, but they would still try.

"So..." Luke started to say, trying to break the silence. "How did this all happen?"

Scarlet didn't know where to begin. For the past week it all had been a jumble in her mind. She started with when she watched those people get taken away from their families and how she went mad and killed those guards. Luke raised his eyebrows in shock but didn't say anything until she was finished.

"But before Drakon killed him he basically said that I was next... and he was right. The day after I went to my house and the guards were there. That's when I took Edith with me and ran away..."

"Scar..." Luke was speechless. "I'm so sorry..." He stopped walking and wrapped his arms around her. She leaned her head against his chest and embraced the hug. For a few seconds they stayed standing there like that, but when they heard a crack next to them in a bush, they resumed hunting.

For the next few hours they hunted with the rain slowing down. The pair could only find two squirrels out of that whole time, but they did find a nearby river if they needed water. Disappointed with their meager findings, they returned to the others and Drakon made a fire with his breath.

I will find my own prey, Drakon said.

Scarlet nodded and started skinning one of the squirrels. There wasn't much to do with the fur, but she tucked it in her pocket just in case and skewered chunks of meat on sticks to cook them in the fire.

"Here," she said and handed the meat off to Edith. "You need this more than I do."

"But what 'bout you, Scar?" Luke asked with concern.

"I'm fine." Before he could protest, Scarlet stood up and left to go for a little walk to clear her mind. To be honest, she wasn't feeling that hungry at all recently. She was beyond exhausted from running away and the trouble she was in for just owning a dragon. She still had no idea how they'd found her out, but she did know that the king had allies. She just had to find out who.

As Scarlet made her way back from her short walk, the sun had set behind the clouds and she was reminded of home. She missed home already, but she had no choice and would continue till she was no longer in danger. Hopefully, that would be soon.

She couldn't help but think of how they were going to do this. She must be crazy for bringing her sister and friend on this trip. However, if she did leave Edith behind, she would be in just as much trouble as she was in. They both were a threat to the king; there was no option with her, she just didn't like having to bring Edith out in the wilderness.

Luke on the other hand wasn't in trouble at all. He was just being stubborn and would not let them go on their own even though they had a dragon with them. Scarlet, however, couldn't help but admit that it was good to have her best friend alongside them. She just hoped that nothing bad happened to him.

After her walk, which took around an hour, and after pondering her life, Scarlet walked back into their camp and saw that everyone but Drakon slept while she was gone. Her footsteps alerted the dragon of someone's presence and he quickly looked around, only to see that Scarlet had returned.

Is something wrong? Drakon asked with concern. *The little sorceress told me you were in distress.*

"Yeah, I'm fine. There's just a lot going on right now," she said and smiled at what Drakon called her sister. He only nodded and Scarlet went over to him to lie down and sleep. Drakon put his wing over her to keep her warm and she instantly fell asleep against his scales.

In the morning, Scarlet awoke on the cold, hard ground. Drakon was no longer there with her. She wasn't too worried as he always did that and so she went to wake the others.

As she picked up Edith to warm her, Drakon came flying over the trees and touched down next to them. Since last night he had grown even larger and was easily double her height.

Master, he said with a hint of worry in his voice.

"What, Drakon?" Scarlet asked. She did not want any more bad news.

North from here is the human's carriage you hate so much. I think they are headed to the village in the distance.

"Can you show me?" Drakon nodded and held out a wing for her to climb onto. "Luke, look after Edith. I'll be back." Before he could reply, she climbed up onto the dragon's back and he lifted into the sky with much force. At first, she was scared of being so high up, but once she got used to Drakon's flying, she quite enjoyed it.

From their vantagepoint high in the sky, Scarlet could see a path that meandered through the woods and saw the carriage Drakon was talking about.

"We need to stop them," she said. She knew that if the carriage reached that village then more people would be harmed. Drakon nodded and dove straight down, crushing it to pieces with the guards running for their lives. Scarlet jumped from his back and violently swung her sword at the enemy. The ones who fled didn't have a clue what was going on. Scarlet took them by surprise and easily ended their lives.

Drakon swiped his claws and bared his teeth at them, injuring three and killing five. Occasionally, fire would leak from his clenched teeth in anger and would let loose a few times on the guards. He tried getting every person that ran from them, but there were too many. They easily slipped from his grasp and Drakon roared in frustration.

"Drakon, we can't get all of them. Could you bring Luke and Edith here please?" Scarlet asked. He nodded and flew back up into the sky. Scarlet wanted to stay down there to see if she could find anything useful. All the guards had now disappeared into the woods, so she didn't bother chasing them down. She did make sure that every guard on the ground was dead and if they weren't, she would make sure they would be.

There weren't many useful things there other than food, which she was happy about, and weapons, specifically the kind of weapons only the guards use. She packed up all the goods that she could carry on her.

While she waited for them to return, she couldn't help but feel as if someone was watching her in the woods. She tried searching for people that could be near her, like those guards, but she couldn't hear or see anything. As she crept up towards the woods, a shadow passed over her from the sky and she saw that Drakon had returned with the others.

"What the hell do you think you are doing?" Luke said as he jumped off Drakon. "I went with you so I could help you. Not just to tag along so you can get hurt and I sit on the sidelines."

"What's your problem, Luke? I had Drakon with me, I wasn't going to get hurt. Do you realize that you had the most important job? I told you to look after Edith so *she* wouldn't be in danger!" Scarlet grew angry that Luke had burst out like that. She could take care of herself just fine.

He looked as if he wanted to say more but instead walked to the carriage to rummage through the supplies. Scarlet only shook her head in exasperation and went to Edith. Drakon didn't even pay attention to the whole ordeal; something had caught his attention in the woods.

As he crept up to see what was in there, Scarlet finished and wanted to leave.

"Drakon, we should leave now and head towards that village nearest to us," she said while pointing in that direction. "It'll take us at least a day to reach."

Luke, still mad at her, walked off without another word and followed the road to the village. Scarlet just shook her head, sighed and took hold of Edith's hand in hers. Drakon decided to fly instead and let them have some time alone.

"Luke!" she yelled to get his attention. She tried to catch up to him as he was walking at a fast pace. "Look, I'm sorry, okay? Next time I will try to involve you, but I just need Edith protected."

Luke stopped to turn back to her, and she could see the hardness in his eyes soften a little, but he still didn't say anything. With Drakon in the air, Scarlet, Luke and Edith trekked along the side of the small dirt road with barely anything said between them. Ever since they had left their home, Edith had grown weaker from lack of food and Scarlet began to worry for her.

When they reached an hour of traveling, Edith could no longer walk and Scarlet waved down Drakon from the sky. When he touched down on the dusty road, she picked Edith up and set her down onto him without question. He flew back into the air, only just below the treetops, and Scarlet walked alongside Luke. She wanted to talk to him.

Luke and Scarlet made small talk as they walked to the village Scarlet had seen when she was flying on Drakon. She wasn't sure just how far it was from them, but they would continue to follow the path till they reached it. She didn't know what to expect to find, or what people were like from other places.

Scarlet repeatedly apologized about what happened as they walked, trying to make him happy again, but he just shook his head and changed the subject. The sun had started to set, and they decided to set up camp for the night near the road. Once the fire had been set and everyone had eaten, Luke and Edith fell asleep, but Scarlet and Drakon remained awake. Something had been on her mind from the time they had journeyed together, and she didn't really have time to enjoy it.

"Drakon," she began. "I want to go for a ride." Other than the time she flew with him to the carriage, she really didn't have time to enjoy it.

Drakon nodded and padded to her side so she could climb up onto his back while also being careful of his spikes. Once she was on, he took off into the air with the cold wind whipping her face. It was much more beautiful to look at the setting sun as they climbed higher into the sky. Scarlet could feel the muscles in his back rippling with each flap of his long, powerful wings as they glided easily for miles. She looked below her without any fear and saw just how thick the woods were. Even with winter almost upon them, the leaves were still full and a bright red. Others remained green, making the forest beautiful.

While up in the sky, Scarlet could see forever in each direction. The way they were traveling, she could see the village in the distance. It was way bigger than Drakonia, and instead of wooden structures, everything was made of stone. To her left, all she could see were enormous mountains linked together to look like a wall of Earth. To her right, the woodlands appeared to stop abruptly, and Scarlet could only see blackness on the other side. She didn't know what to make of it, but by now she was shivering from the coldness of the winter breeze. Drakon sensed this and turned around to head back to camp.

Drakon remembered precisely where they had stopped for the night and dropped off Scarlet. She jumped off his back and decided that she would go ahead and sleep as well. Drakon folded up his wings; he too went in search to lay down and sleep.

Hours later when Scarlet woke up, it was the middle of the night and she heard a horrendous screech that sent shivers down her spine. It was pitch dark, and she could barely see anything. Luke and Edith startled awake after a roar shook the ground they were sleeping on. It was Drakon.

Just beyond their little camp, Scarlet could see flashes of light and saw something that made her skin crawl. Drakon was fighting another dragon. She went to reach for her sword, but she alighted on a pair of glowing yellow eyes staring at her from the brush. She quickly got to her feet just as a massive wolf with broad, powerful shoulders padded out into the open and began snarling. Luke took Edith by the hand and stood next to Scarlet, facing the wolf. It stopped from coming any further, and as they were about to scare the wolf off before it attacked, more wolves snuck into the open behind their leader.

When things couldn't get any worse for them, a different creature came out and Scarlet gasped. A tall figure emerged, walking on its hind legs and looked to be half human, half wolf. It had one arm as a claw with human flesh peeling around it and his opposite leg was that of the hind leg of a dog, but Scarlet couldn't stop looking at its face. One eye could be seen, and the rest of its face swelled up with thick fur. Instead of a mouth, it had a scarred dog's snout. The creature seemed to come out of a nightmare itself.

Just when another roar sounded, followed by more shaking in the ground, the wolf launched itself into the air and was on them in seconds. Luke tried to protect Edith the best he could while Scarlet drew her sword and attacked the creature. Like before, she swung the sword with all her might, but even with practice, she couldn't fight off the beast. It was quick and fierce. There were a few times where it almost knocked the sword from her hands, but she held on and swiped at its jaw. Eventually, Scarlet was able to keep it back just enough for her to join the others.

All at once the other wolves charged forward and joined in the fight. There were too many and all three of them were backing up deeper into the woods, towards Drakon. He was still fighting off the dragon and Scarlet wondered why this was happening. What she didn't see was the half human creature charge towards her on its back legs and plow her over into the undergrowth. She hit the ground hard with the wind being knocked out of her and could only lay there until she could breathe again, which she didn't have time for because that creature was coming right back again.

Luke tried to help Scarlet, but the wolves blocked his path to her and drove him and Edith in the opposite direction. He became covered in scars as the wolves took swipes at him with Edith standing behind him; frozen in fear. Drakon continued to roar in the background.

Scarlet saw the beast approaching her at a quick pace and she struggled to get up. The fall she had taken messed her back up so much that she couldn't stand up in time and the creature swiped her face with the arm that had the claw. Pain seared through her face as the blood trickled down her cheeks. She was lucky that the creature didn't get her eyes. From her place on the ground, she picked up her sword and tried to defend herself as much as she could, but she noticed that she had grown considerably weaker and didn't know how much longer this fight would take to finish.

Not long after, just when Scarlet thought that this would be the end, Drakon finally came and roared an Earth-shattering roar that made all the wolves and creatures turn tail and bolt back into the forest. Drakon was about to give chase and kill them all but then saw his master wounded on the ground. Scarlet had passed out from exhaustion and loss of blood.

9
Scarlet

Chained to the wall, Scarlet tried with all her might to break free, but it was no use. Fear rose inside her when she heard clanging throughout the chambers; the guards were coming. She tried once more to break free, but the chains were very thick and stuck fast into the wall behind her. All she wanted to do was reach Drakon and get out of there.

The door to her chamber opened to reveal the king himself with a sinister smile plastered to his face. Two guards also entered with him and came up to her. Scarlet, gagged, couldn't make a sound and tried struggling against their grip on her. She was weak from lack of food and eventually just let them take her away.

They dragged her through what seemed like miles of hallways in the castle. Her eyes remained closed, but when they entered a dark room, she opened them to see another set of chains and they locked her into those; facing her towards the wall. She slowly turned her head and saw a figure in the shadows, also chained, but her vision quickly faded when she felt incredible pain strike her back.

At first, she didn't feel it; she was too numb and tired. The second time however was even worse, and she screamed through her gag. She then realized what was happening.

Through the haze of pain, Scarlet could make out the sound of chains and shuffling in the background. She didn't pay any attention to it. Her eyes lit up with power as her pupils turned a shade of royal blue. Again, she was weak and couldn't use any of her magic to save her. She hung her head in defeat and let them do their thing as she heard the king's harsh laughter ring through her ears.

Scarlet slowly opened her eyes to bright sunlight and felt something around her mouth. Her heart quickened and she scrambled to her feet, only to find that she wasn't chained up in a dark chamber and what she felt on her face wasn't the gag from her dream. She also realized that she could only see out of one of her eyes. She traced her hand all around her face to find that half of it had been bandaged, and that's when she felt a dull throb from the fierce scratches that the creature had left behind.

Scarlet scanned her surroundings to find herself back in their little camp and found no one in sight. The dream she'd just had unnerved her so much that each sound she heard made her jump in fear. She never had a dream that dark before, other than the dream of her father being captured, but it also didn't feel like a dream. It felt like a memory of hers, but she remembered nothing like that ever happening to her. Ever. Also, she had never seen her eyes like that before. Magic? Perhaps it was just some random nightmare. Or it could be a possibility that what Scarlet thought seemed to be crazy was in fact true. She did believe she had some sort of power in her.

Scarlet gingerly stood up and found that her back was extremely sore from the fall she had taken, and she became super dizzy. Before she fell again, she grasped a tree branch to stop her fall and let the stars fade from her vision. When her dizzy spell faded, she tried walking again and went to find the others.

It didn't take her long to find Drakon sitting on his haunches and facing away from her. She noticed that he had grown to an incredible size, almost exceeding the height of the trees themselves, and briefly wondered just how long she had been out. Drakon heard her approach from behind and stood up on all fours.

Master, he said gently. *You are finally awake.*

Scarlet stared at him in confusion. "What do you mean? How long have I been asleep?" she said; her reply muffled by the bandages.

Two days.

Scarlet gasped. "Two days? But we need to reach the nearest village!" Scarlet didn't like spending any more time here. She had wanted to reach the village as fast as possible.

Drakon nodded as if to agree with her. *But you had lost a lot of blood and we could not move you.*

"Good point." Scarlet went to go sit down next to him. "Where is Luke and Edith?"

Out hunting, he said. *Luke wanted to teach her.*

Scarlet raised her eyebrows in surprise. She was glad her sister was learning how to hunt. Scarlet didn't know how Edith would feel about killing animals for food. She got up and headed back to camp to wait for the others to return.

Before leaving, she remembered the event that had taken place and her scars on her face. "What were those things that attacked us?" Scarlet knew that some of them were wolves, but there was that half-human creature and the dragon Drakon had fought, which should have been extinct.

Siles, Drakon said. *Also known as death itself. Able to change their form into the creature they are cursed with. Infected Siles are permanently stuck between their human and creature form for all of eternity.*

"Wow..." she said with wonder. "So, they were originally... humans?"

He nodded, looking as if he wanted to say more, but then returned his gaze out into the forest.

"How do you know this?"

I could sense it from them. Us dragons are magical creatures.

Scarlet nodded and turned away, pondering this new revelation.

Not an hour later, Luke came back with his bow strung around his back and held a raccoon in one hand and a squirrel in the other. He went to go put the dead animals with the food they had stolen from the carriage. Edith shuffled behind with her head hung low. She looked exhausted.

"You're awake," Luke said. His anger had now dissipated and been replaced with a smirk. "How do you feel?"

Scarlet just shrugged and continued to stare at Edith, who didn't look happy in the slightest.

"You okay?" she asked. She crouched down to her eye level to get a better look at her. She had dark circles underneath her eyes.

She nodded slightly and looked up into Scarlet's good eye. She held out her arms and Edith collapsed in them, burying her face in her chest. She shook as Scarlet hugged her tighter and tried to calm her down.

She began by exclaiming how she felt about Scarlet getting hurt, and then about everything that was happening with them running away. Scarlet had never seen Edith like this, and she could only imagine what she was going through on the inside. Edith had never traveled outside of Drakonia in all her life.

"Hey there," Scarlet said in a soft voice, trying to stop her tears. "There's no need to cry, love. Here, let's go for a little walk." Scarlet gathered her up into her arms, sent Luke a sad look, and walked away with her. Edith couldn't stop looking at Scarlet's bandaged face and realized why Edith was so sad. She had never experienced anything like this in her whole life.

They walked for a little while with Scarlet just holding Edith and soothing her. When they came to a small clearing, Scarlet gently set her down. Edith's attention had been diverted and her tears quickly faded away. Scarlet hadn't seen it, but just a few feet away in the trees stood a deer nibbling on the grass. She stopped immediately in her tracks, careful not to spook it, but Edith seemed transfixed by the animal and slowly walked towards it.

"Edith…" she whispered. Scarlet did not like her getting that close to the deer. Edith ignored her and came upon it. It didn't move at all as the little girl approached, and set her hand gently on its side. At first, Scarlet was about to jerk Edith away from the deer, but then saw that the animal had let her come up to it. They both seemed transfixed with each other.

As Scarlet stood there watching, Edith just continued to stare at the deer. Her face changed into a frown. Eventually, she let go and the deer ran off through the trees. She turned towards Scarlet with a strange look on her face.

"Arius told me what's been happening in the woods," Edith said.

Scarlet gave her a confused look. "Who's Arius?"

"The deer. He said the Siles of the forest are seeking revenge. They sensed your power and went to kill you, but unfortunately you had your dragon with you. They had been driven from their home."

"Why would Arius tell you that? And why kill me?"

"I asked him. He willingly gave me information because he could sense I am a sorceress," she said. "The Siles had taken refuge and had been disturbing the animals who live here. So, he thought I could do something about it. Also, he didn't say why they wanted to kill you. I couldn't really understand those creatures, but I did hear one thought that seemed to run through all of their minds."

"Okay, and what's that?" Scarlet anxiously asked.

Edith looked as if she didn't want to say anything, then decided against it. "King George X."

Scarlet furrowed her brow. "I don't get it."

Edith hesitated again. "I don't know. The king has control over the Siles. If they wanted to kill you then…" She didn't finish her sentence. The two didn't know for sure, but it sounded like the king had both the guards and the Siles after her now.

Scarlet grew silent. Of course, that was likely the case here. It seemed as if he really was out to get her and will not let her escape.

"Scarlet... are you okay?"

She didn't reply. Instead, she decided that their walk would be over. She needed to speak with someone immediately. Scarlet picked up Edith and rushed back to their temporary camp.

It didn't take long to return with her running at full speed. Everything was flooding her mind and she had this faraway look on her face as she placed Edith back on the ground. She snapped out of it when she saw Drakon and Luke packing up.

"Hey, Scar," Luke said. "We are ready to go whenever you are."

Scarlet nodded, but she was too distracted and went up to Drakon. "I need to talk to you."

He nodded and indicated with his head for her to hop on. They took off and Scarlet immediately launched into her questions.

"Why do the Siles want to kill me? How come they were driven from their homes? What do they have to do with King George X?" Scarlet knew that Drakon would perhaps not know any of this, but she had to make sure her suspicions were correct.

Drakon remained silent for a few moments. *I'm not sure*, he said after a while of just flapping his wings in silence. *I don't know why you think they want to kill you, but I do know why King George is involved.*

Scarlet raised her eyebrows in shock and waited for him to reveal more.

Drakon, who looked hesitant to continue, went on anyways. *You saw the dragon I was fighting, right?* Scarlet nodded. *Well... I can sense when other dragons are near and who their masters are. It so happened to be that he is the king's personal dragon servant named Fryvis. I couldn't tell you why they attacked us...*

Scarlet thought about that for a second. "Why didn't you tell me about this before?"

Drakon bowed his head in shame. *Forgive me, master. I wasn't sure how you would react.*

"Aw, you're alright, big guy," she said with a little smirk. She was happy about the little information he could give, and even though she was just figuring out the Siles, she was learning more and more about the king himself.

When Drakon circled back, Scarlet had one more question. "What do animal's names mean to you guys?" She wondered when Edith said the deer's name was Arius and Drakon calling the king's dragon Fryvis. She wanted to know if perhaps their names meant something different to them.

Every creature's name has a meaning that belongs to them. Fryvis means "Champion of the skies," he said with bitterness.

"And what does yours mean?"

Drakon looked back at her and tilted his head. *You named me. My name simply means "The Young Dragon."*

"Oh," she said. She wished she had known there was something to this, but Drakon didn't seem to mind. He turned his head back around and eventually descended into the trees. Luke and Edith were still there talking. Scarlet hopped off and walked towards them.

"Okay, now I'm ready to go."

They finished packing up and when they were done, Scarlet and Luke stayed on the ground as Edith and Drakon took to the sky. There was no more tension between them as they walked along now. What she couldn't stand is the bandages on her face and she began tearing them off.

"Hey, what you doin'?" Luke said with concern. He tried stopping her, but she pulled away and unraveled it all.

"I can't stand it. How does it look?"

Luke smirked a little. "Like you stumbled face first into a briar patch."

"Shut it," she sneered playfully and slapped him lightly on the shoulder. Luke chuckled and they resumed walking alongside the road.

It didn't take long for Drakon to reach the village first, and soon afterwards Scarlet and Luke eventually made it as well. The village was surrounded by towering cobblestone walls with a thick wooden gate as the entrance. It remained open as the villagers walked freely from inside and outside the sprawling community.

"Alright," Scarlet started. "Let's stay here for a few days. Then we'll continue on our journey."

"Where actually are we going?" Luke asked.

Scarlet realized that she didn't tell them what her real plan was. She didn't want to tell them just yet because it would be too risky, and they would not approve. What she really wanted to do was get to the kingdom and *see* the king herself. He sent guards after them, and possibly the Siles, and she wanted revenge.

Instead of answering, Scarlet just shrugged and led them down to the entrance, but then remembered something else.

"Drakon, you won't be able to come with us. Will you be okay here…?" Scarlet didn't like the idea of leaving him behind, but they also couldn't take him with them.

Drakon nodded and gave them permission to go without him. Scarlet, Luke, and Edith all left the cover of the forest and walked onto the footpath. Not many people were out here, but when they entered the village, they were swarmed by many and Scarlet tried not to lose the others.

Scarlet scooped Edith up, nudged Luke with her shoulder, and led them over to the building with a sign that said "Argonian Inn." They must be in Argonia. When they entered, there were less people in there, yet it was still crowded. As Luke went to go rent a room for them, Scarlet and Edith walked over to a little table in the corner and waited to order food, and for Luke to come back.

Luke came and they ate in silence. Scarlet had noticed that when they first walked in, most people had turned to look at them with squinted eyes. Now, they turned back to what they had been doing before and from time to time would occasionally steal glances their way. Scarlet could tell that they knew the three of them weren't from around there.

Once finished eating, Luke led Edith and Scarlet to the room where they would be staying. This room was much better than the rooms at the inn in Drakonia. Edith squealed and ran inside to wash up while Scarlet just flopped down onto her bed with a heavy sigh. She didn't care about anything else that was going on. Once her head hit the pillow, she went right to sleep.

10
Scarlet

When morning came, they all woke up around the same time and decided to go out and explore a little. First, Scarlet wanted Luke to go see Drakon before they did any exploring and see if he was okay. She also told Edith to go along with him so Luke could communicate with Drakon.

"What about you?" he said in confusion.

"I want to check something," Scarlet replied. She wanted to see the village on her own and try to find more information. Luke gave her a suspicious look, but Edith pulled on his arm to hurry and they left to see Drakon.

Scarlet followed close behind and once they left the inn, she went in the opposite direction. Like yesterday, there were many people out and about, so Scarlet decided to stick to the side and try to avoid people as much as possible. Argonia was almost like Drakonia, with all the little shops and the village square, but she could tell that this village was huge and very popular. She couldn't imagine why people wanted to stay here.

As Scarlet walked, she came upon a huge library where she saw people walking out of and entering to see aisles of books. It somewhat reminded her of her old home where they used to have shelves of books that her father would read all the time. He'd sit by the fire that he would make in their fireplace, reach for a random book, and read for hours on end. It didn't matter what it was about; he would read just about anything. Scarlet's eyes grew misty at the memory of her father, so she pushed it aside and continued.

She scanned the books around her and tried to find anything that might help her. Scarlet wasn't exactly sure what she was looking for, but one thing she did know was that she could learn more about dragons. She went in search for the section of the library on dragons to see what she could find out. However, when she came upon the "D" section, she stopped her search and saw a boy her age rummaging through the books. She didn't know why, but something about him had caught her attention; she could feel it from deep inside her.

As if sensing her staring at him, the boy startled and turned to look towards her, which made her gasp at what she saw. The lighting in there was dim, but just enough to let her see his eyes. He had huge, black irises and she could not see the whites of the eyes.

The boy stood there, frozen in the middle of the aisle, pondering whether to run. Just when Scarlet was about to say something to him, he took the book he was holding and bolted for the door. Scarlet wanted to find out more.

"Wait! Come back!"

Edith held onto Luke's arm as they left the inn and headed towards the entrance to the village. He could tell that she was afraid of being swept away from him and into the crowd. As they approached the entrance, Argonian guards lined the side every couple of yards against the cobblestone wall up to the big doors. Luke had noticed them yesterday but didn't think much of them till now. They must be overprotective here because even in Drakonia, there had never been this many guards to protect them.

As they left, they avoided the guards' stares and started over to the spot where they had left Drakon the night before. They didn't find him there, but there were giant claw marks on the forest floor and they assumed that Drakon had gone somewhere to feast on prey. Luke began to look for him.

"Drakon! Where are you?" he said just below a shout. He didn't want people to hear them; they were too close to the village. Edith and Luke heard nothing but the rustling of the trees in the wind. They ventured farther with Edith remaining silent by his side, focusing intently on finding Drakon, but they could not find him.

After what seemed like forever, Edith grabbed Luke by the wrist.

"Wait," she said. "I hear something." Edith dragged Luke along in a different direction and saw Drakon, who had grown even more overnight. Immediately they could tell something was wrong. He was covered in deep gashes from what seemed like a battle, and these wounds were fresh.

Drakon growled low and long but Luke didn't know what he was doing. It seemed that Drakon was communicating with Edith and she could understand. It was like that for him when Luke heard Scarlet speaking to Drakon. As Luke looked on, her face changed from happy to worrisome.

Finally, she slowly turned towards Luke. "They're coming."

"Who's coming?" Luke asked.

Edith didn't speak for a long time, and when she was just about to, they all heard loud rustling coming from deeper into the woods. Drakon reared up and growled, this time much fiercer. Luke peered around him to see smoke billowing from a distance through the trees. At first Luke didn't know what everyone was so worried about, then as he looked on even more with Drakon growing restless and Edith beginning to pace, he saw flickers of light coming from that direction.

"It's the bad people," Edith said in worry. "Drakon got badly hurt. They're setting this part of the forest on fire!"

Luke raised his eyebrows in alarm and sure enough he could hear the crackle of the fire along with shouts from the guards.

They had to get out of there. Without warning, Drakon charged forward into the trees to attack yet again. Luke turned to Edith.

"Edith, you need to get out of here. Go find Scarlet and tell her that we need to leave. Now."

Edith nodded and without another word, she ran back to the village. Luke turned back to see Drakon already amid battle and ran to join him. When he drew closer to the smoke, Luke took out his knife to defend himself against the guards. He couldn't see much through the smoke, and his lungs seared with each breath he took, but he continued to try to search for someone to fight.

To his left, Drakon was barely visible in the smoke, roaring at the enemy, and just when he turned around, a hulking body slammed right into him. He hit the ground hard with the wind knocked out of him and he quickly got back onto his feet just in time to block an attack from a spear. With the knife still in his hand, he freed himself from the man and whipped his arm around to sink the knife into his gut. Luke pulled the knife back out while the man staggered and clutched at his bleeding stomach, yet he did not fall. He charged forward, making Luke dodge his next attack and landed into another man's grasp.

Luke tried to do the same with this guard, but this one was way faster and soon Luke was being prodded at all sides by the spear. He tried defending himself with his knife, but it appeared to be useless. The guard swung the spear at him, catching it in the face, and as he covered his wound in pain, the guard he had stabbed returned.

As Luke struggled with the two men, Drakon rushed forward and knocked down several guards into the flames. The fire licked at his scales, yet it had no effect on him as he weaved his way around the trees and breathed more fire into the midst to completely ward off the enemy. Once they were distracted, Drakon flew over to aid Luke and flung him onto his back to fly to safety.

Edith ran from Luke and Drakon with the crackling of flames filling the forest, but really all she could hear were the voices inside her head. This started a while ago; when they first began their little journey. At times she could rarely hear these voices—unless there was silence—while other times they were so loud that she could barely hear anything else around her. This was one of those times. The forest was waking up.

She could never make out what any of them were saying, and she was too worried about telling Scarlet. Edith did not want her sister to see her as a crazy sorceress, so she blocked all of that from her mind and continued through the forest to warn Scarlet.

It didn't take her long to exit the woods, and when she burst out of the forest, there was no one to be seen. She ran for the gate, down the street, and hit head on into a person and fell flat on her back.

"Oh!" the person Edith hit exclaimed. He turned around to look at her but froze when he saw her face. Same could be said with Edith when she saw his eyes. Large, deep irises stared back into hers from the face of a boy about Scarlet's age. His face transformed from casual to fear in a matter of seconds and he ran in the opposite direction of her, all the while pushing away someone else as well. It was Scarlet.

"No! Stop!"

11
Scarlet

Scarlet entered the now somewhat empty streets of the village. Just down the road ran the boy she was chasing.

"Oh man…" she whispered to herself as she watched the speed at which he was running. With trepidation, she gave chase, then soon lost him around the many twists and turns in between building after building. Instead of trying to follow him, she decided to hurry back and head to the village gate to block him from escaping. She knew that the boy may not leave—or maybe he will—she just had to try and catch him.

Scarlet didn't know why but something about him intrigued her. His eyes were very strange, and she just had to find out who or what he was. What she did notice was the little amount of people that were out and about; they seemed to be unfazed by him.

After retracing her steps, she came back out into the streets and headed towards the entrance. Sure enough, just as she drew closer to the gate, he popped out of nowhere and started slowing down after seeing that he was no longer being chased. To prevent her from being seen, she quickly hid off to the side all the while maintaining her hurried pace.

As he came closer to the gate, he passed by one more building and that's when she made her move. She quickly stepped into view, wrapped her arms around him, covered his mouth, and forced him away from the gate and from the prying eyes of the Argonian guards. As Scarlet dragged him away, he began kicking at her legs and made every attempt to break free and cry for help.

When they were far enough away, Scarlet let go of his mouth, but not his arms.

"Wait. Just listen to me. I'm not trying to hurt you. I just want to talk."

The boy looked as if he was about to yell, then pursed his lips and nodded.

"Okay… good. You're a Sile aren't you?" She didn't know what made her ask that other than the fact of his eyes.

The boy did not move, and his face relaxed a little. "And you're that girl with the dragon," he added with a thick accent.

She raised her eyebrows in surprise and let him go. He didn't run but instead grinned from ear to ear.

"You're famous among us creatures. In fact, there's an award for your head."

"Why?" Scarlet's heart skipped a beat when she heard this.

Instead of answering, he put out his hand for her to shake. "I'm Jay."

She looked down at his hand with contempt. "You threaten me and now you want me to shake your hand?"

Jay pulled his hand back sharply with a hurt expression on his face. "That was no threat. I was merely letting you know. I'm not like most Siles you know."

"Then answer me. Why?"

Jay sighed reluctantly. "I could get in a lot of trouble."

"Nothing new I see."

Scarlet's statement confused him, but he kept going. "Don't you know though? You must know that owning a dragon is against the law of the kingdom. The king doesn't want you guys in his world. Dragons hold incredible power."

This was nothing new to Scarlet. This was all she was getting from people, yet one thing wasn't right to her. They would continue their journey to the kingdom.

Jay smiled and put his hand out once more. "Let's try again. Hi, I'm Jay."

"Scarlet." This time she shook his hand with some hesitance. She still didn't fully trust him.

"You gave me quite a scare back there. If I had not known that you were the dragon girl, I would've decked you. You know, you and I have a lot in common. I'm being hunted down just like you."

"Why? Aren't you a Sile? Why would they hunt you down?"

Before he could answer, someone hit him full on from behind and fell onto the street. Jay turned around and glanced at her, but one look into her eyes and he freaked. He immediately turned around and pushed Scarlet over.

"No! Stop!" Scarlet wasn't done talking to him. However, when she saw the person on the ground she gasped. "Edith? What are you doing here? Where's Luke?"

Edith had a sort of stricken look on her face that worried her. "We're being followed. Luke stayed back to help Drakon fend them off."

"Oh no...." Scarlet grabbed Edith by the wrist and left the village. She was stunned by the amount of people that came running and screaming from the direction of the woods. Just when Scarlet began to wonder, Drakon burst out of the forest with Luke riding on his back, roaring fiercely, and right behind them came a horde of guards flooding in and trying to spear him down. Scarlet picked up Edith, ran as fast as she could to Drakon, and grabbed ahold of his scales on his leg as he flew over her. He lifted unexpectedly and Scarlet almost jolted off and back to the ground. She held on even tighter and they were off, leaving every guard on the ground.

Fear coursed through Scarlet whenever she looked down and thought of falling. Edith was even more afraid than she was, so Scarlet kept her composure and held on to her tight. Occasionally she would look behind her and see a blur following them, but she didn't think much of it as the thought of falling clouded her judgement.

Eventually, the village blinked out of view with Scarlet and Edith still dangling from Drakon's legs. When they were far enough away from the angry guards, they finally landed in a different part of the woods with Drakon panting. Scarlet realized that even though he had grown incredibly in the past week, he was still a baby and carrying all three of them had put quite a strain on his wings. Feeling bad, she walked over to Drakon, told him to rest, then walked over to Luke. Edith was already with him and Scarlet saw that he was injured.

"Luke…"

He looked up at the mention of his name and smiled. His face had been scratched up and his left eye oozed blood from a cut. His hands were also bloodied and one of his fingers bent at an odd angle. Every injury on him looked painful. "Hey Scar…."

"What happened to you guys?"

"Try fightin' two hulking masses at the same time while your best friend's dragon burned everyone else to a crisp…" There was amusement in his voice as well as pain as Edith checked his finger. He tried to pull it away, but Edith gripped his wrist harder and snapped his finger back into place.

"AGH! How the hell is she doin' this??"

Scarlet and Edith smirked at each other. "Our mother used to teach us about healing and medicines. It's what she did for a hobby," Scarlet said. Again, just thinking about her parents brought tears to her eyes, so she bent down to help take her mind off it. Edith handed her some bandages that were left over and began to clean his eye. When she lifted his eyelid, the sight of it startled her. The whites of his eyes had taken a red shade from the blood, but that's not what concerned her. Just above his bottom eyelid, right on his eye, a large cut just barely perked into view. A lot of damage had already been done to it.

"Luke... can you see out of this eye?" Edith asked.

Luke didn't say anything and looked between Edith and Scarlet. Scarlet gasped and Edith squinted at him. "Just what I expected." His left eye did not move at all with his other. It was like the eye was dead.

"What? What's happening! What's wrong with my eye?!" Luke started to get frustrated when both didn't answer. Scarlet didn't know *what* to say that could put him at ease. All she knew was that he would never be able to see out of that eye again.

Scarlet couldn't bear to look at him, and so decided to let Edith tell him the news. She walked back to Drakon—sadness and guilt filling her chest for bringing them along—and looked out through the trees. She saw a bird just sitting there on a log, staring at her. Something about the bird seemed to weird her out and its eyes looked... familiar.

"Wait. Jay?"

The bird that Scarlet was staring at was a blue jay, and what happened next baffled her. It flew straight to the ground, blinding Scarlet with a bright light, and a person then stood in front of her. Jay smirked back at her. "Hey, what's up?"

Scarlet couldn't say anything. She was surprised to see him there. Drakon heard what happened and immediately bounded to his master's side.

"Woah there," Jay said with his hands up. "Don't worry, I'm good. Not evil."

You're a Sile, Drakon said with a growl.

"Uh, what?"

"He says you're a Sile," Scarlet translated.

"Yeah... but I'm not like them, remember? Like I said, I'm being hunted just like you guys. Wow, this is such a strange group. A dragon, Dragon Master, sorceress, and a human."

"How do you know what I am?" Edith asked.

Instead of answering, he began begging. "Oh, please let me come with you! If you're traveling, then I want to travel with you! It would be so much better than being hunted on my own. I can help you fight them! Plus," he added with smugness. "You would barely know that I was there. No Sile can talk in their form."

"I don't know..." Scarlet was unsure about him still. He was supposedly the same creature that wanted her dead and they had only met today.

"Maybe he should," Edith said. "I believe he's telling the truth."

"Oh yeah? How do ya know," Luke said from a distance. He was still sitting in the same spot with his eye bandaged up. He seemed to calm down the tiniest bit after learning that he was blind in one eye.

"I just do." Edith had that strange look on her face like she had sometimes when she used her powers. Perhaps it had something to do with her sorceress skills.

Scarlet hesitated, then sighed. "Alright... he can come with us."

Jay smiled, turned back to a blue jay, and flew over to Edith's shoulder, making her laugh. Scarlet smiled and they all settled down for the night.

12

ALEXANDER

After years of being held captive, Alexander was dragged from his cell every day to do a daily job for the king. This time he was to report to the king's own throne room to be his *personal slave.* He was disgusted at what his life became and wondered if he would ever leave this hell hole.

They dragged him through the same halls he had memorized for the past years of being trapped there. The castle would be a wonderful sight to behold if he weren't a prisoner there. It made him miss his childhood friend, and his family, even more.

Alex and the guards made it to the room where most of his nightmares originated. Right there in front of him sat the king with no expression on his face. The guards unchained him and left the two alone. Alex just stood there waiting for his orders.

"Your first order of business is to clean my windows. I can hardly see out of them these days."

Alex didn't say a word when he detected the smugness in his tone and went to pick up a rag. He wasn't thinking straight, so without realizing it, he sent a withering look towards the king that he would soon regret. King George quickly stood up, making Alex flinch and wait for the beating, but it never came. A knock on the door stopped the king in his tracks and he went to go answer it, which relieved Alex immensely and he managed to slip away to do his job.

As he worked on the windows, a group of men came in, followed by their leader that happened to be part wolf and part human. Alex learned a lot about these creatures back in his village. They were Siles and the leader was infected.

“Gentledogs,” the king said with a smirk. “Any news regarding those… escapees?”

The group of men looked at each other—not liking the king’s joke but having no other choice about what he said—and the man next to the leader stepped forward.

“Your Highness, Roue has the dragon girl’s blood in his possession. Unfortunately, he and Fryvis could not stop them from escaping. The dragon you told us about has seemed to grow incredibly large in only a matter of days. Even Vixen, our dragon Sile, hadn’t grown like that.”

“No, he wouldn’t have. Dragons are powerful beasts and your friend there is a Sile. Two different creatures. It doesn’t matter if Vixen has dragon blood in him, it is completely different. Fryvis on the other hand is a real dragon. He has grown to full adulthood in a matter of weeks.”

The speaker nodded and stepped back into the group. The king turned towards the leader. “Roue, the blood I presume is where I told you to put it?”

Roue nodded and growled something to his comrades. Throughout the whole conversation, Alex had paused in his work and stood there eavesdropping. Hearing that an actual dragon had been born and someone like him was out there gave him a surge of hope for the future. He wondered who it was.

“Good. Now, there is business I need to attend to. If you don’t mind,” the king said, motioning them to leave.

The Siles turned around without another word and left the room. The king approached Alex, who had started to clean the window again, and stopped inches away from him.

"Come with me," he said. Without waiting for a reply, he turned around and left the room. Alex looked around him, wondering whether he should try and escape, but then realized that he wasn't strong enough and if he dared to try, he would not get far. He'd be captured yet again and possibly killed. He sighed and reluctantly followed him.

King George led him through a series of hallways he had never seen before, and eventually made it outside into the garden. Alex gave him a suspicious look, wondering why they were here, but the king paid him no attention. People that passed by them would immediately stop, bow, and continue. It made Alex gag at just how much respect the king received.

They walked through the garden and onto the other side of the castle. This must have been where the other cells were located. They stopped at a door with two guards in place and when they saw the king approach, they snapped to attention and opened the door. Inside it was all dingy and musty; Alex scrunched up his nose at the smell of mold and rotting flesh. Smelled worse than his own cell.

"People who are stuck here have committed serious crimes. More serious than yours surprisingly. I just need to have a little discussion with one of them and you can go back to doing your job."

Swell, he thought to himself. As they passed by many of the cells, the prisoners looked up and begged to be let out. It was hard for him to watch all those people and not be able to do a thing about it. When he was out of here, he swore to kill the king himself and free all these people.

Finally, they stopped at one specific cell that couldn't be seen through and had metal, bolted hinges. Alex wondered who in there could be so dangerous. He opened the door and inside were two people; a girl that looked to be about eighteen years of age, and a man who hid his face from view, making it hard for Alex to determine his age.

"Darling, I have one question to ask you," the king said. The girl lurched forward but was held back by a chain around her neck, and her eyes flashed with fiery rage. Literally. Alex gasped when he saw her eyes change from pitch black to a bright orange in seconds. The king didn't even flinch.

"Why would I do anything for you? You were the one who put me in this awful place," she snarled.

The king sighed. "Do you want me to kill that girl for you or not?"

She froze and the anger left her eyes. Alex grew confused.

"Darling, I would like you to help me with something."

"Okay… and what is that *Your Highness*?" she replied sarcastically.

He smiled. "If you want me to take care of the one who turned you, then I need your full allegiance to the kingdom. I have all Siles at my disposal and you would make a great addition. How would you like to come and join my ranks? I can guarantee your freedom if you choose to accept."

She sneered, but Alex was no longer listening. He became distracted by the man next to her. Alex made sure the king wasn't paying attention and crouched down next to the man. He had turned his head a little to see what was going on and his eyes alighted onto Alex's face with recognition.

"Who are you?" Alex whispered.

The man turned more towards him and tried to talk, but his voice was completely lost. Obviously, the man knew of him, but Alex had no idea who he was.

"Well, well, well. Looks like you two have finally met again."

Alex lifted his head up sharply to find the king staring at them with a grin. It seemed the two were done conversing, leaving the girl even more agitated than before. The king didn't seem to mind.

"Let's go. We're leaving." He left, followed closely behind by Alex, and he didn't look back. As the door locked, the man in the chains was left behind with a tear in his eye.

13
Scarlet

After a restless night of paranoia, Scarlet and the gang continued their journey. It had been a day and a half since they fled Argonia and since they found Jay. She wasn't happy about bringing him along; he happened to be the same type of creature as those who had attacked them just a few nights beforehand, but Edith insisted that he wasn't lying about being good. Scarlet didn't understand how her sister would know this, but she trusted her, and so Edith kept Jay on her shoulder as they trekked along.

The distance they had traveled on Drakon had cleared most of the forest and the trees thinned out, only to reveal ice-capped mountains. Luke and Edith both groaned when they saw that these mountains went on for what seemed like forever and Scarlet sighed loudly.

"Alright... so there are mountains blocking our path," she stated to the others. "Maybe Drakon can fly over and see how thick the mountains are to see if we can manage to climb over them?"

Drakon nodded and flew up and over the mountains. While they waited for him to come back Scarlet began planning with the others.

"Only two people can ride on Drakon's back. If the mountains are too treacherous to pass, then we need him to transport us over and onto the other side. Edith and Luke, I want you two to go first."

"What? Why?" Luke said in irritation. He no longer had the bandage on his eye, but after traveling for a couple of days, a milky white sheen had covered it. He was upset and was still getting used to it. "I can't just leave you here on the ground alone, there are guards on our tail!"

Scarlet just shook her head. "Luke, please do this for me. I can't have Edith on her own; it's dangerous out here. Plus, I won't be alone. I'm keeping Jay here with me."

"Oh, that's even better..." Luke replied. He looked as if he wanted to argue with her, but everyone's attention had been diverted to Jay as he lifted off from Edith's shoulder and flew the short distance to the base of the mountains. When he descended, Scarlet saw him fly and perch onto a rickety sign that she could've sworn wasn't there before. They ran to him and got a better look at the sign. It read:

GVIY JA OCZ YZVY
E - z
WZRVMZ OCZ BCJPGN VIY OCZ IZXMJHVIXZM
OCZ KVOC TJP OMVQZG DN V YVIBZMJPN JIZ
OPMS WVXF IJR

"What the hell is this??" Luke exclaimed. "This is nothin' but gibberish!"

Jay shook his little bird head and flew to the ground where he could shift easily back into human. "It's code."

"Code for what?" Scarlet asked.

Jay shrugged. "Dunno, but I've only seen it as a code for creatures. You know, like Drakon and I."

"Well, whose code is this one?"

"I don't know... There is a total of twenty-five codes. Mine, the Siles, is number one."

As Jay spoke, Scarlet turned back to the sign to see it glowing slightly blue. She crouched down to see the letters fizz out and reappear in a different spot. Finally, they all stopped moving and she read a completely different thing.

"'Land of the dead,'" she read aloud. The others had already stopped talking and froze when they saw her face. "'Beware the ghouls and the necromancer. The path you travel is a dangerous one. Turn back now.'"

"Scar... your eyes," Luke said in dismay.

"What about em'?"

"They just turned blue..." Edith said. Even Jay seemed concerned.

At their words, Scarlet froze, and chills ran down her spine. Just like what she saw in her dream! She didn't know what to say and everyone was looking at her with suspicion. Just when Luke was about to say something else, Drakon came back down from the sky, distracting them and giving her relief from their stares.

The mountains are not as thick as it may seem. Drakon said. *I'll be able to take two of you at a time, but I don't think we should stay here for too long. Those guards could be upon us in minutes.*

"Drakon's right," Scarlet said. "Luke and Edith will go with Drakon, and Jay and I will start heading through the mountains. Once you guys are safe on the other side, Drakon will come back, find us in the mountains and bring us the rest of the way. Okay?"

Everyone nodded and Luke and Edith hopped onto his back. Edith seemed to forget about the mystery of Scarlet's eyes, but Luke on the other hand still wanted to say something. He didn't get a chance as Drakon took off into the air. However, Jay was right there and asked, "Do you have magic...?"

Scarlet sighed. "I don't know anymore... All of this stuff is just getting to me and making things even more confusing."

Jay gave a little smile and glanced down at her sword to see it glowing. "Can I see that?"

Scarlet looked down, pulled out her sword, and held it up for him. "It's been glowing for a while now. Nothing special."

Jay gasped. "You're from Drakonia aren't you?"

"Y-yes," she stammered, confused. "Why?"

"That's the Drakonian blade. You do hold magic! That jewel

there in the blade is The Royal Jewel of Drac. This jewel was created by the sorcerer Drac. Before he had passed, he, along with other sorcerers and sorceresses, had instilled most of their magic into this Earth and the creatures who reside here… That includes dragons. The jewels were made by him, the actual blades were created by other powerful beings. I don't actually know who but…"

Scarlet looked at her sword with newfound surprise. "What? Really?"

Jay nodded. "It's why the king wants to behead people with power and made the dragons go extinct. Since they are magical beings, they can give their masters power, but when a dragon is killed, their master's magic dies with them. That would never happen to you though. Even if they kill Drakon that sword you possess will always give you magic."

Scarlet wondered how he knew so much, but then remembered that he was a Sile—a magical creature himself. One thing was bugging her, and she needed to ask it. "What if I lose this sword?"

Jay shook his head. "You've touched the jewel. Once it glows you will always be its true master. Nobody else can take that away from you." Then he added nonchalantly, "Well, unless you're killed of course."

"Well, that's nice." Aside from that last part, Scarlet smiled, and excitement stirred in the pit of her stomach. It quickly changed to fear as they both whipped their heads around in the direction of pounding footsteps coming from the woods.

"Oh no, they're coming." Scarlet grabbed Jay by the hand and they began their trek up the mountain; all the while forgetting about the warning from the old sign.

At first the mountain inclined gradually, making it an easy climb, but when they rose above tree level, it became much steeper to climb and snow blanketed the ground. They had nothing warm enough to get them through this hike except the clothes on their backs, so they were shivering. Jay went into bird form to see if he could warm up and travel a farther distance, but that didn't work as the wind kept blowing him away at fierce speeds, so he stayed on the ground.

Scarlet looked down and could see nothing except trees, so when they made it to the top of the ridge they were on, they took a mini break and huddled together to stay warm.

"Maybe we should stay here and wait for Drakon..." she said through clenched teeth.

"No way. The guards are still coming. We need to keep moving."

Scarlet hesitated, then nodded and continued up, but they realized that it was just flatland for miles.

"We must be in a ravine," Jay said. "Look."

Scarlet looked up to where he was pointing and saw the mountains rising on either side of them.

"Let's stay in this ravine for a bit so the wind can be blocked, and we can save our strength," Scarlet said and Jay, even nervous about those guards approaching, agreed. It was just too cold for him.

The snow grew thicker as they ventured further into the ravine. Scarlet couldn't stand the cold anymore and her fingers and toes went completely numb. Jay seemed to be doing a bit better than her, but his cheeks were rosy red, and his lips turned a shade of blue. If Drakon didn't come by soon they were both going to freeze to death.

Ten minutes passed and they finally reached the end of the ravine, showing a very large cave entrance, and Scarlet was tempted at the sight of it.

"Let's stop here," she said.

"I don't know..." Jay seemed hesitant to enter the cave.

"Oh, come on. We can warm up in there. Plus, maybe the guards will pass this cave."

"Yeah, but what about Drakon?"

Scarlet only shrugged and ran into the cave with Jay

reluctantly following. Something was tugging at Scarlet to enter and she couldn't help herself.

In the cave, there were stalagmites of ice hanging from the ceiling and pools of water on the floor. It was still cold in there but at the same time a lot warmer than outside. They moved deeper into the cave and settled down for a bit.

While Jay tried to get dry, Scarlet examined the cave from her spot on the ground and noticed strange markings on the sides.

"What's this?" she asked. Before Jay could respond, Scarlet hopped up and walked over to get a better view. They looked like chicken scratch to her, but a little over to the right of her was a code. It appeared to be exactly like the one on the sign. It read:

E - z
GJYPGPN OCZ HPOZ
XVQZ JA YZVOC
333 333

Before Scarlet could translate the words, a loud bang came from the back of the cave, startling both of them. She drew her sword out and crept closer to the sound. Slowly, a green light made its way into view and fear leapt into her heart. A dark figure with little green flames flickered around it and made its way out from the darkness. When he lifted his arm, a bony hand revealed itself from a black cloak and Scarlet and Jay screamed in terror.

14
Luke

Throughout the whole trip over the mountain, Drakon, Edith, and Luke were blasted by strong gusts of wind that knocked them back and forth in the air. It had seemed like forever, but they finally made it over and Drakon dropped them off in the nearby woodlands. Right when Luke and Edith jumped off his back and onto the ground, Drakon immediately took off yet again to pick up Scarlet. Luke noticed his scales were ruffled up, and not just from the wind.

As if reading his mind, Edith nodded. "Drakon doesn't like leaving his master behind. He's gotten… irritable without Scarlet."

Luke couldn't help but feel the same way. He hated leaving her behind, especially with a Sile. The guards were hot on their tracks and Luke wanted to be there with her to fight them. It was the reason he first came on this trip. He didn't want Scarlet to get hurt, or worse.

They walked out of the woods to find a large meadow with a wide variety of flowers, and far off in the distance they spotted another village that they had seen from the sky. Edith grew excited and frolicked around in the tall grass. Luke bent over to get a better look at the flowers.

"How are these flowers still alive? It's almost winter," he asked himself. Edith only shrugged and continued to frolic towards the village. They made their way there while Edith randomly picked at the flowers she really liked and put them in her hair. She was adorable, and suddenly Luke had the strangest feeling of guilt claw at him about something happening to Scarlet's little sister. He knew that she was in as much danger as her sister, but this journey would kill just about anybody. He swore that he would protect them at the cost of his life.

Eventually they made it and the village seemed almost cozy to Luke. Not too big, not too small, just the perfect size. Even the people there seemed nice and didn't stare at them as if they were animals, like in Argonia. Edith couldn't contain her excitement and wandered around the different shops. Luke followed close behind and made sure he didn't lose sight of her.

As she ran around with the people gawking at her, Luke didn't pay attention and saw something amazing in one of the shops. On display was a unique dagger dotted with red rubies.

Luke was mesmerized by it and decided to go in and see how much it cost. By the looks of it, the dagger seemed super expensive, but when he walked inside and asked the lady how much it was, she replied that it was free. That caught him off guard. The woman's face held a strange expression, almost like fear. Luke froze for a second, as if pondering its value, but was then overtaken by the fact that it was free.

Luke told the woman that he would take it, and when he grasped its handle, a weird sensation fell upon him. Suddenly he was thrust into a new environment. Luke spun around wildly at his new surroundings; taking him by surprise. He was standing in the mountains again, but it wasn't the mountains they had just traversed. These huge cliffs rose so high into the sky that he couldn't see the top, and huge stalagmites covered every cliff in sight.

As Luke calmed down, a figure emerged from the thick snow. At first, he didn't even notice it, but when it drew closer, Luke could make out its red eyes in the white snow. He realized that the figure was a wolf. Luke had a hard time seeing it because the wolf's fur was snow white. It was the most unusual sight ever, but Luke didn't stay there for much longer.

Waking up from his daze, Luke quickly scanned his surroundings. He was back in the little shop and no one had seemed to notice his episode, except the woman, who just stood there with a relieved yet guilty look on her face.

"Blood Dagger," she said randomly. "Good one to own."

Luke looked down and an overwhelming surge of electricity coursed through his body. He *wanted* this dagger. He started to shiver uncontrollably, and his body dropped temperature in seconds.

Without another glance at the woman, he left the shop in great haste. Just outside, Edith waited for him next to the building. Luke began to warm up a little but kept the dagger in the palm of his hand.

Edith hopped up from her spot on the ground once she saw Luke and ran towards him. When she saw his face, she could tell something was wrong, and then she spotted the dagger in his hand. She went from smiling to fear to stone-faced in seconds. Luke had the dagger.

15

Scarlet

Scarlet pushed Jay out of the cave as she tried to escape whatever was trying to grab ahold of her. The hand that reached out for her looked to be an arm from a skeleton and she couldn't see its face from underneath the dark hood. Even stranger, the green fire that covered it did not seem to be burning in the slightest.

Jay screamed again. "Scarlet! You led us right into the necromancer's home!"

"Huh?" she said, confused.

"The necro's home! Remember the sign? This is his land!"

Before she could reply, the necromancer grasped her shoulder, sending horrified chills down her spine, and she shrieked. His eyes from underneath the cloak started glowing bright green and Scarlet felt searing pain scorch her shoulder but managed to pull free.

They ran out into the snow, only to find that they were trapped between the guards and the necromancer. Scarlet swore under her breath and turned back towards the cave entrance. The figure did not follow them out, but instead stopped just before exiting, raised his arms, and the ground beneath them shook. Everyone, even the guards, looked around uncertain of what was happening, and something grabbed ahold of her ankle. She looked down to see a grotesque hand clawing at her ankle.

She screamed and kicked at the hand. Apparently, the same thing was happening everywhere else because many of the guards were freaking out. Jay immediately changed and flew out of danger.

"Well thanks!" she yelled up to him. She ran away, but all around her the corpses were rising and coming for her, and they were a lot faster than she thought. There wasn't anywhere for her to run; it was either through the guards or try to climb up the cliff. There was no way she would go through the guards, that was suicide, and so she tried to climb the cliff. Two things she noticed. One, the cliff was covered in snow that had hid the ice from view. After a couple attempts at climbing up pure ice, it was impossible. Two, the guards were a lot more scared than she was. Each one tried attacking the dead with their weapons, but they were highly outnumbered and ran in the opposite direction. Another route was clear for her. However, now it wasn't necessary. Scarlet saw Drakon fly across the sky and land right on the dead. He breathed fire on them and instantly incinerated them. The necromancer was nowhere to be seen, but Scarlet wasn't paying attention to that and hopped right onto Drakon's back, escaping that horrid place.

The flight over the mountain felt short but frigid. The winter wind whipped at Scarlet as she told Drakon everything that happened. The wind was so strong at this height that it was hard trying to hang on. Drakon remained silent for most of the time, then told her where he had dropped off the others. He flew over to that spot after clearing the mountain and let Scarlet off.

I will be here until you want to leave again. I believe your friend and sorceress went to the village just outside of these woods, he said as he indicated the direction they had gone. Scarlet nodded, gave him a reassuring pat on the shoulder, and set out for the village.

When she left the woods, a blue jay landed gracefully on her shoulder, and she scoffed. "Now you come back for me."

Jay just stared at her through his little beady eyes but didn't respond. Scarlet continued with him on her shoulder and saw a small hamlet in a meadow of tall grass and flowers. The place looked comfy enough to stay at for a bit, but now Scarlet became too cautious and worried about their safety, so they would rest until night fell and continue their way. She then realized that she still hadn't told any of them about her plans. They were just following her blindly. She would have to tell them later.

The village they entered wasn't anything like Argonia. There were no guards or stone walls, and the people there seemed nice. One priority of hers was to buy a map so she could know where the kingdom was located. Jay still sat on her shoulder as she walked by many people and shops. One of them was a dagger store, and she saw Luke and Edith standing at the entrance to the shop, but something was off. Luke held a beautiful dagger in his right hand, which he continuously stared at with his face a ghostly sheen of white, and Edith stood in front of him, trying to get his attention.

"What's going on ,guys?" Scarlet asked.

Luke snapped out of his reverie but still had a vacant look in his eyes. Edith blew out a frustrated sigh. "There's something wrong with that dagger. Ever since he found it, he won't answer me, won't listen to me, and won't even *look* at me."

"That's odd," Scarlet mused.

Luke looked back down at his dagger and said in a distant voice, "I'm fine. Just need some rest..."

Scarlet grew confused by the way he was acting, but Jay caught her attention when he flew off her shoulder and onto the ground across the street. Then, when no one was looking, changed and motioned for everyone to come over.

"Scarlet, you said you wanted a map. Well, here's one," Jay said. Scarlet looked to where he was pointing and saw a huge map of Kaggaegia, where Ixaemithia resided, along with some other land called "Boukasia". This was perfect. Scarlet went in, bought the map, and looked it over.

"Okay, so Argonia is right here," she said as she pointed to its location. "And here are the Imperial Mountains, which we just went over. The village closest to them is 'Renu,' which is the one we are in now. The kingdom is way over here and the closest village to us is not for another one hundred miles." Scarlet glanced at Luke and added, "Let's stay here for one night and then continue in the morning. I'll go tell Drakon to keep watch for any guards coming, though I doubt it since they fled from the mountains."

"How come?" Jay asked.

Scarlet looked up from the map and glared. "You would know if you hadn't left me behind."

He smirked and shrugged. "Hey, if you had a means of escape, go for it."

Scarlet could just shake her head but didn't push it and soon everyone agreed with the plan. She left to go over it with Drakon while the other three went to go find a place to sleep.

Scarlet ran on weak legs through hallway after hallway, not knowing where she was, and with people running for their lives next to her. She tripped over her own legs and was knocked around by the other people, but she continued until she finally reached a huge room with a throne. She ran to the wall as fast as she could and held out her hand. A streak of violet lightning flew from her hand and struck the wall, leaving dust and debris smacking her right in the face.

Standing on the opposite side were a group of ten guards whipping around to see what the explosion was. Scarlet didn't give them a chance to react. She snapped her wrist at one and the guard closest to her burst into flame. He fled, screaming, and didn't get far before collapsing onto the ground. The other guards glanced at each other nervously, but then raised their muskets and spear-like weapons to attack Scarlet. She didn't let them get far either. Even though she was weak, everything she had learned gave her strength and she effortlessly burned each guard's hand to force them to drop their weapons. Then, with both hands, she shot out a massive fireball, sending the rest of the guards flying and hitting the wall, knocking them out.

Next, she stepped over the bodies and sent another streak of lightning towards the wall that left a hole to the main lobby. She couldn't see any more guards but there were even more people in the lobby, trying to flee. Scarlet tried to get through. It was nearly impossible when no one cared about trampling over you, so she looked behind her to find another way out. At the top of the grand stairs, there was an enormous white wolf with a black stripe running down its back. It stared at her with sharp, multicolor eyes—one black and the other a bright emerald, and long, white fangs protruding from its jaws. Before Scarlet could run, the enormous beast pounced over a flight of stairs and landed squarely on her chest; sneering right in her face.

Scarlet startled awake and sat up in her bed with wide eyes. They had rented a room from a tavern for the night to let Luke get some rest. All four of them had to share a two-bedroom room, so it had been difficult to sleep while having to share a bed with someone.

The nightmare she just had seemed to be the same as the others, though the wolf was new; she didn't know what to make of them. She didn't think much of it when she noticed that Edith was not next to her in bed. She dressed, woke the other two and headed down to the tavern to wait for them. There she found Edith talking with a woman at one of the tables. Scarlet noticed that Edith was covered in mud, especially in her hair, making it look darker than usual in certain areas.

"Hey, sis," Edith said from the table with a smile. "This is Kehlani. She could tell we were new and told me some pretty cool things. Kehlani, this is my sister, Scarlet."

Scarlet held out her hand for the woman to shake and sat down next to Edith.

"I was just telling your sister about life outside the village. Your group seems nice and I wanted to tell you about the dangers you could face by leaving this village," Kehlani said with kindness.

"Dangers?"

"Yes. I'm not sure which way you are traveling, but if you keep going through the meadows, you will come across some dangerous animals. Alas, I have even lost a daughter to them. Found her body in the thick grass with a bite mark on her wrist. Turns out she had been bitten by a very venomous snake."

Scarlet glanced at Edith uneasily. "Is there a way to avoid them?"

Kehlani had tears in her eyes as she shook her head. "Sadly, these snakes are only here, and this meadow goes very far. You may have to head to the woods near the mountains, but there's no avoiding this meadow."

Scarlet sighed. "Sorry, but we can't turn back now. I guess we'll just have to be careful."

Kehlani nodded and wished them good luck. Around this time Luke and Jay came and sat down with them, with Scarlet eyeing both of their bed heads. Luke seemed to look a little better, but he still had that vacant look in his eyes, and whenever Edith glanced at him, her smile slipped with her face showing no emotion at all.

16
Alexander

A few days after the Siles had come to visit the king, Alex was removed from his cell once again. This time the guards brought him in the opposite direction of where he usually went, and they entered a different set of hallways he had never been in before. After years of doing this, he had lost hope for ever escaping this wretched place, and during these moments he would think almost exclusively about his family.

So much had happened to him in his life and sometimes he couldn't stop thinking about his wife. An image of her pushed its way to the forefront of his mind and tears sprang to his eyes. The last time he had seen her she had been hurt badly, and he tried to protect her. He couldn't when they overpowered him and dragged him away. Now he wasn't sure if his wife survived, or if his children were hurt as well. He may never know.

After many other hallways, they finally reached a door that led to outside. At this part of the castle the trees overtook the area and blocked it from view. It was a perfect place to hide something you did not want anyone to see.

They dragged him further across the big plot of land and to the back where a massive stone building stood. The front of this building had been replaced with iron bars, and in the darkness, two huge purple eyes stared at him. The guards told him his job and left to go back inside the castle. A chill ran down his spine. *Feed the dragon.*

Alex looked around but couldn't see anything with which to feed the dragon. The extremely large creature looked to be getting restless in its small cage and Alex got a glimpse of its body. The dragon had huge, purple ruffled scales and sharp claws that could easily rip someone to shreds.

While he searched for the food, he heard growls coming from the creature. *Another human to come to me today… Master is using them as slaves. A pity. They'd be better off dead.*

Alex stopped his search for the food and banged his hands on the bars, making a harsh clang that jumped the dragon. "Just so you know, I was also a Dragon Master, so I can hear you. Your master is nothing but rat dung. That *rodent* doesn't even know what he's doing half the time. I suggest to you, *dragon*, that you stop growling and mind your own business," Alex sneered. "Now, you want your food or not?"

The dragon circled around and poked his face out towards him to reveal very spiky horns with long whiskers and sharp teeth. He didn't say anything but whisked his tail through the air like a whip and slapped what looked to be a hidden door on the side of the building. Alex opened it to reveal a fresh dead carcass of an oversized raccoon in there. He nodded his thanks to the dragon and grabbed the carcass. The dragon eyed it with greed as Alex brought it out and threw it into the cage where he devoured it whole.

Despite the dragon being rude to him, Alex didn't like being rude back. "What's your name, dragon?"

The dragon looked suspicious at first, then turned back to him from his meal. *Fryvis.*

Alex nodded. "Fryvis. Champ of the skies. Nice name."

Fryvis tilted his head. *Who was your dragon?*

Alex hadn't thought about his dragon lately. He missed her so much and just the thought of her hurt him. "Sessyl," he whispered.

Giver of life.

"Yes.... She was a precious creature. Would never hurt a living thing."

Frvyis' eyes softened with sympathy. For once the dragon wasn't cranky. *What happened to her?*

Alex didn't reply. That was a long time ago. His memory of that event was crystal clear. He watched his dragon be murdered right in front of him and felt his magic die with her. Alex wasn't sure if he wanted to tell Fryvis that his master was the one who killed her. Dragons never tend to harm or kill their own kind unless commanded, so telling the dragon could go two ways. One, he could lash out from the death of his own kin, or two, he could still lash out at Alex for holding contempt for his master. Either way, Alex didn't want to become food, and he wasn't sure he could trust himself to hold it together if he did tell Fryvis.

As Alex struggled to answer, they heard a bang from behind them, startling them both from the conversation. The same guards came back with another man in their arms. He realized that it was the same man from a couple days ago when the king brought him into his cell along with the strange girl. Fryvis, seeing more company, turned back into the darkness.

"Clean the dragon's cage," one of the guards said to the man. They walked off and left him with his mouth agape. As he tried to find supplies to clean the cage with, Alex decided to go and help him.

"Hey there. My name is Alex. Let me help you." Alex went to the other side to see if there was another secret room, and sure enough there seemed to be a closet on the side. He opened it and handed off a rake to the man while grabbing a shovel and other supplies for himself. Alex opened the cage and told Fryvis to stand back. Then gently pushed the man in when he stood outside the cage; frozen in fear.

"What's your name?" Alex asked.

The man opened his mouth to try and speak, but his voice was still lost. Alex just waved him off and told him what to do. Fryvis was getting agitated for having two humans in his cage, but Alex reassured him and stayed far away as possible as to not disturb him more. Alex and the man began scooping up the dragon's feces and bedding.

They worked silently for a half hour just cleaning and Alex watching the man. He seemed rather new here. Not yet all dirtied up from labor, but he did seem to have a bad limp and kept tripping over his own feet. Alex repeatedly helped the man up and continued shoveling and throwing the nasty bedding out to the side of the cage.

At one point, the man fell so hard to the ground that he startled both Fryvis and Alex and did not get back up. Alex rushed to his side. He was gasping for air.

"I…am so…sorry," he said in a barely audible voice. "It is… my anxiety…I…" His voice was lost once more.

Alex furrowed his eyebrows. "No need to apologize, my friend. This is no place for someone like you. Here, let me help you up and you can take a break outside."

The man nodded and Alex helped him out so he could sit down and take a breather. Once he knew that he was settled and calm, Alex went back inside to finish up on his own. That man reminded him of someone. A close friend of his since childhood. He too had anxiety and so he knew how to handle someone with it. Of course, this man wouldn't get far in a prison like this with his disability. Perhaps he could help him just as he had with his own friend.

After finishing with cleaning the cage, Alex exited and locked it up once more. Then he put back all the supplies they had used. When Alex returned to the man, he had relaxed some and swept his hair from his face with a tremor in his hands. He gasped when he saw the man's face and his shaking hands. He recognized the face staring up at him and had just been thinking of that very person, his childhood friend. Alex smiled.

17

SCARLET

The sun beat down on the four as they traveled through the thick meadow. Scarlet had told Drakon to fly out of sight and to the woods nearest to the next village they were heading for. Of course, it would be hard to find him, but he reassured her that he will be looking out for them, and since he had better eyesight than any of them there, that would make it easier for him to spot them.

Scarlet told each of them to be on the lookout for any poisonous animals that could be hiding. Jay had transformed and was now flying to get a better view. Edith kept next to her, looking quite fearful, and Scarlet noticed that Luke didn't care. She thought that getting good sleep at the tavern would have helped him, but now he seemed ghostly in the sunlight. What was even more odd was that he held that dagger in his grip like his life depended on it. Scarlet would have to talk to him later.

As they walked on, with Edith's hand in hers, Jay would randomly dive bomb from the sky and into the grass, then come back up again. She had no idea what he was doing, but Edith had caught her attention. She was walking next to Scarlet absentmindedly as she looked out across the meadow, as if trying to hear something.

"Everything alright, Edith?" Scarlet asked.

She nodded slightly and took off running through the field.

"Edith! Wait! Be careful!" Scarlet gave chase to make sure she didn't come across any snakes that could kill her. Luke looked up to see what the commotion was, but quickly lost interest and stared back down at his dagger.

After a few minutes of trying to catch up with Edith, she slowed and approached a group of large rocks sticking out of the tall grass. Scarlet finally caught up and grabbed Edith's wrist.

"Edith, you could get yourself ki-"

"Shhh!" Edith ripped her wrist out of Scarlet's grasp and slowly creeped around each rock. "Here kitty… I won't hurt you, Kioko."

Kioko? Scarlet thought with confusion. She didn't say anything more and continued to watch Edith crawl around on the ground and hold up her hand. That's when Scarlet saw an animal crawl out and rub its head against Edith's hand.

"Edith… that's a lynx."

"Yup. I heard Kioko and wanted to see him. He actually likes me." Edith then gasped as if she'd just thought of a great idea. "Can I keep him?"

Scarlet bent down next to her and took a closer look at the lynx. "I don't know… Aren't Lynx's supposed to be dangerous?"

"No. Not really. Just don't corner one and you're fine," she said with a chuckle.

Scarlet still was unsure, but when she took another look at Edith's face, she sighed. She didn't like making her sister sad. "Alright… fine."

Edith hopped up excitedly. "Yes! Come on, Kioko." She picked up the wild cat, which immediately snuggled against her chest, and they moved back to where Luke was. However, one look at him told Scarlet that something was wrong.

"Luke? What's wrong?"

Luke looked up at Scarlet and tried to talk, but instead his good eye rolled to the back of his head and he collapsed onto the ground, shaking. The sisters immediately sprang into action and started to examine him. Even though Luke had been looking bad all day, something else had happened to him. Edith set her lynx down on the ground, who obediently sat by her side, and flipped Luke over. Foam had formed around his mouth as he struggled for breath; his leg convulsing more than his entire body. Scarlet ripped his pant leg and saw blood cover his calf.

"Edith! We need water," she said in panic. Fear clutched at her chest as she thought of losing him. She tried to clean it off the best she could to see what was causing the blood flow, but it kept coming and she couldn't get a good look at the wound.

Edith turned towards her lynx and asked the cat where to find water. Kioko took off with Edith giving chase and Jay came down from the air to see what was going on.

"What happened to him?"

Scarlet didn't say anything as she kept trying to clear the blood. Finally, the blood slowed a little, and what she saw did not relieve her one bit. "Snake bite!" If Luke had been bitten then the snake was still close by.

Jay didn't say a word and searched through the grass for something as Scarlet looked around for the snake. There wasn't much for them to do as she waited for the water, and they had no clue how to get rid of the venom. Jay came running back with a lot of little green leaves cupped in his hands.

"Here. This is Cissus. They'll help with his venom, but they won't completely get rid of it. We will need help with that part."

Scarlet grabbed the herbs from him and waited for Edith to come back with the water. By now Luke was getting worse. His body shook even more, and his eyes remained closed. What worried Scarlet was his leg because it stopped moving and has now swelled to incredible size.

As they tried to stop his shaking, Edith came running with a clam shell in her hand that had been filled with water. She slowly cleaned his wound and Scarlet used her clam shell to mash up the Cissus to put on his leg. Once the herb had been applied, the three sat back and watched, nothing else to do, as his convulsions continued for a minute, then slowed.

Scarlet sighed in relief and asked Edith where she had found the water.

"There's a lake past those rocks we found Kioko in." Speak of the devil, Kioko's ears perked up and pounced in the tall grass, only to reappear with a long snake in its jaws.

"Good boy, Kioko!" Edith squealed. The lynx happily padded towards her and laid down to eat the snake.

"We should bring Luke to the lake and rest there for the night," Jay said. "This heat will not help him at all with his venom."

Scarlet agreed and Jay gently picked up Luke. He didn't even move a muscle. She was worried that Luke wouldn't make it. They would have to wait and watch.

That night, all four of them settled down on the small beach next to the water and made a fire. Luke, still unconscious, laid beside the water with Edith playing with Kioko. Scarlet restocked the fire every so often and Jay sat next to her silently.

"Jay, I've been meaning to ask you, why do you want to help us? Don't the Siles want to kill me?"

He remained quiet for some time before answering her. "I hate the king as much as you do. He uses the Siles like puppets to do his bidding. When he took my friend away… I've become rogue. I disobeyed all Ixaemithian laws to find her. It's why I'm being hunted down. They see me as a threat. That's why I want to help you guys. I want to kill the king and get my friend back."

"Who was your friend?"

Jay smiled, as if remembering her. "Aki. A bird Sile like me. We used to travel everywhere together." He paused, then added, "Despite being hunted down, why do *you* want to kill the king?"

Scarlet stared into the fire with hard, cold eyes. "He killed my mother and took my father away."

"How do you know it was him?"

“I recognize an Ixaemithian guard when I see one.” Scarlet didn’t say anything else, which left them in an awkward silence. To make it less awkward, Scarlet stood from her spot on the ground, walked over to Luke, and sat down next to him to keep watch for the night.

18

LUKE

Luke opened his eyes to find himself in a new landscape. It was the mountains again. Not the ones they just traveled over, but the ones he saw with the wolf. He walked around to search for new things. Ever since he took that dagger off that lady, he had been feeling under the weather. For a day a major pounding took residence in his head and he could hear nothing but screams. Whenever he felt the dagger in his hand, paranoia usually took over and he worried so much about losing this weapon for some reason. Sometimes he would feel like he was going crazy.

Luke walked past cliff after cliff as the heavy snowflakes fell from the sky. The view was getting hard for him to see and the snow grew even thicker as each second passed. When the snow completely covered his view, he stopped walking and tried to see around him. He didn't notice a different wolf sitting right next to him. He didn't see it since its pelt was white as snow. What was different about this wolf was the black stripe on its back and it had mismatched colored eyes. One as dark as night and the other an emerald green.

"Who are you?" Luke asked. The wolf didn't answer him and instead cocked its head with squinted eyes. Blood dripped from its jaws and onto the white, fluffy snow.

"What the hell?" Luke backed away quickly, but now the wolf steadily climbed to its feet and morphed into… Luke. He stared at

himself from afar with confusion and noticed that there was a dagger in his chest. The blood ran down quickly from the wound and each breath he took the blood bubbled around the dagger. The sound was even more horrifying. The slapping of the blood against his wound made him queasy and the sight of his own mouth filling up with blood made him vomit. That was when he was thrust into darkness and random words spewed out through his head, rendering him disoriented.

The words continued as if in some strange language, making his head fuzzier with each vowel, and he thought he'd pass out… in his own dream. They looked to be similar codes to the one he and his friends came across when traversing the mountains. He had no clue what they meant.

When the words stopped scrolling through his mind, the darkness faded and he found himself on the streets of his hometown, Drakonia. Luke looked on in horror as the layers of smoke enveloped him. Buildings crumbled around him and flames erupted into the sky. Screams echoed in the distance and blood covered the pavement in pools.

When the smoke cleared, the tower that used to hold meetings for Drakonia was no longer there. Just in front of the base of the fallen tower sat the same wolf with an evil glint in its eyes. Behind it, a man appeared from the smoke with all sorts of weapons at his disposal. He was like a walking arsenal.

"Master Xirgrath," a voice said from behind Luke. He turned around to see another man, but this person had peeling skin and red, drooping eyes. It looked as if he'd emerged out of a nightmare.

"Speak, General Algor," said the man with the guns. Luke could only stare in confusion as the monster walked up to him and bowed his head.

"The portal is reaching its highest point in power. Soon you will be able to cross worlds completely and continue with the plan."

Xirgrath nodded and addressed the wolf personally. "I hope you know what you are doing here, young Edhisu."

The wolf glanced up at him and uttered a low, guttural growl with such menace that the monster known as General Algor whimpered in fear and bowed lower to the ground. Xirgrath, however, wasn't moved by it.

"You summon us for help running this kingdom. If we are to work together then I need to know that you can handle this."

Edhisu didn't reply, but instead began to blur in front of Luke's eyes. As the smoke clouded his view once more, he saw Edhisu change into a little girl. However, Luke couldn't get a good view as he was thrown into darkness once more.

When Luke opened his eyes, his vision blurred, and his head throbbed in pain. He groaned and tried to move, but his whole body ached, and his leg was on fire. A figure came into view as he tried to rub away the blurriness.

"Don't move, Luke," a voice said from above him. It was Scarlet. Luke tried to speak, but he realized his throat was too parched and before he knew it, he blacked out once more.

19
Alexander

Alex sat in the cold, dark cell, waiting to be let out once more. Just a few days ago, the king had moved him to a different part of the castle and now he was closer to his friend. When he had first figured out who he was, Alex was so happy and wanted to ask him many questions, but his friend could not speak well, and they could not talk to each other.

Alex stood up to stretch his legs, which made a lot of unnecessary noises due to the chains and he saw his friend's cell. It was a lot different than the other cells, since they had bars and that one didn't. It made it impossible to look through and see to the other side.

What was also different were the people. He didn't have many neighbors from the part of the castle he came from, but now he made a few new friends in the wee hours of the day. Just next to him was a man who had come from a village called Argonia. He had said his name was Ace and he had watched his entire home burn down to the ground.

"It was very strange," Ace said earlier that day to Alex. "First thing in the morning news had spread that strange newcomers had come. It didn't even take a day before somethin' bad was to happen. I wasn't there to see it, but apparently there was a dragon that barged into the village and it looked like it had belonged to those newcomers."

The Dragon Master, Alex thought to himself. "And what did they look like?"

"Well, there were three of 'em. Two girls and a young man. All had blond-ish brown hair, tall, except one of the girls who looked around the age of ten. They looked rugged and out of place in Argonia."

Alex nodded and let Ace continue with his story.

"Then that night when they had left, even more things got out of hand. Ixaemithian guards had come and burned down the whole village! And then…." His voice trailed off. Alex looked and saw tears begin to pool under his eyes. "And then I had to watch my friend die. It was awful. That's when they dragged me here..."

Alex had no idea what to say to help his newfound friend's pain go away, but Ace did not say anything else and had turned away to reflect on how bleak things were for him now. That's when Alex decided to leave him alone. He knew how it felt the first time he had been put in here.

Now Ace slept in the next cell over and his other neighbor was awake. A woman who apparently came from the exact place where Alex used to live.

"Shame," she said while glancing over at Ace. "I can't imagine what you all have gone through."

"Well, why were you put in here, Isabella?" Alex asked.

The woman turned to face him in the dark cell with a small smile. "My daughter. She is a Sile. In fact, she's here right now. Over in that cell." She pointed towards the cell where his friend was also locked up and Alex gasped.

"That's where my friend is. That girl with him is your daughter?"

Isabella nodded. "She wasn't born like that. Got turned at a young age. She just happened to be really powerful, so I was brought into this situation."

Alex raised his eyebrows in surprise, but when he was about to ask another question, he saw guards approach his cell.

"Here we go again," Alex said to Isabella with sarcasm. She laughed, but the guards didn't say anything. They just opened the cell and silently took him out and through to the other part of the castle. This time they didn't even tell him where they were bringing him, which he thought was weird. Eventually he did know where they were taking him, and suspicion took over once they opened the huge throne doors and sat him there on the floor. The king smiled and stood in front of his enormous throne.

"Alexander, I would like you to meet someone."

As his suspicion continued to grow, King George stepped aside to reveal a white wolf with one black eye and the other an emerald green. When it sat down, Alex could see a long black stripe run down its back.

"Alex, this is my partner, Edhisu."

"Alright... And why show me?" Alex always had thought the king was dimwitted.

"Because of this." The king motioned his hand towards the wolf, which stood up and walked over to Alex. Then, the wolf blurred and right in front of his eyes transformed into a human, but not just any human. A little girl took its place and there was no innocence in her eyes. She had a dagger in one hand and a small pistol in the other. She happened to be dressed like every jester in this castle; a kabuki mask over her head, heavy makeup done on her face, and a purple jeweled dress with a shawl draped around her shoulders.

"Alexander, I just wanted to show you what she is capable of. She knows who you are and requested for your presence here." He had a sort of evil grin on his face as Edhisu came closer and closer to him. He stood up and tried to back away but hadn't realized that the guards had chained him into the ground.

That did not worry him. What scared him more was the little girl running full speed at him with the dagger poised up and ready to strike him. So, the king wanted to see him fight Edhisu. Well, it wouldn't be much of a fight if he was helpless to do anything. Thankfully she saved him from that by cutting his chains loose.

At first, he thought the girl was trying to free him, but then realized that the king was still smiling and Edhisu looked as if she wanted a challenge. His chest filled with dread. Being stuck there for years had taken a toll on him and he could see that the young girl was very agile and flexible.

She walked away from him, grabbed a sword from the wall and threw it with incredible strength at Alex. He caught it before it could slice him and glanced down at it, thinking, *she wants a fair fight.* Alex would be ready, even though he did not feel comfortable fighting a little girl.

Immediately after throwing the sword, she pulled out her pistol and shot off a bullet towards him, which he easily deflected. Then she lifted her dagger and with great speed tried to land a blow on him, but he soon remembered his training from his past and even though he was rusty, he still managed to block all her attacks. With every swing of her arm, or kick to the stomach, Alex managed to either dodge her every attack, or defend himself with his own attacks. Edhisu wasn't getting anywhere.

The girl sighed in frustration and lifted her hand up towards him. Just when he started to wonder what she was doing, the handle of the sword grew warm in his palm. At first, he didn't notice the growing heat, but then was forced to drop it when his hand sizzled and burned from grasping the handle. He looked up with confusion, then realized what had just happened. Magic. Edhisu has magic.

Alex began to panic as she drew him further away from his sword and continued to try and land blows on him. He could only keep this up for a short time, and when he grew tired, he couldn't block her every attack. The dagger pierced his arm, sliced his cheek open, and eventually plunged into his leg. He grunted in pain and fell to the floor, but not before Edhisu pulled out her pistol and shot him right in the stomach.

He collapsed in shock as the blood pooled around his body and his skin grew warm. His throat felt clogged and with each labored breath he took, pain seared through his stomach and lungs.

This wasn't a fair fight at all, he thought to himself, and with that, he blacked out on the throne room floor, defeated.

20

Scarlet

The next morning, Scarlet woke up from lying next to Luke and looked him over. Scarlet had tried to speak with him the night before, but he was so out of it that he had fallen asleep and threw a fit again. They needed to get him to the nearest village, quick.

When she saw that he was okay for now, she looked around and only found Jay sleeping by the fire. Edith was nowhere to be seen. Fear trickled into her heart as she frantically searched around the lake. Something might have happened to her.

She didn't have to worry long. She spotted Edith behind a rock beside the lake with Kioko. The feline played with the torn-up skirt that her sister was wearing as Edith stared into the small clump of trees with a vacant look. Scarlet put her hand on her shoulder and Edith jumped in alarm.

"Edith? Are you okay?"

Her sister stared at her, as if tired, then nodded. "I'm fine. Just couldn't sleep." She stood up and they both walked back over to the others.

Jay was now awake and crouching over Luke, who twitched slightly.

"We need to get him help, fast," he said in concern. He picked Luke up and they all headed out again. It didn't take long until they passed the small canopy of trees and to the next village on their map since they had already trekked through the meadow to get there.

"Okay, this here is the village 'Glemm Grove'," Scarlet said as she scanned the map. "Maybe we can find some help for him there." They all agreed, and they came upon the grand gates to the village. Before she could follow the others in, she remembered that she had to meet Drakon here in the nearby woods. She went in search for him.

She had no idea where to look, but she scoured the entire woodlands surrounding the village for him. The trees there were very different than from the trees they had traveled through those previous days. Huge, thick yellow and orange leaves hung above her head with the rays of the sun leaking through and hitting her skin in pleasant warmth. It would be the perfect place to live without a care in the world.

Finally, after traveling further into the woods, she found Drakon, and boy was she surprised. The young dragon looked to be a fully grown adult and his tail was long enough to wrap right around his body easily, the wings spanned hundreds of feet apart, and his hulking body covered a great amount of space in the woods, barely able to fit in between the trees. Large, blue scales grew around his neck like a rough-edged mane, and his face had grown small horns, making him look even fiercer.

"Wow," Scarlet gaped. "I didn't know you guys grew that fast."

Drakon nodded. *I presume everything is alright.*

"Not exactly." Scarlet told him everything about Luke and his bite. He didn't seem concerned in the slightest.

I can heal wounds.

"Really?"

Drakon cocked his head to the side as if it were obvious. *Yes. I am a magical beast. Remember the human's injury?*

Scarlet thought back but couldn't remember what he was implying. Everything was a blur from the moment they had left Drakonia.

He shook his massive head. *I can heal wounds. Just bring him to me.*

"I'll try. I already told the others to find someone in the village to help him."

Drakon nodded and Scarlet left him and promised to be back in a day. She retraced her steps through the woods and made it back to the village. This one was slightly different, but very much the same with every shop she walked by. She didn't see the others on the streets.

Scarlet decided to just wander around and hope to find them soon. She entered each shop to see what they were selling. Even when traveling, she still loved to shop. There wasn't much that was being sold other than clothes and jewelry.

Not a lot of things in this store interested her, so Scarlet walked into the next store and found her sister with Jay on her shoulder. *That was quick*, she thought to herself. A smile spread on Edith's face as she gazed at the dress in her hands. It was a small, cotton pink dress laced with bright red, jeweled straps and a beautiful little train on the back. When Edith looked up from the dress, her eyes brightened even more.

"Scarlet! Can I please have this dress? It's so beautiful!"

Scarlet walked over and crouched on one knee to look her in the eyes with sadness. "I'm sorry, love. I have no money left."

Edith cast her eyes downward and reluctantly put the dress away. Scarlet grasped her hand and led her out of the shop. By then Jay, in his bird form, fluttered about and pecked at Scarlet's hand.

"Ow! Jay! What are you doing?"

He continued to peck, and when no one was looking, he changed.

"Scarlet, I wanted to tell you where Luke is. I found an old friend of mine that would be able to help him."

"Who?" she asked.

Jay smiled. "Kagura. A witch."

"A witch? Jay, how did you find someone like that so quickly? And can we even trust a witch?"

"Of course, Scarlet. I've known Kagura for quite some time. I did a lot of traveling in my time as a Sile. She was one of the friends I had made. I didn't know she lived here until Edith here used her little magic and found a witch here called Kagura. That's when I knew I had to bring Luke to her."

Scarlet looked down at Edith next to him and gave her an approving smile. Edith smiled back and Jay led them away into the dark corner of Glemm Grove. Laughter could be heard from deep inside the alley and Scarlet noticed people sitting on the sidewalk covered in dirt and dressed in torn up clothes. Fires in trash cans were placed between them, keeping them warm.

"Too poor to live a normal life," Jay explained sadly to them. As Scarlet continued to gaze at them, she grew thankful that her family were never that poor. Even though they could not afford food for themselves, at least they had a roof over their heads.

Once they passed the poor, Jay walked up the steps of a house and knocked on the door. There was no reply for a minute or so, but then an elderly woman came and answered the door.

"Jay! *Es bueno verte de nuevo! Quien es esta otra chica?*" the woman said.

Scarlet stared at her in confusion for she did not know what she was saying, and Jay saw her reaction.

"Oh! Uh… *Lo Siento*, Kagura. *Mi amiga*, Scarlet *no habla tu idioma. Ella es novia de Luke*," Jay replied to the woman.

Kagura smirked at Scarlet and with little hesitation she switched languages. "Friend of Jay's. It is good to see you all. Please come in. Your friend is doing wonderfully."

As Kagura led them into her home, Scarlet whispered to Jay, "What did you just tell her?"

He smirked. "I simply told her who you are and that you don't speak her language. Also, I told her that you are Luke's girlfriend."

"Wait. No. I'm not his girlfriend."

"Really? Well it seemed pretty obvious. I see how Luke stares at you all the time."

Scarlet had no words to say and Jay's smirk slipped away.

"Here we are. You guys are free to stay here for as long as you want."

They walked into a room that was colorfully refurbished. They found Luke laying down on one of the couches.

"The venom is almost completely distilled from his system. He just needs time to rest now."

Scarlet went to go sit down next to him and put the palm of her hand on his forehead. He was hot. Edith, with Kioko, went into another room and Jay stayed to talk to Kagura. Scarlet stayed by Luke and Kagura started to clean up the room by using magic. Objects that were on the ground floated up and took their spots back on the shelves. That's when an idea struck Scarlet.

"Kagura. Is it ever possible to teach someone magic?"

Kagura looked up from what she was doing and smiled. "Why, yes. I've had many students before in my lifetime."

"Would you… you know… consider ever teaching me?"

"Are you a witch too?"

"Not exactly." Scarlet wondered if it was safe to tell her what she was. Then again Jay trusts her so maybe she should. "I am a Dragon Master. I own a dragon."

"Oh! So, you do hold magic. When would you like to start?"

"Oh, um… possibly tomorrow. It's a bit late for today."

Kagura nodded and offered her the couch next to Luke to sleep on. She and Jay then went into the other room to talk some more, leaving Scarlet sitting there for a second more, then she moved to the other couch to rest a while before eventually closing her eyes and falling asleep.

21
Scarlet

In the morning, Scarlet opened her eyes to find a young woman on one of the couches.

"Oh, um, hello." Scarlet didn't know who the woman was.

She only smiled and Jay came walking in.

"Kagura, where is the best place to eat around here?" Jay asked the young woman.

"Wait, that's Kagura?"

Jay glanced over at her, as if wondering what the problem was, then he remembered. "Oh right. Since she's a witch she can turn herself to a younger age each day."

"Okay… so how old are you then?"

"Let's see… It's kind of hard but… I'd say I am five hundred two."

"Five hundred two! You must have seen a lot in your life."

"Indeed. I have lived through wars after wars, saw my loved ones perish, and see old friends die. This magic isn't a blessing. It's a curse, and I deeply regret doing this to myself."

"Then why don't you just stop?" Scarlet wasn't trying to be rude; she was just really confused about this.

She smiled slightly. "It's not that simple. If I were to stop then it would be a most terribly slow, painful death that I do not wish to endure. All those years I have added to my age would surely catch up to me. I was naïve before I learned the full extent of my powers. If I could go back, I would not have messed with my age from the start."

"Oh." *That's dark*, she thought to herself.

Kagura just waved her off. "It's nothing. The only way I want to go is if someone tries to kill me. Now that will be swift, quick and with no pain."

For some reason Jay laughed when she said that, but Scarlet thought it sad. It sounded awful to be alive for so long and to experience so much pain. She didn't think she could ever handle that.

Kagura, as if sensing Scarlet's discomfort, changed the subject. "So, Scarlet, when would you like to learn magic?"

"Oh right! Today would be great. I just have to uh… see my dragon first before I do anything else."

Kagura nodded and Scarlet asked her to watch Edith while she went out. Jay would also be leaving to go get something to eat as he kept complaining about how hungry he was. They decided to leave together.

As they left, Edith came from the room she was sleeping in and saw a younger version of Kagura sitting on the couch with a cup of tea in her hand. She could tell that it was Kagura because of her power. She had started to see people's auras now and hers was black with silver streaks. Scarlet's aura was a royal blue wisp and Jay's was the color of the sky. When she looked to Luke, however, his aura felt threatening. His color was more of a blood shade red than anything else and often gave her the chills.

Kagura looked up from her tea to see Edith standing next to Luke with wide eyes. She cleared her throat to get her attention and Edith snapped her head around, as if distracted.

"*Me entiendes?* 'Do you understand me?'" Kagura asked the little girl.

"*Si, puedo hablar todos los idiomas.* 'Yes, I can speak all languages,'" she replied. "My sister doesn't know that. She thinks I can only talk to animals."

"Very impressive. You are a true sorceress."

Edith blushed when Kagura said that. "I heard you wanted to teach my sister magic?"

She nodded. "A Dragon Master cannot learn magic on their own, unlike witches and sorcerers. Your magic will come in time, but Scarlet needs a little push."

Edith wanted to say something else, but Luke caught her attention. She turned her head towards him and was instantly thrown into a new landscape.

"Kagura!" Edith shouted. Snow had begun to cloud her vision, but just a few feet in front of her she saw Luke. He was glaring at a creature next to him. A wolf almost as tall as Luke stared at him with beet red eyes. He was yelling at it.

"Who are you! What do you want with me!?"

The wolf gave no reply, but instead turned its head to look at Edith. She held her breath, but it made no advancement towards her. Instead the same exact words began to repeat through her head.

BloodNightBloodStalkersNightStalkersBlood...

The words were like a jumbled mess in her brain, but she also knew what they meant. They were creatures she had read about once before. Powerful demons that went by the name of "Blood Nightstalkers." That's when she realized that Luke was in danger and they would not go away unless someone else took possession of the dagger and controlled the demons themselves...

Just as fast as it came Edith was thrust out of the snowy landscape and found herself laying on the floor of Kagura's home. Kagura herself stood over her in concern.

"Are you alright. young one?"

Edith rubbed at the back of her head. "Yeah... I think I need to lay down for a bit."

The witch nodded and led her back to her room to lay down.

That afternoon, Scarlet came back to Kagura's house after discussing with Drakon what to do. She had told him that she planned on staying in Glemm Grove for a few more days to learn magic. At first, he was skeptical about this so-called "witch" that Jay randomly had brought up. Scarlet reassured him that Kagura was a fine witch and that nothing bad would happen. Still, Drakon had his doubts and worried for his master.

Now once back at the house, they immediately jumped into Scarlet's training.

"We will need to move somewhere else to do your fighting," Kagura said.

"Fighting? I thought we were learning magic?"

"Yes, but magic will not always help you defend yourself. That's where fighting comes in." Kagura led her away and across town. Along the way people were smiling and waving at her like they all knew each other. When they reached the other side of the village, they stopped just outside a barn.

"This is my friend's barn. We will need the extra space for your training."

Kagura led her into the massive barn filled with hay. There were no animals in there and no other structures. It was a perfect space to practice fighting moves.

"I'm going to teach you some moves. They may be easy or may be hard. It depends on the person's own ability of their 'fight response'." Kagura showed her the first move and Scarlet repeated it. It was the "block" maneuver where Scarlet held her arms out in front of her and would be able to block any attack that came her way. Then she showed her some other moves, like the standard punch and kick, roundhouse, elbow punches, and—Scarlet's personal favorite—knee kicks. They practiced all these moves with their correct stances for a while. Scarlet wasn't having a hard time, she'd just never fought before. However, she was a quick learner.

When Scarlet successfully performed a few times without fumbling, Kagura decided to have them start with a simple fight. The first thing Kagura did was move her body into a roundhouse kick, which Scarlet learned to block with her forearm. Then Scarlet kept the same stance as Kagura slinked around her like a cat, trying to find an opening to Scarlet's defense. While that distracted her, Scarlet decided to throw in an attack of her own. When she wasn't looking, Scarlet effortlessly whipped her leg up in the air, spun her whole body like a dancer, and made foot to head contact with Kagura, but made sure to pull away at the last second to not hurt her as much. Kagura only swayed on her feet and was soon back on her, nodding her approval. Scarlet was exhilarated. She had never been able to do that before.

Eventually, they were able to increase speed. Kagura switched tactics and landed punches onto Scarlet, but lightly as to not hurt her. She dodged almost each one, as well as blocking them, and landed a specialty of her own. A knee kick. This continued for an hour and Scarlet was building up a good sweat. However, after another half hour, Scarlet was getting tired. Kagura saw this.

"Okay, you've had enough basic training for today. You are doing wonderfully. How do you feel about now moving onto magic?" Scarlet nodded eagerly. Kagura smiled. "Then for that we will need to be outside; we don't want to ruin this barn. It is now time for you to learn Earth magic."

They left and moved into a field next to the barn with tall weeds flowing in the wind. Buildings from Glemm Grove stood out across the hill and Scarlet could see people walking about, minding their own business. She admired the view from her spot on the hill.

"With Earth magic you need complete concentration on what you are going to do. You can create mountains, hills, cliffs… or walls if you prefer," she said with a smirk.

"Walls?"

"Let's say you are in a battle and your enemy has guns. You can create a thick wall of Earth that can stop any bullet. With it in place you could then attack with your magic and they would not be able to reach you without having to get close to you or aim around the wall to attack. It slows down all your enemies." Kagura then went to explain how to cast spells. "For beginners like you it is best to hold out your hand in the direction you want to cast your magic. If you were more advanced in magic, then you could easily cast spells with just your mind.

"For the magic to actually work you can either say the spell in your mind, like for Earth magic it is just 'Earth' to make land rise, or to cast a wall you say 'Earth, Wall'. You can also make ravines by saying 'Split Ravine'. Basically, you can think or say whatever you want, and it will happen, but I find it easiest to say or whisper the incantation.

"Other spells are more complicated, but you have nothing to worry about. Dragon Masters are only able to perform the elements of the universe while witches and wizards can move objects, change appearances and age, cast spells, and play with elements. A sorceress, or sorcerer, can almost do anything they put their mind to. It somewhat makes them more evil than they appear."

"My sister isn't evil," Scarlet blurted out in defense.

"Oh no, your sister is such a great young lady. Sorcerers are born well behaved, yet the possibility of infinite magic corrupts people. Your sister looks to have a pure heart, but time will only tell if the magic is too much for her to handle."

Scarlet couldn't imagine her sister ever being evil. She was just such a sweet, innocent little girl and always liked to help people. She hoped she would never see the day.

Kagura saw that she had distracted Scarlet, so she showed her what Earth magic is. The hill they were currently standing on began to rise steadily towards the sky.

"Wha…?" Scarlet felt the ground move and shake underneath her feet. She didn't know what was going on at first, but then she saw the town disappear. Now she could only see sky.

"Look down."

Scarlet did as she was told and saw that the hill had risen and now a steep incline led to the village.

"When changing your landscape, it is easier than creating your own land. Try to move this hill back to the spot it was at before. Remember, just concentrate, use your hands, and utter the spell."

Scarlet concentrated, outstretched her hands, and whispered, "Earth, Down." She waited to feel the rumbling underneath her feet, but nothing happened. She tried again, this time concentrating so hard that a small headache formed in between her eyes, and she felt the hill move this time. The movement made her lose concentration, so she tried once more, managed to keep it together and eventually moved the hill back in place.

"Nice. I recommend you try your Earth walls now. They will come in handy for later."

As Scarlet practiced her Earth magic, Jay and Edith came from the village and were seeing how she was doing. Luke was awake and being propped up between the two. He looked ghostly pale in the afternoon sunlight and as he clutched onto Edith, her face wore an expression that told Scarlet that she was not happy.

"Why have you brought him here? He is too weak to travel back now, and we were just about to leave," Kagura said in disdain.

"Well then I guess we should stay up here for the night," Jay replied. It was almost as if he had planned for that to happen. Both Kagura and Scarlet looked skeptical for having Luke up there; there wasn't much they could do but to keep him up there.

While they all entered the barn, Scarlet was the only one who stayed outside and kept on working with her Earth magic. She wanted to get this down and soon nothing would be able to stop her from continuing with her plans.

22

SCARLET

First thing in the morning, Scarlet and Kagura woke up before the others and headed out. She wanted to bring her to a perfect environment for her next lesson on elemental magic. Water. Kagura had told her that there was a river near the barn where she could practice her water element. Scarlet, however, still needed practice on creating these elements out of thin air.

At the bottom of the hill, a small river flowed gently among the reeds and when she put her hand in, the water was refreshingly cold.

"The next two elements are very simple. With all magic spells, concentration is key. You already have a little bit of Earth at your fingertips, so concentration isn't new for you.

"Now, let's try to reverse the direction of the water. Remember to use your hands to help you out."

Scarlet did as she was told, and Kagura was right. Water magic was easy. In no time she reversed the water and now it flowed steadily upstream. She then told her to try and create water in thin air. Now that she could not do so easily. No matter how hard she tried, she just couldn't do it. It was only after her tenth attempt that she managed to make a little stream of water fall from her hands.

"Hmm. I see that you have a hard time with the concept of creating magic out of nowhere. Which is normal," she added quickly. "It'll just be a little hard to control the less major elements that are involved with water."

"What's that?" Scarlet asked.

"Ice and Lightning. They can both be used as weapons. You can either pull lightning from the sky and shoot ice from your hands, or again, create both on your own with your hands. You can only pull the lightning if there is a thunderstorm, but other than that you'd be good to go. Let's not focus on those two. We will skip right to air magic and then focus on those afterwards.

"Air magic is the simplest thing you can learn for magic. All that is needed to do is to pull the wind from the air and control it. Or you can move the air itself to do stuff for you. For instance-" Kagura motioned her hands and began to levitate branches up from the ground. Apparently, she was just using the air for that. Scarlet was impressed.

"Your turn." She dropped all the branches back onto the ground and Scarlet followed her instructions. Kagura was right. This was easy. On her first try she was able to do that; plus be able to control where they were going. To challenge herself more she used the air magic and controlled larger objects, including the water itself. Kagura was impressed.

"I think that's all you can learn for today. I want you to save your strength for the hardest magic to learn. We should do that tomorrow. For now, you should practice what you know now and then we will go home." Scarlet nodded and they walked back to the barn.

By now the others were wide awake. Edith sat on the ground and played with Jay, who shifted back into a bird. Luke just sat there against the barn wall, looking as if he wanted to die. Scarlet sat down next to him and talked for a little bit, but he still seemed out of it. Even before the snake bite Luke had been acting very unusual and she had no idea what was going on with him. She decided to leave him alone and took Kagura's advice on practicing. She really wanted to get good with magic.

As Scarlet practiced making lightning, Kagura was off to the side watching Edith. She had told Scarlet that Edith could be evil, but the longer she watched her, the more convinced she became that her little sister couldn't possibly be evil. The girl was just too pure and happy. However, Kagura still had her doubts. Edith in her opinion had a chance of being corrupted in the future when she became a young lady. Just by watching her, a flashback clouded Kagura's head; one that made her deeply sad.

A young Kagura Jarsdel and her friend Amelia Raynott wandered around in the Forest of the Dragons. It was a time of war and turmoil—the Kaggaegian War. The best friends were reckless and had found their way into a particularly gruesome battle. The Battle of Echo. Named after the famous sorcerer, Echo. Amelia's lover.

All over the ground there were blood and bodies who had fallen in battle. There were two lines of fighters, Ixaemithian soldiers and the Boukasian knights; their neighboring land. At the forefront of the battle, a handsome young man on a black stallion with weapons of all types stood face to face with the king of Ixaemithia, King George I. The young man was no other than Echo himself. His eyes lit with intense power.

"I'll give you one more chance," the old king said to Echo in irritation. "Leave now or I will kill you and everyone you love. Surrender and I will let them live. But not you."

Echo sneered in reply. "I have done nothing wrong. Your reign over this land is troublesome. You are killing off every magical being in Ixaemithia, so you forced me to make a choice. It's life or death now."

"You brought Boukasia into our affairs. Now they will have to answer to me." Then the king added something else to make Echo's blood boil. "How can your ancestors be proud of you. They were sadistic, evil creatures and you are nothing like them. I'm surprised you call yourself a sorcerer. You don't have the courage to be one."

"At least they didn't kill at random like you! Sorcerers never killed for fun!" Echo grew so angry that thunder clouds had begun to form above their heads and the ground cracked. "They had chosen Amelia and I to be one instead of you!"

That made the king even more irritated and he lashed out with the sword that had been at his side. He managed to catch Echo with it in the arm, making him lose its mobility, but he retaliated by swiping his other hand out in front of the king, and using his magic, he effortlessly slit his throat. He fell off his horse and writhed on the ground; blood pouring from his neck and mouth. The Ixaemithian soldiers ran to help their king, but Echo maneuvered his horse in between them, and a huge crack split the Earth; making it hard for them to get to George.

"Nobody is going to help this devil live. You either leave me to be in charge now, alongside Boukasia, or you go right ahead and kill me. If you can." That seemed to set off all the soldiers and they went to search for a way to get over this massive crack to kill Echo. He saw what they were doing and returned into his line to fight.

Kagura had never seen anyone so angry before. It made her unsettled to be there and she tried to get Amelia to leave with her. She wouldn't budge. Her face was stone cold, and her mouth formed into a grimace.

"Amelia… I want to leave. Echo will be fine, but we can't get caught." Kagura tried and pleaded with her, but she wouldn't move, wouldn't say anything, and wouldn't even look at her. She had never seen her soft-hearted friend like this before.

When Kagura continued to nudge her, Amelia finally came to, but not as the same person. She stood up, lifted her hand out towards the Ixaemithian soldiers, and they all began to scream in pain.

"Amelia! What on Earth are you doing?!"

She kept her hand poised at them and eventually they fell one by one, dead. Kagura became even more alarmed and tried to stop her. By now the other soldiers, including Echo, had noticed what was happening. Amelia snarled at her from her nudging.

"Get away from me, witch! You are no match for me. You're a weakling." With that she pushed Kagura off with so much force that she flew several feet away from Amelia and landed hard onto the ground. She didn't even try to get up after that. She wasn't the same person anymore. Evil had corrupted her, and she was no longer her Amelia. Kagura took one last look into her eyes and only saw hatred. She had lost her friend forever.

Kagura came back into the presence with a tear running down her cheek. No one seemed to notice, they were all watching Scarlet, and Kagura gently wiped the tear away from her newly formed wrinkles. That memory of the first Kaggaegian War still puzzled her to this day. She didn't know how sorcerers are corrupted; she just assumed it was the almost infinite magic pulsing at their fingertips. After she had lost her friend, Kagura never saw Amelia again. It wasn't until decades later that she had found out that Amelia was captured and executed for her crimes. It broke her heart.

Kagura was distracted from her feelings when Scarlet accidentally cast a thunderstorm and a stray lightning bolt struck down right next to her, making her yelp in fear. They all ran back to the barn once the rain started pouring from the sky.

"That... did not go as planned..." Scarlet said with a chuckle. Kagura went to go help her and she finally managed to create a clear bolt of lightning. She cheered excitedly and Kagura praised her, but she also noticed that Scarlet had begun to sway on her feet and knew that she needed to stop and save her strength. Her and Jay took her by the shoulders and led them all back to the house.

Once there, they set her down on one couch while Luke went to lay down on his couch and Edith went into her room with Kioko. When Luke's head hit the pillow, he immediately fell asleep. Kagura walked over to the fire pit, lit a fire, then left, looking as if she had something on her mind. Scarlet and Jay were the only ones left in there. Jay was strangely quiet.

"You were really good out there..." he said at one point.

"Thanks. Still a bit rusty, but I will get there." Scarlet thought his behavior odd, but she didn't worry too much about it.

Jay nodded silently and stared straight into her eyes, making her freeze in place. He remained that way for a while, just staring at her with his big black eyes. Scarlet was about to ask what was wrong when suddenly, he closed his eyes and with quick efficiency planted a kiss on Scarlet's lips. That took her by surprise, and she froze. They were there a few moments, lips firmly pressed together, and Scarlet looking around the room, trying to figure out what was going on. Then Jay pulled back, as if regretting that he kissed her, and with a flushed face he walked away quickly in embarrassment. Scarlet sat there, dumbfounded, and wouldn't move for minutes.

When she finally did, Jay did not come back and Scarlet, confused, decided to try and sleep but couldn't now that the kiss was on her mind. She didn't even know that Jay, whom she had met randomly in Argonia, and was a Sile, was in love with her.

23
Alexander

In the darkness of the castle, Alexander opened his eyes for the first time in days. A sharp pain had taken residence in his stomach and the only thing he could smell was blood. That's when he remembered that he had been shot. He scrambled to his feet, but when he did that, his stomach clenched, and the bullet wound opened back up and sent intense pain throughout his body. He involuntarily screamed.

Ace, from the cell next to him, yelled out his name, but Alex couldn't stay awake any longer. After the pain was too much to bear, he threw up, then blacked out.

The next day, Alex opened his eyes once more with the same throbbing pain and he could hardly keep himself awake. He was gasping for air as he laid on his side; his face planted against the ground. He has never experienced this type of pain before and he was having a very difficult time. Eventually, he blacked out yet again.

Finally, he woke up and found that most of the pain had dissipated. Isabella, on his other side, looked at him with concern.

"You have the spirit of the dragon within you," she said to him.

Alex gingerly lifted himself up and looked at her in confusion. "What... do you mean...?" His voice felt scratchy from disuse.

"Well, there is no possible way a person could survive a wound like that."

Could it be true? he thought to himself. *Could I have the spirit of Sessyl in me?* "Do you think so?"

"No doubt. You have been unconscious for many days with your wound bleeding steadily. Nobody went to help you. Ace and I would have if we weren't stuck in these cages."

He only shook his head. "Don't worry about it... To be fair, I'm even surprised that I am not dead yet."

"What happened? They took you away healthy and dragged you right back here looking dead. No one said a word as to what happened."

Before he could reply, the guards came to his cell and opened the door. Alex panicked. He wasn't sure if he could stand, let alone walk with his wound. He wasn't given much choice. They forcefully grabbed him by the arms and shoved him outside his cell. He looked back to see Isabella watching them take him away with fear in her eyes. He tried to smile to reassure her that everything was going to be fine, but even he doubted himself. It seems like they were now treating him worse than before and they reopened his wound, making him clutch his stomach as he walked.

Blood seeped through his fingers and he saw stars, but he forced himself to continue. He could only assume that they were treating him this way because he had survived that whole ordeal with Edhisu. He had no clue who she was, or what she is. All he knew was that she had magic.

After a few minutes, he knew that they were taking him to the king... again. *What does he want now?* he thought with anger. Alex was getting tired of seeing him. He was the only one who was ever really the king's personal slave; he'd been sent there so many times, sometimes to his "death," and after all that he did not want to even see his stupid face.

When they walked in, there were people swarming around and the king himself stood on the steps of the throne with a grin. A few feet away from him sat a girl in a chair facing away from Alex. She had long, blonde hair, and was covered in blood. She wasn't screaming, but she squirmed in her seat as one of the men stepped closer to her with a pin needle in his hand. Alex knew this process. Anyone who was deemed "extremely dangerous" would have their voice taken away. By doing this, they would insert that needle right in the neck to damage the vocal cords. Once the needle is firmly in place, the speaker can no longer talk for as long as it is in there. He thought it barbaric and unnecessary, but there was nothing he could do. If he tried to prevent this from happening, then he would be sentenced to death. He wanted to survive for as long as he could.

Alex couldn't take his eyes off the girl. She looked to be around eighteen years of age and her face was distorted in pain. She had deep scars on her face and arms and when the man inserted the needle into her throat, her face changed from pain to straight up panic. It made Alex sick to his stomach and he could no longer watch.

The guards took him away from the girl and towards the other side of the room to do his chores. When they left, he began to do them, but looked back at the girl again, who was now standing. Tears streamed down her cheeks yet there was fire in those eyes. That's when he knew that she was exactly like him.

When the guards told her what to do, she didn't give a second thought, walked up to one of them, and spit right in his face. His immediate reaction was to slap her, which she did not take lightly. She slapped him right back and then turned to the other guard to punch him in the stomach; making him double over in pain. She then tried to make a break for it but did not get far. More guards came in and tackled her to the ground. She tried to scream but the needle prevented her from making any noise.

Eventually they were able to take her away. *Poor girl*, he thought. She did seem recognizable to Alex but couldn't seem to put his finger on it. He was sure he had never seen her before.

For now, all he could do was do his chores, which was to clean his windows once more and to dust his entire room until everything was "sparkly clean." His golden throne also had to be cleaned for his pleasure. Alex did everything without arguing and at his own pace. His wound hadn't stopped bleeding and he was getting a stomachache. It made it harder for him to work.

Later, when he was done with everything, they brought him back to his cell and sure enough the girl had a cell right across from him. She looked very depressed yet determined as she sat next to the bars with her hand glowing bright orange against the iron. She can do magic as well. When Alex had passed her, she looked up from what she was doing, caught him staring at her, and sent him a glare that looked as if she wanted a challenge. Alex held up his hands, as if to say he did not want any trouble, then held a finger up to his mouth and nodded. Alex could see determination and a lot of rage pent up inside of her and he wanted to help her.

The girl looked as if she understood him and relaxed, all the while trying to burn the iron bars to escape.

24

Scarlet

The next morning Scarlet and Kagura were in her friend's barn once again to do more training. Her mind was clouded with thoughts from the previous night. She didn't know that Jay had feelings for her. It was all very strange to her and she didn't know how to handle that situation. She did not see him at all like that, but maybe she held some sort of feelings for Luke and wasn't trying to look for anyone else. She never thought of him like that before.

Kagura was just beginning the lesson on their next element: Fire. She began explaining the basics of Fire magic, but Scarlet wasn't paying attention. As she thought about Luke and Jay, she didn't notice Kagura had stopped and was glaring at her with impatience, or the little streak of lightning pass from her finger to zap Scarlet's shoulder.

"Ow! What was that for?"

"Scarlet, there seems to be something on your mind. What is it?"

Scarlet hesitated at first, then decided to tell her. "Jay and Luke are in love with me. I never saw Jay like that, and Luke has been my best friend for years. I've just never thought of having someone in my life before."

Kagura gave her a look of sympathy. "Many young people are different from each other. You are still exploring your youth. It just shows people that you are a young, independent woman who doesn't need anyone in her life. Don't let those two boys get in your way. You will be ready when the time is right."

"Thanks, Kagura." Scarlet felt a little relieved to hear that from her.

Kagura nodded and they resumed their training. "Now back to your magic. We've learned three of the major elements. What we haven't learned is fire. I saved the hardest for last."

"How is fire hard? Air magic was a breeze-" she chuckled to herself at the pun. "And Earth and water required the same level of skill. What's different about fire?"

"Fire burns. Creating fire out of thin air will burn. You will need to build immunity to the flames. That is why I saved it for last. You need a lot of strength for fire magic."

"Let's get started then," Scarlet said with a smirk.

The first thing Kagura did is flick her wrist towards a medium sized container that looked to be a large metal trash can and placed it on the ground. Fire flickered up on its own from inside it.

"Creating fire from a distance will cause you less physical pain than if you were to cast it in midair. So, that is what we are going to do today, and if we have time at the end then we can start the process of creating fire in the palm of your hand.

"First thing you need to do is concentrate on creating fire, just like with the other three elements. One major difference is the concentration to place the fire. If it materialized in a spot you did not intend it to be placed, then there would be a drastic cost following afterwards. Just relax, take deep breaths, and focus intently on the spot you want to place the fire. For example, place it right over there." Kagura pointed next to her fire and Scarlet saw another container that hadn't been there before.

Something about what Kagura said threw her off. If she placed the fire in the wrong spot, then she could literally burn down this entire barn. Taking her advice, she took a deep breath, focused on the empty container, and whispered the word "fire." Nothing happened. Scarlet tried again. Still nothing. That's when she remembered and sighed in frustration. Kagura had told her that it would be easiest to use her hands when performing magic. Using just the mind was only for advanced magicians.

So, trying for the third time, and feeling stupid, she whispered the word "fire" again. This time something happened, but nothing good. The fire managed to land right in the container, yet she threw too much, and it ended up spilling out onto the wooden floor. Almost instantly it caught fire and spread rapidly across the floor to the hay structures in the corner of the barn.

"Oh no!" Scarlet began panicking and didn't know what to do. Kagura, on the other hand, reacted quickly and extinguished the fire with water magic. Scarlet sighed in relief.

"Whenever that happens, do not panic. You have the power of the elements within you. Use them to your advantage."

Scarlet nodded and practiced repeatedly to try to place her fire in the right spot. There were a few times where she got it perfectly right, but other times she didn't. At times, if she was growing tired, she made huge mistakes like: placing fire far away from the bin, placing it right next to it, setting the hay on fire, almost hitting Kagura with it, or managing to blindly shoot fire right from the palm of her hands, which seriously took her by surprise. If she wasn't focusing enough, crazy things could happen with this element if she wasn't careful enough. So, as her strength escaped her body, the fire grew more difficult to control. When she looked down at her hand, a small, burnt spot appeared at the center of her palm. Kagura saw this and halted her.

"That's enough for the day. We don't want to overwork your magic. We also don't want to burn this barn to the ground. We'll keep practicing each day for as long as you stay."

Scarlet thought that sounded good, even though she wasn't sure exactly how long they were going to stay, and they started cleaning up. What they didn't notice was the barn doors were open to reveal several people, but not just anyone. Scarlet looked up to see dozens of Ixaemithian guards rush in and point muskets at them.

"What in the-" Kagura was interrupted by a guard who quickly ran over and shut her up by slamming the butt of his gun against the side of her head, knocking her unconscious.

"Hey! Don't do that to her! You're after me! Not her!" Scarlet had to think of a way to get out of there. She had thought that these guards were way behind them. She had badly miscalculated, and now she was in trouble.

The guard that had hit Kagura now came after her, but another guard shouted for him to stop. "Do not harm her, imbecile! She is needed for the king's work."

"Oh? Like I'll ever work for you!" Before they could do anything else, Scarlet thought quickly and used everything she learned. The strength she had lost before now came back tenfold. She was being attacked and she wasn't going down without a fight.

First, she distracted the guards with water. She didn't want them to fire off shots at her, so when she drenched them, she used her Earth magic to create a barrier to protect her and Kagura from them. Once the wall of Earth was in place, she pelted the group of guards with bursts of fire, stopping them in their tracks.

"Like hell with it! This thing doesn't deserve to live!" one of them shouted. He broke off from the line and fired stray shots at Scarlet, who was able to dodge them by ducking back behind the wall. Before he could fire any more, Scarlet peeked around and concentrated on bringing all her energy to her hand, creating a ball of electricity, to throw at him.

"Are you numb?! You know the reason why he needs her! If you kill her then you will answer to the king himself!"

The rogue guard immediately lowered his weapon at the lead guard's warning, leaving a perfect distraction for Scarlet. When they all had begun arguing with one another, the pent-up energy in her hand was finally released and a bolt of lightning shot into her enemies. It was a much greater impact than she thought it would have. Every one of them burned to a crisp.

"That was easy." Scarlet stepped over the charred bodies, made sure there wasn't any still alive, and ran outside. She was met with a whole other battalion. Scarlet froze, and quickly tried to make a run for it back into the barn. However, as soon as she turned her back to them, an explosion met her right to the face. The blast rang through her head, making her dizzy and go blind. Another explosion came right after, knocking her off her feet. She tried to get back up, but the explosions detonated right next to her, leaving her unconscious.

It seemed forever that Scarlet was trapped in the darkness of her own head, but when she came to, she found herself in a new setting, with strange men standing in front of her and a needle being inserted into her neck.

25

Scarlet

Scarlet woke up from lying on the cold, hard floor in a dark, rank room. At first, she panicked; she had no idea where she was. Then she remembered what happened the other day and only slightly relaxed. She gently got to her feet and looked around. She was placed in a dingy cell with other people who looked to have been captured as well. As she looked at them, they all remained still and silent, as if they had no life in them anymore. It made her mad that no one else was as angry as she was for being put there. They had no personalities at all, except for one person. It was the first slave she had met there. He was the only one she interacted with and seemed to hold as much anger as her. He was located across from her.

All day and night, Scarlet tried again and again to escape the bars. Her and Kagura hadn't learned about the other part of fire magic; where she could build her immunity to flames. Since she was stuck in this place, she would have to learn and experience it herself. She had begun her escape by painstakingly burning the iron bar to break apart. It was slow going. The bars were so thick that she barely made any progress, and what was worse was how the fire was affecting her. Scarlet's whole hand carried burns just from trying to melt the bar. She had no idea how she was going to build immunity, but to stop her hand from burning off completely she would take breaks, cool off with water, and build her strength.

She hated how the guards continuously came to her cell. Usually they wouldn't say anything, but other times they would enter her cell, grab her, and bring her to a place inside the castle. This was one of those times. They came in, grabbed ahold of her arms, and dragged her out.

Whenever they brought her out, she was showed the view of the castle. Everything was so fancy and expensive. It made her angry to see the king's extravagant wealth juxtaposed to the abject poverty of most of the people in the kingdom. Everything was encased in gold and Scarlet could see that he had horded an abundance of food for himself and his court. When she thought of the court and jesters, she couldn't help but feel the same way. Just by the way they dressed in fancy jewels and suits, they seemed to be as rich as the king himself. It was disgusting.

After going down every hallway imaginable, they led her outside and the sunlight hit her eyes like fire. She hadn't seen light in a long while due to the dark environment in the castle. She wondered why she was brought out here. Then she realized they were bringing her to a closed off area and deep into the woods. At the end of the enclosure, Scarlet could see a gate with a grand cobblestone building beyond it. They unlocked the gate, pushed her in, and closed it back up. They didn't even say a word.

Okay... now what? Scarlet looked around and got a better view of the stone building that had bars at the front and to the side of it. Inside was dark, but she could barely make out a creature with large, purple scales fluctuating in the sunlight.

Oh no... It was a dragon. She wondered why they'd brought her here. However, them bringing her here made her learn more about the king. He was a Dragon Master too. He was exactly like her. When looking at the dragon, it made her think about Drakon and the others, and tears sprang to her eyes.

As she tried to keep tears at bay, the gate opened from behind her once more. She glanced over and saw two different guards carrying a man. The same man she had met the day she got there. He had short, brown hair, brown eyes, tall, and was covered in dirt from being in the cells for so long.

Scarlet could see the guards did not care for him at all. They shoved him onto the ground, hit him, then left. He stayed there for a bit, breathing hard. Scarlet could see his face scrunched up in pain and him gripping his stomach. He stayed like this for a while with sweat running down his face profusely. To Scarlet, it looked as if he may be carrying a fever.

Eventually, he managed to stand and went right to the cage. He didn't notice Scarlet at first, but when he entered a compartment on the side and brought out supplies, he looked up and froze. Scarlet tried to speak, then remembered they had put a needle in her neck, preventing her from talking. The man stared at her a moment longer, then realized who she was and relaxed.

"You're new here," he said without question. She nodded and was surprised that she somewhat recognized his voice. He carried the same accent as Liam. Perhaps he came from the same place as her Godfather did.

"You'll get used to things around here. Just follow the rules and you won't get punished."

Wonderful. This place couldn't get any better. The man told her what to do and they began working. Her task that he gave her was to make sure the dragon had fresh bedding. There were so many questions she wanted to ask about this place, but the horrible people had to take her voice away. She would just have to go with the flow.

When he unlocked the cage, the dragon became distressed and scratched his scales off from the bars.

"Easy there, big boy," the man said, then to Scarlet, "We'll need to clean out his cage. Watch out for him though, he is a bit cranky." He gave her a shovel and they started to clean up the bedding.

This is disgusting. Scarlet wasn't sure how many times this cage has been cleaned out, but they didn't do a very good job at it. Hay and feces were flung all over the place. She hated this so much. It made her hate the king even more.

As Scarlet was cleaning, she accidentally backed up into the dragon, and the creature recoiled at her touch.

You human weaklings are always screwing up. Master should have you killed right away.

Wow, you're rude. Scarlet could hear other dragons. She thought she could only hear Drakon. Then again, he had told her she could speak the tongue of the dragons, so it was possible.

The man from the other side of the cage stopped what he was doing and gave the dragon a stern look. "Fryvis, don't be rude to the young lady. Just remember, your master is also a human weakling."

Sessyl would be the exact same way, human. How were you ever a master of a dragon? You don't know anything about us.

A Dragon Master? She glanced over at him and saw all expression leave his face. It seemed he was trying to stay calm while addressing the hotheaded dragon.

"I know plenty about you and your kind, Fryvis. It's how the master treats their dragon. I treated mine with respect. How did your master treat you?" Without waiting for a reply, he set down his shovel and left the cage. Fryvis rolled his eyes and snorted smoke into Scarlet's face. She silently choked on the smoke and followed him out of the cage.

She saw him leaning against the wall, looking as if he was in pain. Scarlet looked closer at him and saw blood leaking out of the corner of his mouth. She tried to shout to warn him, and yet again she forgot and tapped his shoulder.

"Hmph? Is there a problem?" Scarlet pointed to his face and he went to go dab at it, but then she saw his hand that was on his stomach come away sticky with blood. When he saw her face, he chuckled. "Don't worry. It's just a bullet wound. Nothing too serious. Though, I had to come out here because I'm feeling drastically sick. It's fine. I've been feeling like this for a week now. Ever since that battle..." He drifted off in thought until he noticed her still standing there. Scarlet raised her eyebrows, but he only smiled and walked back into the cage. Scarlet stayed outside, reminiscing on what her life had become for her. Meeting these new people and seeing how affected they were under the King's barbaric rule. It was one more reason to continue with her plan.

26

LUKE

Chaos ensued after the initial explosion took place in Glemm Grove. At first Edith, Jay, and Luke were unaware of the events, but when they heard screaming in the village, they started searching for Scarlet and Kagura. Their immediate thought was to check the barn where they had been training. It was in complete ruins. Jay and Edith scrambled to get a better look while Luke trailed behind them, gasping for breath. Once there, many people surrounded the area and searched through the debris. Jay joined in and eventually found a body hidden under the shrapnel. His face fell.

"Kagura!" She looked ghostly pale and was cold to the touch. When he pulled her whole body out, they could see she was missing limbs from the explosion, which made them sick to their stomach. Edith, however, did nothing and stared blankly at Kagura. There was no surprise, no sadness, and no anger in her expression. For once in her lifetime she grew silent and stayed that way for a long time. There would be no changing how she felt now towards the world and other people. Kioko stood beside her, sensed his owner's mood, and pawed at her leg.

Luke did not care at all for Kagura. When he saw all the debris, he had begun to frantically search for Scarlet. She was nowhere to be seen. All he found were scores of bodies that had been Ixaemithian guards scattered all over the ground, and that's when it dawned on them that what happened was on purpose and that Scarlet was in danger. This knocked him right out of his reverie.

"I… am going… to kill… ALL OF THEM!" Jay seethed. He charged after people at random and made loud threats. Luke ran over and tried to calm him down the best he could, but Jay easily escaped his grasp, transformed, and flew away. He didn't come back.

"Great…" Luke whispered. Now they didn't have Scarlet nor jay, and they did not know where Drakon was.

That was soon not a problem. After finding the bodies and Jay freaking out, they heard more screams in the direction of the woods. Luke looked up into the skies and saw a massive figure flying towards them. The people had already fled and Drakon touched down in front of them. Luke's head filled with roaring as Drakon, a lot bigger than the last time he had seen him, roared with fury and broke everything in sight.

"Drakon! Hey! Calm down!" Luke tried to get him to settle down, but he wouldn't and decided to set things on fire. As Luke continued, Edith, still quiet, walked over to the distraught dragon, and began to speak with him. He had only ever heard Scarlet speak the tongue of the dragons, so it was still weird hearing Edith speak like that. After talking to him, she turned towards Luke.

"He says he heard the explosion and went to see if we were alright. Then the guards tried to enslave him. He managed to get away, but he was too late. He feels as if it is his fault."

"Don't beat yourself up," Luke said as he walked over to pet him. "It was all of our fault. We got a little too careless in the end. We will get her back."

Drakon said something to Edith so that she could translate back to Luke.

"'Unless she's dead.'"

“No, she’s not dead. They won’t kill her. They’ll capture anyone with magic and use it. I wonder why they didn’t try to take you Edith.”

She only shrugged, but their attention was diverted to Drakon. He started sniffing the air, then walked towards the wreckage with his eyes glowing slightly blue. When they looked over to where he was staring, a blue mist seeped through. They moved it aside to get a better look and gasped at what they found.

The Drakonian Blade lay glowing on the ground. Luke picked it up and felt its weight.

“Scarlet’s sword.” Then he came up with an idea. “This is how we will find her. She may be captured, but with its magic, we might be able to get her back.”

They all agreed, hopped onto Drakon’s back and took off into the sky.

27
Scarlet

Each second Scarlet spent here in the castle drove her mad. What was even more insane was she *couldn't talk*. Every day in her cell she would try to make her voice be heard in the deafening silence, but it was no use. She wanted to tear her hair out in frustration.

Her escape wasn't going so well either. She had underestimated how thick the bars were, and fire barely made an impact on them. They only seemed to scorch the surface of the metal. She didn't know what to do, and it made her even more frustrated.

Some nights in the castle, she would silently cry. Her plan had gone horribly wrong and nobody in this entire place would give her any hope in escaping someday. The only friend she had made in here was the man across from her, and she didn't even know his name!

On one of her roughest days, she thought that she would be let out to do more chores. Nope. About a hundred guards entered the prison and went to one cell each to take out the prisoners. They first had started on the line of cells opposite of her, and she could tell this didn't happen often because each prisoner's face, including her newfound friend, betrayed shock and confusion. They all bumped into each other as the guards led them out of the cells, through the hall, and out the door; all in single file.

When removed, it was her row's turn. Scarlet could hear complaints all around her but they were immediately quieted by lashings from the guards. One by one the doors all opened to release the prisoners. If they refused to leave their cells, the guards would go in, hit them, and drag them out into formation. When her door opened, she didn't hesitate. She saw what had happened to the people who refused to leave. She didn't want that, so she followed orders.

Scarlet didn't know where they were taking her; it soon led to outside. Scarlet's immediate response was to close and hide her eyes. She had not seen the sun in many days. When she'd adjusted to the brightness, she looked around at her surroundings. People sat on each side of them; a wooden structure stood in the middle and what she saw on those structures made her freeze in fear. Nooses of all sizes hung down from wooden poles with a guillotine placed in the middle. Many people tried to escape the guards' grasp but were unsuccessful.

They are going to hang us! She began to panic as they lined them up. They loaded them below the ropes and prepared them for the hanging. Her breathing became ragged and she begged silently to the sky for her not to die. As they prepared the first set of people for death, they set the next row in front of the nooses, making them next in line to die. The rest of them were left standing to the side, waiting for their turn. Many prisoners were crying hysterically as they tightened the ropes around their necks. Scarlet tried to stay calm, but it was hard when she was seeing people getting ready to die.

Once they were prepped for the hanging, King George, amongst the crowd, stepped forward onto a pedestal and addressed them with a booming voice. "Ladies and gentlemen! It is time for the next execution! As you all know, I have protected these lands from the many generations of criminals, like the ones you see before you now, to maintain order."

Scarlet raised her eyebrows. What he was basically saying was that once his prisons were full, it was time to clean up for the next group. She suddenly felt sick to her stomach and almost collapsed in a cold sweat.

"These criminals, as I've said in the past, have committed crimes such as: stealing, resisting, law-breaking, and the most horrible crime there is." He paused for dramatic pause as the crowd shouted angrily at the prisoners. He stared down at the prisoners in glee. "That crime, as you all know, is the law of magical creatures. It states that no person may help, or own—" he said while looking at Scarlet, then to her friend, who seemed to be just as angry as her, "—any living being with extraordinary power that no person can handle themselves. I banned these creatures for a reason. To protect the people and to grow as one!"

Scarlet couldn't help but simmer in rage. The king was blatantly lying to his own people. He was categorizing them as horrible people, when really, he was just like them. Firstly, he had his own dragon that gave him his own magic, and secondly, he didn't want to protect his people. Scarlet could assume that the reason no one could own a dragon was because he did not want anyone to be more powerful than he was. It made sense if he was to have a dragon and they couldn't.

"So, I ask you now to enjoy this spectacle! Watch the low-life criminals of this planet die and your safety increase! Guards!" he turned to them after his speech was finished. "Raise the prisoners!"

Scarlet watched as the guards moved behind the nooses and grabbed a rope that was hooked to the ground. When they unhooked it, they began pulling the rope, causing the prisoner's feet to leave the ground. Scarlet's anxiety rose with the prisoners as she saw them struggling in midair, and she could no longer watch. She looked to her friend instead and saw his jaw was set as he watched the spectacle. His eyes were hard, and he did not move. To Scarlet, it looked as if he was enraged.

As Scarlet looked anywhere but at the hanging with her anxiety continuing to rise into outright panic, each hanging was completed no more than three minutes at a time. With every group gone, the guards would pick the next one in line. By now the king was gone and the crowd was wild. At this point, Scarlet was aggressively shaking.

However, as they went, knights in metal armor had begun picking random people out of the large group and dragging them beyond the stands of people. When Scarlet and her friend reached the front of the group, they grabbed him by the wrist and yanked him away. His face showed outright panic. Then they came up to her and removed her from the line.

What are they doing? They led all the picked prisoners away from the nooses and guillotine, and away from the people. Scarlet visibly relaxed. Maybe they weren't going to kill her after all. Instead they brought them to a field surrounded by Ixaemithian knights with weapons poised out towards them, as if to keep them in the circle they were now beginning to form. In the middle stood the king with a sneer.

"You're probably wondering why your time hasn't come yet. To be honest there is so much more you could give me, including entertainment. Let's play a game."

Scarlet and a few of the prisoners rolled their eyes while others quivered in fear. Her friend gasped when a figure emerged from behind the king. A little girl with a mask and a long, purple dress walked up to the prisoners with confidence.

"This here is Edhisu. She is a young, talented girl and I am going to put her to the test. Even though killing people is quite fascinating to watch, it is even more interesting to watch people fight someone with more experience and die."

Scarlet took a closer look at who the little girl was, but it was hard to see because of the mask. She did notice that she had long, dirty blonde hair with a black streak in her bangs.

“I had fought Edhisu a while back… She may look innocent now, but when you start to fight, she can be a real pain in your ass. She’s the reason why I’ve got this damn bullet wound in the first place,” her friend whispered to her. Scarlet raised her eyebrows in surprise. She did kind of look innocent and small. How much damage could she do?

After the king was done with his lecture, he left and Edhisu stared down all the prisoners. She cracked her knuckles and motioned her hands towards the knights. Their weapons rose up from their bodies and landed at the prisoners’ feet. She didn’t speak and motioned for them to pick up the weapons to fight her.

“Pray for mercy,” he said in her ear. That left her unsettled. A loud horn sounded and Edhisu charged full on into the group. She was quick, agile, and flexible. With the first five slaves she was able to kick the weapons out of their hands in under six seconds. Others retaliated and tried to fight her back. That included Scarlet’s friend. He had picked up a revolver and charged at the little girl with fury in his eyes. Scarlet, on the other hand, did not want to fight anyone and stayed near the back.

As he fought Edhisu, he first tried to kick the weapon from her hands, but she continued to dodge his attacks easily. After being unsuccessful, he then took swipes at her with his revolver. He didn’t want to shoot his weapon if he didn’t have to. It looked like he would need to. She was beating all the prisoners with ease.

Many other prisoners, to Scarlet’s amazement, showed unique power when fighting the little girl. Some reminded her of Kagura and her abilities. They tried every element they could to defeat her, like magically picking up the fallen weapons off from the ground and using their minds to throw them at Edhisu or using the elements of the universe to try and take her down. The girl blocked each attack with her sword, deflecting lightning bolts and daggers that flew at her every which way. Scarlet was beginning to think they had specifically picked them due to their magical abilities. She just didn’t know why they all had to fight.

When they all joined in at once without using their powers, Scarlet's friend got distracted from being bumped around all over the place and didn't see Edhisu come at him with a long, sharp sword. She pulled back her arm and just as he was turning around, he managed to fire a shot off, hitting her square in the shoulder, but she still ran him through his stomach with the sword. He gasped and fell to his knees as blood ran down from his mouth and onto the grass.

"Not again…" he groaned before blacking out. Scarlet panicked but didn't move from her spot as she watched the rest of the prisoners get slaughtered in front of her.

When everything went quiet, Scarlet was the only one left standing and as Edhisu walked over to her, she scrambled to pick up a weapon, yet the little girl didn't attack. Instead she stopped in front of her, stared at her for a second, then turned back around and left the bloody arena. Scarlet felt like breaking down, but she held it together and quietly walked over to her friend and knelt next to him. He looked quite dead. However, when she felt for a pulse, she gasped. He was still alive.

28
Luke

As the day went by and the sun shone brightly, Luke and Edith had a hard time fighting the wind while Drakon flew quickly across the sky. It was hard seeing below them, and Edith only focused on trying to hold Kioko in her arms.

They could only guess where the kingdom was located because they had lost the map and were navigating on their own. They hadn't been able to find Jay either ever since he threw a fit and took off. However, Drakon's keen eyesight was sure to find him.

When the clouds passed, Luke once again looked over to see if he could find anything. Nothing. All Luke could see were the dozens of trees littered all over the place. At some point, the trees thinned out to reveal a large mass of blue. It was a body of water, but Luke had never seen so much water in one place. He had no idea where they were.

When he looked back up, he noticed birds flying up and landing on Drakon's tail. They had no trouble staying aboard on his fast whipping tail. Their beady eyes stayed on the two like they were watching them. It kind of creeped him out.

Edith had also caught sight of the birds and raised an eyebrow in curiosity. As she looked on, her face changed from curiosity to dread and as soon as she tried to warn Drakon, he suddenly roared and they were pulled from the sky.

The fall to the ground didn't take long and Drakon squealed as they hit the ground hard. Luke flew from his back and through the dirt. When he lifted his head up, a blade pointed down at his face.

"'ello there, *human*," a voice sneered from above him. A man with a spear in his hand glared down at him. "Look 'ere, boys, we got ourselves mo'e prey tah eat. Woohoo! An' look at tha'! Look at tha' dragon pelt! Tha' was an easy catch, Archie!" They all snickered, and Luke grew angry.

When they went to pick up Edith, she stood up and walked towards them with an air of confidence in her step. The creatures immediately backed down. She then spoke to them in a weird language. The man that had held the spear to Luke was now taking a knee and bowing his head. The others did the same.

"What's going on...?" Luke quietly asked her.

"Well, I'm a sorceress and they are Siles. They are afraid of me."

"Oh..." Luke was still confused. Something else was going on. "Well...why did they pull us from the sky?"

She shrugged like it was no big deal. "They see a dragon; they will catch it. It just happened to be good fortune for them to find a human upon its back. However, it was also good fortune for you that I was here to stop them from eating you."

It was surprising to Luke that creatures like the Siles knew her power and how Edith knew what their reaction would be.

As soon as Edith turned back and finished speaking with them, she walked into their territory without a care in the world. Luke thought it odd, but something else caught his attention. Drakon still laid on the ground in pain. His leg set at an odd angle and blood pooled around it. A chain looped around his ankle, causing him to grunt in pain.

"Drakon..." Luke hurried over and tried to remove the chain. It was stuck fast in his scales and each time he tried to pull it out, he ended up hurting him even more.

"I am so sorry, Drakon. I'm not a great healer. I'll tell Edith." He ran off to find her, but she was already gone.

Where could she have gone now? He thought. All around him there were normal looking people mixed with an endless assortment of different creatures. There was one specific creature that looked half human and half wolf. The weird, humanoid figure caught Luke staring at him, making him quickly look away at his snarl. He searched the other spots of the camp; she was still nowhere to be seen.

He eventually gave up and walked back to Drakon. He only slightly worried about her but knew that she was fine because of her abilities. He knelt next to Drakon and tried to put him at ease.

Luke walked amongst the Battle of Drakonia like a ghost in a dream. People everywhere were fighting for their lives against slaves and Ixaemithian guards. Leading the charge was the wolf with the black stripe. Edhisu stood with an evil glint in her eyes and watched a girl cry on the ground. Luke glided over for a better look and saw who it was. Scarlet's long, blonde hair draped over her shaking shoulders and she was hugging a body. Her cries for help could not be heard. Literally. She would open her mouth to scream, but no sound would come out. It made her rip her hair out of her skull. As she saw Edhisu looming over her, she let go of the body, and when he looked down at it, Luke's vision blurred, and his chest exploded with pain. He cried out, fell to his knees, then blacked out.

When he came to again, creatures were hovering over him and fire flashed into his line of sight out of nowhere, blinding him. He screamed as more pain enveloped his whole body and the light made his eyes burn. When the pain was too much, he blacked out again, this time forever.

Luke awoke from sleep in chills. A headache battered his head and he still felt the throbbing pain in his chest from his nightmare. These dreams were getting worse and worse, and he hated it.

As the sun neared the horizon with an orange hue, he stood up and found Edith close by. She was focusing intently on bandaging her shoulder, which was dripping with blood.

"Edith! What happened to you?" Luke hurried over to her.

She looked up in alarm, then saw who it was. "This? Oh, I went hunting with the Siles. You know, to use my sister's skill. Then I accidentally slipped and fell onto a sharp stick. I'm fine though."

"You went hunting with the Siles?"

"Yeah. Well, I wanted to go out and made the Siles come with me because, you know, they are afraid of me."

"Okay… well now that you are back, I need you to help Drakon so we can get out of here."

"Sure." She finished bandaging her shoulder and then went to go help him. Luke was about to follow her but saw something in the corner of his eye and went to go see what it was. There was a cage with a blue jay inside and it kept trying to escape. Luke took a closer look and recognized the bird.

"Wait. Jay!?" Luke ran over to Jay as he transformed. The cage was big enough to just barely fit a human. When Jay changed, he had to press his legs up to his chest and scrunch his shoulders to his body. He gave Luke a cheeky grin.

"Hey… how's it goin'?"

"Jay? Why are you in this cage?"

"Well, I am wanted by the Siles. Even though I am one of them!" He shouted in defiance. The creatures didn't stop what they were doing, but they did glance at them suspiciously and growled. Luke hurried to quiet him down.

"So anyways, I was flying, and they pulled me down! All I wanted to do was reach the kingdom, but noooo I HAD to get captured."

"Settle down, Jay. Look, we were heading there as well, and they hurt Drakon. We are safe though; apparently, they won't hurt us because of Edith. She says they fear her."

"They should be. She could kill them in a hundred ways. Just don't know how they knew she is a sorceress."

"Thinking the same thing. Something is going on here and I don't know if I like it, but we must get going. They have Scarlet, so we need to get her."

"Sure, but you need to get me out of here as well. I ain't built for this cage."

"Of course. I don't think they'll let me take you that easily. I'll have to wait till it's dark."

"Good. I'm starting to get a cramp from sitting like this," he said with a grin. With that he shifted back into a blue jay. Luke turned towards Drakon and promised to be back when the sun went down, which wouldn't be much longer.

When darkness finally came, Edith managed to remove the chain from Drakon's ankle. Luke had remained awake by that time and he told the others what he would be doing. Not many creatures were roaming about as he made his way towards Jay. It was hard to see in the pitch black, but a dim campfire off to the side gave enough light for him to find the cage. Jay was wide awake and chirping loudly to Luke. He told him to be quiet and fiddled with the cage. Jay tried to help, but his little beak couldn't do much so instead he waited patiently. Luke didn't have a key or anything good to break the lock. He did have a sharp stick and tried to pick it.

As he did that, without leaving his position he started searching for the key. The stick he was using broke and he cursed under his breath. He threw the useless stick away, stood up and quietly walked around.

As he moved farther away from the fire, it became harder and harder to see. However, he was able to make out the dark outlines of many structures. As he drew closer, he found the structures to be made up of logs and housing the Siles. The key had to be among the creatures. What he didn't notice was the fact that he had just entered the circle of many mountain lions.

Luke froze and placed his hands over his mouth to cover his panicked gasps. He didn't dare move in case he woke any of them. However, he caught a glimpse of something reflecting the light from the far away fire in one of the mountain lion's jaws. A key. It appeared to have come loose and now rested in its saliva.

Hesitating, Luke reached down and picked at it. The saliva dripped heavily from it, making Luke gag. Forgetting to be quiet, Luke hurried out of the circle and back to the cage to let Jay out. He flew to the ground, shifted and cheered. That woke up every creature in the whole camp.

"Are you stupid? We need to get out of here. Now!" Luke shouted at him.

They both ran back to Drakon and Edith to leave. All the different types of Siles in that camp began to howl and scream as they ran. It sent chills down Luke's spine.

When they got back, Luke picked Edith up, set her onto the dragon's back, and climbed on himself. Jay decided he would fly.

As Drakon took off, one of the Siles, the human and wolf hybrid, bounded over to them and latched onto Luke's ankle. He screamed in pain and fell off Drakon. Jay scrambled to help him, but now the entire camp was filled with growling creatures. Drakon flew up, deposited Edith in a safe place, flew back and went to help Luke. Jay flew up to Edith, and they both left the camp in a hurry.

While Luke was being pulled back by the beast, Drakon decided to breathe fire on the lot to reach Luke. By now his ankle had become numb and his one good eye clouded with dirt as he kept getting dragged along. He tried everything in his power to stop it, but it was no use. The thing held on very tight.

Just when he thought it would pull him out of sight, Drakon flew over, landed squarely on the creature, breaking its neck, and quickly grabbed Luke in his jaws. Once Drakon was able to fly both to safety, the creatures didn't give chase. Instead they noticed their dead leader on the ground. They whimpered and ran off into the woods. They were finally safe.

As Luke sat in Drakon's jaw, the feeling of passing out was strong. He did eventually stare out into the sky in a daze and let Drakon take him to wherever. He was too exhausted to deal with anything right now.

After hours of travelling through the sky, Drakon finally landed in a small, wooded area in unknown land. In the distance glowed a huge castle with tons of beautiful lights on the ground; he was already fast asleep.

29
Scarlet

Scarlet felt a flutter of hope in her chest at the prospect of her friend surviving his wound. She didn't dare remove the sword; she didn't want him to bleed to death.

She helped him out by trying to stop the bleeding, but the knights that had been surrounding them in the fight walked over to them and pulled her away. She tried to scramble away from them, but they held on tight and began dragging her friend and the bodies away. Scarlet motioned to the knights that they needed to feel for his pulse. When they didn't notice her, she kicked the knight that was holding her to get his attention, which she soon regretted. He threw her onto the ground, pulled out his whip, and hit her. The first few blows were incredibly painful, yet she was determined to keep her friend alive and managed to run back to show the knights with her fingers to her neck to check his pulse. She didn't want them to think he was dead and bring the body to burn. Finally, one of them listened to her and felt for his pulse. Her eyes widened.

"It can't be…" she said to her fellow knights. "He's still alive."

"How?" the one that had hit her said.

"How should I know?" she replied harshly. "If he is still alive then he can still be useful to the king. Pick him up! And bring him back to the castle! As for you." She glared down at Scarlet. "You'll be brought to the king."

Scarlet was confused, but the two were picked up and dragged back to the castle. Once inside, the two were immediately separated and went down two different hallways. When they were out of sight of each other, Scarlet hung her head.

Scarlet and the guards eventually made their way into the one room she'd had nightmares about. The throne room. This was where they had stuck the needle in her neck. In front of her sat the king and Edhisu stood right next to him.

"I'm surprised you aren't dead like the rest of 'em, but she insisted on keeping you alive. We do have uses for you and your magic, so this is good. Edhisu will escort you through the castle."

The little girl stepped over to Scarlet, took her by the hand, and led her out of the room. Scarlet felt like running away. She had underestimated the girl before. Edhisu could, and would, kill her in a blink of an eye.

The castle was enormous. She had only seen a portion of this place, but as Edhisu took her everywhere, she saw all kinds of fancy people and rooms. People were dressed in expensive dresses and suits, which had been bejeweled with beautiful rhinestones. Other people were dressed like Edhisu. They had masks on with less fancier outfits and weird hairstyles. A couple of them didn't have their masks on and revealed their faces to be covered in heavy makeup, and Scarlet would never be able to tell who they were.

Edhisu eventually brought her to a massive ballroom. There were people swarming around with huge needles in their hands, and when Scarlet saw, she panicked. Around the room slaves were being poked and injected with these needles. When some of the prisoners were done with their injections, the guards took them back to their cells. When they passed her, Scarlet could see that they were out of it and a new tattoo had been cut into their faces. She would consider it beautiful if it weren't for the profuse bleeding on the whole side of their faces. They were made up of neat intricate swirls that connected to their left eyes and the corner of their mouths. When the bleeding stopped, they dyed the brand red, to make it stand out longer. Scarlet continued to stare at them as Edhisu brought her to a chair and strapped her down. She then left.

Scarlet looked around to see if she recognized anyone, which she did. Her friend sat across from her, unconscious, as they sculpted the brand onto his face. She looked at his stomach to find the sword no longer there. Instead a very bloodied bandage wrapped around his body. They had decided to keep him alive.

Nobody was there for her just yet and being bounded to the chair, she decided to take as much in as she could. Her friend's tattoo was nearing completion and another person came to inject him with a strange, clear liquid. It woke him right up and he gasped for air. At first his eyes were vacant, then he realized what was happening to him and tried to escape his bonds. When his eyes alighted on Scarlet, he stopped. His expression changed and his eyes brightened in recognition.

Scarlet watched as the guards took him away quickly and moved on to her next. They carried over an empty syringe, which made her feel uncomfortable, and easily slipped it into her neck. It didn't feel at all like the pin needle they had stuck in there to keep her voice away. This needle made her dizzy, but she was able to focus on what they were doing to her. Dark royal blue liquid came out of her, and before she could freak out over it, they put her to sleep.

When she woke, she sat in the same seat with the room empty, except for the men still working on her. They had just finished branding her face and now started unhooking her chains. Edhisu came in, along with two other guards and they walked over to Scarlet. One of them spoke to her.

"Now that your magic has been removed, you will be treated just like any other slave in this here castle. We will escort you back to your cell so you can get some rest and be ready for your king's orders by morning."

Scarlet stared in horror as they explained to her that she had lost her magic. *Was that the blue liquid?* The two guards picked her up and made their way back to her cell.

When they got there, the others that were guarding stopped them in their tracks.

"You have to bring her to the new cell. She can't be in her old one," a female guard said to them.

"And why is that?"

"King's orders. Follow them," she said sternly.

The guard holding Scarlet seethed in anger, but only slightly grumbled and continued his way to put her back. They passed her old cell, her friend, and brought her to the "new" cell. She had glimpsed it before from her spot in there but never really got a good look at it. The cell was made completely out of iron with iron deadlocks. When they opened it up, Scarlet saw a girl with long, black hair chained to the wall. She couldn't see her face.

The guards chained her to the wall and left. She felt like passing out, but before she did, her hand began to sizzle. She looked down at it and was filled with confusion and joy. She still had her magic.

Scarlet continued to look down at her hand. If they squeezed it out of her, she shouldn't have it. Then suddenly she remembered her conversation with Drakon. She would always have his magic as long as he lived. Then she remembered her conversation with Jay. Her Drakonian Blade also held magic, even if she did lose it, which she just realized that her sword was not with her and was still in the village. She would never lose her magic.

After having been locked up in her new cell, Scarlet soon found out why they had moved her. The morning after, King George had personally come to her cell. He was not happy. Apparently, they had found out that she had been trying to escape by burning the bars of the cell. She found out when the king came to her and harshly beat Scarlet right there in the cell and she couldn't even make a sound. The girl that was sitting next to her looked up from bowing her head and watched with defeat in her eyes.

As the king beat her, Scarlet tried to protect herself, but she couldn't. He just kept going and going and she received severe bruises all over her body. A trickle of blood ran down from her mouth, as well as her newly branded tattoo, and after one final blow, he cracked her skull open. Her whole head exploded in pain as she grew dizzy and lightheaded. When the king was done, he left without saying a word.

Scarlet laid on the ground, sobbing, as she cupped her head in her hands and tried to make the headache go away. The girl beside her looked on in pity and moved closer to her.

"Hey there… everything will be ok. You will get used to how things run around here. What is your name?" Her voice was silky sweet and comforting. Scarlet looked up and motioned to her neck, saying she couldn't speak.

"Ah, you're one of those people. I'm not exactly sure but I think you can get that thing out of your neck. If you tried, though, they would kill you."

Comforting. Scarlet moved her hands from her face to see the girl better. She looked to be around her age with clear smooth skin, deep soulful black eyes and the corners of her lips curled up in a little smile.

"My name is Aki. Wish I could know your name."

Scarlet jumped up in excitement. She knew that name. Jay had told her that he had a friend who had been captured by the king. Her name was Aki.

"What? What is it?" Aki sat up in alarm as she stared at Scarlet who was having trouble keeping calm. She so badly wanted to explain everything to her, but she couldn't. She would just have to leave Aki in the unknown.

Aki sat back in silence and began playing with her hair. It was silky smooth and reached to the ground easily. When her hands touched her hair, it changed color. Wherever her hand went, the black brightened to orange. Scarlet watched in fascination as her hair changed back to black. She then played with her hand. Her fingers were also changing colors and shape. At first her hand sizzled and increased in size. Orange feathers replaced her fingers and grew all along her forearm to form a wing. Scarlet remembered that Jay had told her that Aki was a bird Sile. A phoenix. Scarlet wanted to see her transform fully.

When she formed her other arm into a wing, a loud bang startled them both and her wings grew back into arms. A couple of guards came back and roughly picked up Scarlet and brought her out; they didn't even glance at Aki. When she stood up, her head throbbed even more, and her vision blurred. She was in no shape to walk.

Not being able to object, they brought her to the top of the castle and into a closed off room with huge windows overlooking the kingdom's ground. There was a table with stacks of paper on it and two other people in the room. One was her friend she recognized, who glanced at her, smiled, and then saw her face. His cheerful attitude immediately disappeared. The other person was a man with shaggy hair that blocked most of his face from view. He didn't even look at her.

The guards left her again without saying a word and the three of them were in there doing nothing. Her friend and the man were speaking a language Scarlet could not understand. They seemed to be writing something down on the pieces of paper that were in the room.

Since they didn't give her any orders to follow, she wanted to see if she could write something of her own for her escape. Maybe she could slip the piece of paper out of the window for someone to see on the ground so they could know what was being done to her here in the castle. It may not work but it was at least worth a try.

She picked up a piece of paper, found a pen, and wrote a note:

> *Whoever is reading this please help me! My name is Scarlet Shookram and I am a prisoner here in the castle! They are beating us and keeping us imprisoned in here! Please help me. I did nothing wrong... Please!*

As Scarlet wrote this, a tear ran down her cheek and she began to cry openly in the room. Her friend looked over from writing on the paper and his face scrunched up in pain, as if he could feel her anguish, but he didn't say anything and continued writing. Scarlet just wanted to disappear.

When her crying fit stopped, she stood up, walked over to the window and went to find a place to stick the note through. The window was open a little bit; she could see the tiniest crack on the side where it opened. She tried to stick it in there, but before she successfully did, her friend and the man got up, walked over to Scarlet, slipped the piece of paper into her pocket without her noticing, and walked away.

30
Luke

When Luke woke up, the sun shined down onto his face and he found Edith wrapping his ankle. His whole body ached from being dragged on the ground from the previous night. He waited for Edith to finish wrapping his wounds before slowly raising himself into a sitting position. He winced as he used his aching muscles. Next to him were a pile of clothes with a strange looking mask on the top.

"What the… what is that?" Luke asked aloud. Edith looked up from what she was doing and shrugged.

"Dunno. Jay and I went to the kingdom and found everyone wearing those. You and Jay will have to go in, dressed in a disguise, and try to find Scarlet. Unfortunately, we could only get one of those outfits; we were almost caught. So, Jay will be dressed differently than you."

"Wait, we reached the kingdom?" Before he let her answer, he rushed to his feet, which surprisingly held his weight, and peered through the trees. It was noon and he could see the castle with little houses surrounding it. Part of the castle had been obscured by the forest. Around the small buildings, people were bustling about doing their day-to-day activities.

Edith began pushing him through the trees and towards Jay. At first, he did not recognize the person standing in front of them, but when he turned around, Luke saw his tan face and pitch-black eyes peeking from behind a grey mask that covered his mouth, and a black hoodie. His eyes crinkled up in a smile.

"Looks like we both won't be recognizable. You match though, so if I get into any trouble at all, you leave me behind. Scarlet is more important."

Luke nodded and put on his own outfit. It was hard to see through the mask, especially with just one eye, but he still managed to walk around easily. They then left for the kingdom and planned. When Jay wasn't to be on the ground, he would fly around looking for Scarlet while Luke stayed on the ground to gather information about what was going on there.

Just before they came into full view of the kingdom, Jay shifted and flew out of sight. Luke lowered his mask over his face and walked into the village. He saw people he had never seen before, with fancy jewels embroidered on them and beautiful outfits. Luke was officially jealous.

He passed by delicious looking food that made his stomach grumble loudly, but he had no money and reluctantly continued. When he made it to a specifically massive alleyway with tons of people fooling around and drinking, Luke saw out the corner of his eye a commotion with a group of people. A little girl around the age of five wearing the same mask as his ran around people's legs and waved a piece of paper in her hand. Either they were too drunk or did not care, they just ignored and pushed her away, making her stumble to the ground in defeat. Luke walked over to help her up. She saw his mask and began to speak a language he did not understand.

"I-I'm sorry. I don't understand what you are sayin'."

She froze for a second, then handed him the paper and pointed up to the castle. Luke opened it up and read what was inside. There was short, neat handwriting dotted with a couple drops of blood, and a name caught his attention. It was Scarlet! She had written a note for someone to help her! She sounded desperate and lonely. Luke could only guess what horrible things were going on in there and it made him furious.

"Thank you," he said to the little girl and hurried off towards the castle. He searched for a way in and saw the grand entrance with guards on each side, eyeing him.

"Who might you be, jester?" one of them asked him.

Luke's heart jumped in fear. What was he supposed to say? He was not from around here. He did not even know if they had a system in place or if he was supposed to remove his mask. Also, Luke had no clue how to speak the language the jesters spoke. Are all of them like that? He felt like running as fast as he could from there.

"Ugh, one of these jesters. Hodge, remove his mask."

When his buddy stepped up, Luke straight up panicked and fled from the entrance. All he could hear were the guards yelling from behind him. He didn't look back.

Meanwhile, when Jay had flown from the trees, he had immediately headed towards the castle. If Scarlet was being held captive, then she would be there. He just had to figure out where she was.

From the height he was at he could see the entire Ixaemithian kingdom. And he loathed it. He'd had deep, powerful anger directed towards them every day of his life. First, they took his best friend away. Then they took his mentor's life. And finally, they took the girl he had started to have feelings for, who had chased him through the streets of Argonia with determination in her eyes, and who was the bravest person he had ever met, away from him. Tears leaked from his eyes. He would right all the wrong that had been done to him. Starting today.

Jay didn't waste any time in going through the whole kingdom, he went straight to the castle's entrances. There was a huge window at the top that he could see through, but no one was in there, so he tried another entrance. The main doors were guarded, so he didn't want to risk it and go near them. All the other entrances were the same and there were barely any windows in this castle. What he did find was a large opening to a huge garden. He flew in there and landed on the archways.

Many prisoners were working on planting flowers and watering them. It seemed to him that they were sprucing up the place for some event. Some were uprooting flowers to be cut and placed for decorations. Others were replanting the areas that had been uprooted. Jay had never seen the inside of the castle before, but he could tell that decorating for an event was new for them.

Jay looked up from the prisoners gardening and saw two guards bringing another prisoner out. It was Scarlet! She had been beaten badly with dry blood caked to the side of her face. One eye was slightly closed and bulging, and the bottom of her lip was cut open. Jay's heart picked up speed, but he waited for the guards to leave and then made his move.

31
Scarlet

For the next few days, Scarlet has been healing from her wounds she had received from the king and been planning her escape. Someone had to have seen that note she wrote—either if they didn't want to help or did not find the note, she would continue anyway. Her plan included saving her strength to draw magic. She had noticed that ever since they drew that liquid from her body, her magic had weakened but hadn't completely vanished.

For now, she would wait and follow the rules. Today that was for her to garden with the other prisoners. The king wanted the castle to look "pretty" for an event Scarlet knew nothing about. She couldn't help but roll her eyes when she heard this.

When they brought her to the garden, she saw other girls of her age planting the flowers and watering the grass. A few jesters roamed about while the "fancy" people laid around in laziness and watched the prisoners work with scorn. Scarlet wanted to give them a dirty look, but was afraid that she would get another beating, so instead she minded her own business and started to plant the flowers.

Once Scarlet fertilized the flowers, the insects and birds swarmed around her. They kept getting in her way and she had to swat at them. There was this one particular bird that paid more attention to her than the others. It was a blue jay and each time she swatted it away it would always come back and peck at her. When it continued to do that, the bird decided to go fly up onto her shoulder and peck her face. Scarlet was getting irritated.

When the bird was unsuccessful getting her attention, it flew over to the flowers she was planting and looked her straight in her eyes. Scarlet was confused for a second, then realization hit her. She quickly, but gently, picked him up and brought him into a corner of the garden where they couldn't be seen. Jay shifted into a human.

"Hey, Scarlet. Your face looks rough. Having a good time here?" he said with the sound of a grin on his face. He was covered in all black except the cloth covering half his face.

Scarlet just stared back at him in irritation and pulled out a piece of paper she had taken from that room. She began writing something down while Jay looked on in confusion. When she was finished, she handed him the note.

"'I can't talk so I have to write. They stuck a needle in my neck to prevent me from speaking."

"What the hell is wrong with this place?"

Scarlet only shrugged and took back the paper. She told him everything that has happened in the past few weeks. Then she asked him how she would escape.

"Well, Luke is out and about trying to find a way in while disguised and I am here. Drakon and Edith are hiding in the trees. If you're strong enough you can use your magic to break yourself out of here. Unfortunately, I can't do much to help you, only to find you and report to the others. Hopefully, Luke will be out there to guide you back if you manage to escape."

Scarlet nodded and before Jay was to be caught, he shifted and flew away. She quietly walked back to the garden. By now more guards had appeared and were chatting with each other. She managed to hear a few of the conversations, and it filled her with dread.

"Did you hear?" one of them asked the other. "The king is bringing all of us, plus the prisoners, on a charge to attack Drakonia. He's going to take them down. He won't say the reason why, only that that village is important."

Scarlet's heart froze in place and she stopped what she was doing. They noticed her and whipped her to start working again.

"What are you doing? Get back to work on planting those flowers. The big ceremony needs to be spotless." Then they left. Once Scarlet saw them leave, she stood up, walked over to the nearest wall and lifted her hand up to it. She wasn't going to let the king go through with his plan.

Someone who was admiring the gardens from their seat glanced over at her and shouted, "Peasant! What you doin'! Are you stupid?"

Scarlet looked over her shoulder as the anger built up inside her. She instead moved her hand over to her and with little energy she struck the woman with a bolt of lightning; leaving her unconscious in her seat. By that time all the prisoners looked up to see what was happening and cheered. The guards came running in when they heard the commotion and tried to stop Scarlet. Before they could reach her, she blew up the wall and ran for her life.

When people heard that explosion everyone began panicking. It was just like the dream she had a while back. She blew up wall after wall as her anger continued to grow and she plowed through the fear-stricken people. The one person she did not want to come across was the king. Or Edhisu.

Without realizing it she had blasted her way into the throne room. It was empty. She took one look at it and quickly blasted the next wall. Guards were there lining up, ready to fire at her. She didn't let them have the chance and sent them up into flames as they screamed in agony. By now her strength was beginning to fade.

Finally, she made it to the lobby. Tons of people were running around trying to escape the castle, and the figure she had remembered from her dream was right there in reality. The wolf with the black stripe. It glared down at her with menace and padded its way to her like the Grim Reaper in disguise. Its powerful muscles rippled as it walked down the steps and up to Scarlet. It almost seemed… human.

Scarlet prepared herself to fight the beast, but the wolf stopped mere inches from her. It then shifted into an actual human and standing before her now was the one girl she did not want to come across. Edhisu. Scarlet didn't even give it a second thought and just booked it out of there. She knew the girl's strength and since her own strength was fading, she did not want to pick a fight with her. Unfortunately, Edhisu wasn't going to give up that easily.

Scarlet ran out of the castle and down streets she had never been through before. She occasionally checked behind her back to find no one there. However, once she rounded the corner, she plowed into someone. Edhisu had gone a different direction to stop Scarlet. When she noticed who she ran into, she scrambled to her feet and ran in the opposite direction, but it felt like something was grabbing ahold of Scarlet's neck and choking her. All the air rushed from her body and she dropped to her knees once more. The pressure made the needle poke deeper inside her neck and she soon tasted blood. She looked around to face Edhisu and found her hand raised towards Scarlet with massive twitching all through her arm. She could tell the little girl was using a lot of strength to choke her out.

Just when she thought she would pass out in suffocation, a boy came up and knocked the little girl out stone cold. He wore the same mask as her and had rugged brown hair. When he reached down for Scarlet, she cowered back and mustered up the last of her strength to defend herself. He saw what she was doing and backed away.

"Hey, Scar, it's okay. It's me," the boy said. He lifted his mask and she saw Luke behind it with a huge smile on his face. "I know it's rude to hit a little girl, but man was she haunting my dreams." He picked her up and Scarlet buried her face into his chest. She burst into tears and relief filled every limb in her body. The nightmare was over. For now.

Luke cradled her in his arms for a few minutes, and when she calmed down, he let her stand up and led her to their temporary camp. He told her everything that had happened; from being trapped at a Sile camp, escaping with a minor ankle injury, to Jay and Luke disguising themselves to rescue her, and him being chased by guards. He chuckled at that memory.

"When they realized I wasn't a jester, they chased me all the way to our little camp where Drakon easily killed them. They were stupid."

Scarlet silently laughed and wanted to ask how Drakon was. She missed her dragon. She was so relieved to find all her friends here and she couldn't wait to see her sister again.

Luke looked to her in confusion when she didn't reply. "Are you okay? You haven't said a word since I found you."

Scarlet stopped and stared at him. She forgot all about that. Scarlet must have grown accustomed to not talking. She would have to tell him on a piece of paper.

When she pulled the paper with her writings to Jay, another piece fell out. She picked it up in confusion and opened it up. It was a letter to her. She read it over and her chest tightened in panic. Without Luke knowing what she read, she burst into tears once more and made a break for the castle.

32
Luke

"Scarlet! Wait!" Luke ran for her after she broke down and freaked out. He had no idea what was going on with her or what happened to her, but he needed to get her back to the others. Scarlet was going to get herself into even more trouble.

Before Scarlet could escape him, Luke caught up to her and wrapped his arms around her, stopping her in her tracks. She sobbed, kicked, pulled at his hair, and screamed. She did not make a single sound. That really unnerved him. He waited for her to stop and then carried her away. She just went limp in his arms in defeat.

When they did reach camp, which was made easy because no one else was around to stop them, Drakon was there pacing with his nostrils flared and smoke rose from them. When he saw his master, her purred and wrapped his tail around her. She still didn't move. Luke took the note from her hand and read it himself to see what made her freak out so much. It read:

Hello there, Scarlet. You may not know me, but I know you. My name is Alexander Shookram and the man with me is William Ransier, your Godfather. I can't believe I didn't recognize you before; perhaps because it has been seven years since the last time we saw each other. I should have known better. You look exactly like your mother.

Now, don't you worry about me. Most likely by the time you read this you will be long gone from the castle. Don't come back for us. You have already suffered enough, and I don't want you to be in danger anymore. Live your life in peace, try to stay out of trouble, and always remember the good moments in your life; you will need it to keep your head above water.

Well, with that I bid you farewell, daughter of Elena.

Alexander, your father.

Luke teared up when he read this. He remembered her dad from a long time ago. The memory was a bit fuzzy, but when they became friends, he met her family every day. Her parents were loving people; her dad was always quiet and loved to read about folklore while her mother could heal anyone with her amazing, gentle skills. She was the sweetest woman he had ever met. She had been named after the Drakonian goddess, Elena. Scarlet's Godfather William, also known as Liam, would come by every day to see them. Luke was surprised that he was also captured here. Scarlet's whole family had been ruined and now he understood why she freaked out so much.

Luke handed the note back to Scarlet and found Jay perched in a nearby tree. Edith was nowhere to be found. Jay flew down and then told him what was wrong with Scarlet. She couldn't speak. They had removed her voice by inserting a needle in there to cause her pain. That made Luke angry.

"I overheard some of the Ixaemithian's talking. Apparently, King George is planning a ceremony tonight. I don't know what it is about though," Jay continued.

"I heard that too, but I hear they are planning an attack somewhere. That's what the ceremony is about," Luke added.

Scarlet overheard and she nodded. She then pointed to Drakon, and then to the west of her. Jay didn't know what she was talking about, but Luke had an idea.

"Drakonia?"

She nodded.

"Why would they be doing that? Drakonia is a simple village. It's harmless!"

Scarlet only shrugged and looked down. Then she noticed someone was missing and looked at them with a question in her eyes.

"Edith? I don't know where she is. Drakon, tell her the last time you were with her," Luke said.

Drakon gently growled to her and her face went pale. She wrote furiously on the paper and handed it to Luke, which he read aloud afterwards.

"'Drakon says she wanted to go hunting hours ago and never came back. What if she got caught? We need to go to Drakonia to warn them of the attack, but we can't leave her here either.' I say Jay does a flyby of the area to see if he can find her."

Scarlet shook her head furiously. Jay stepped up and went along with Luke's plan. "I agree with that. If the king *has* to have a big ol' ceremony, then that leaves us extra time to head back. It's your hometown, Scarlet. Don't let everyone there down. I will stay back if I can't find her."

Scarlet hesitated while Drakon and Luke both agreed. Jay continued.

"And when I find her, I will bring her back to you. Don't worry about our transportation; I have a few friends who will be willing to help, and she can show us where you live."

Scarlet still hesitated and Luke tried to convince her. "What about my family, Scar? I don't want them dead. We have to go."

Tears ran down her cheeks again, and she reluctantly nodded. They all hopped onto Drakon and got ready to take off. Before they could, Scarlet remembered something and tore off a little piece of paper and wrote down a name. She then handed it to Jay and took off.

33
ALEXANDER

Alex had seen many things in his life, but today just seemed crazy. First off, the king having a ceremony was unheard of. If he was holding one today, then something big must be going on. When things were getting ready throughout the day, that was when the madness really began. The girl he had initially thought was a friend still had her magic. He so desperately wanted to escape with her, but not yet. He still had plans to follow through with to completion.

He could not believe that Scarlet, his daughter, was here. He also couldn't forgive himself for not realizing that it was her. She looked exactly like his wife, Elena, and yet he had no idea. It was all so crazy.

Now, even with everything in ruins, all the prisoners came together to hear the king's words of "encouragement" for them. Standing next to him was his best friend, Liam. He had told Alex that he had been captured right when Scarlet ran away. He had no idea how, or why. All he knew was that from the moment they did, they would be in big trouble. That included Alex's youngest daughter, Edith.

"*Alexein*, what do you think he wants?" Liam asked him just as nervous as ever.

"I don't know, *Guglielmus.* You shouldn't have to worry though. Whatever he wants shouldn't have to involve us."

Or so he thought.

When the king appeared in front of everyone, they all gasped when they saw his face. He was covered in tribal paint.

"My fellow prisoners! I have exciting news to share with you! You may hate me now, but after you do this one last task for me, I will set you free."

Alex rolled his eyes. That was a bluff. There was no way he would allow most of these slaves to be released. However, the others seemed to believe him.

"The events that have taken place an hour ago make me even more sure I should follow through with the plan. I want to take all of you, plus my soldiers, across Ixaemithia and attack Drakonia. That dragon girl lives there and has escaped. She will be heading there as well."

Murmurs flooded among the prisoners and Alex's heart sank. He had many friends there; he hoped Scarlet would get there in time to prevent any deaths. He and Liam exchanged glances.

One slave spoke up above the others. "But how do you know where she traveled to?"

The king smiled. "Oh, don't worry about that. I have my ways."

For some reason that made Alex unsettled and he shot him a suspicious glance.

"We will attack tomorrow morning, and I will need a few personal slaves to help me along the way while the rest of you follow my soldiers and attack the people. Some of you are the least dangerous so you will fight. The others who I deem dangerous will stay with me.

"Now, the names I say will come up here and stand by me. Those are the ones who will not fight and will instead do errands for me. Guards, as I say them, and if anyone rejects this notion, force them up here and make them cooperate."

Everyone quivered in fear and the guards standing next to him nodded in agreement. The king said aloud the names of the prisoners he wanted by his side. A few of them couldn't even move because they were so afraid, so the guards would come down, shove them up towards the king and take out their whips. Alex looked for his friends Ace and Isabella, but sadly realized where they were. They were dead. They died in the battle with Edhisu.

As the king went down the list, he eventually announced Alex's name. He froze, then steadily walked up next to him along with all the other prisoners. Liam's name was not called. His best friend looked up at him in a frenzy and looked as if he wanted to run up there with him. Alex motioned for him not to and to keep quiet. He listened.

"Alright, prisoners. The rest of you will be assigned by the guards. This group will follow me," King George said and led them away. They were brought outside where a horde of Ixaemithians crowded around to hear their king's words. They were more afraid than anything about what was happening right now.

"My fellow comrades!" he introduced. "You may be wondering what is going on right now. I assure you everything is fine. An extremely dangerous prisoner has escaped and is on the run, but I will promise you protection."

Alex wanted to say, "My daughter isn't dangerous! You are!" But instead he kept his mouth shut and his gaze forward. The Ixaemithians sent looks of respect towards their king and glares of disgust at the prisoners beside him.

"Before I can do that, there is someone I would like to introduce you to." He backed up and made room for one more person. Edhisu. Alex had never seen the little girl without her mask or makeup before. She had long, dirty blonde hair and brown eyes. One eye was beginning to swell and bruise.

"This here is Edhisu. She has helped me through thick and thin; I think you should trust her as well. She can give you protection and leadership while I am gone."

Murmurs ran throughout the crowd as they looked uneasily at each other. He raised his hands to calm them down.

"Please, please. I will only be gone for a short period of time while I take care of that dangerous prisoner. With Edhisu as leader she will keep you calm and safe while I am away."

One man stood up from the crowd with a confused look on his face. "But she is just a little girl. How is she supposed to keep us safe?"

As the king was about to speak again, Edhisu walked up and addressed the man herself; boy, was Alex surprised to hear her voice.

"What is your name, sir?"

"Uh, Remi, ma'am."

"Hello, Remi. Your king has trusted me every day since I've been acquainted with him. If you wish, I can show you how I can protect you and your loved ones." She hopped down from where she had stood, walked up to the man, and motioned for him to hold out his hand. When he did, she showed him that her hand was empty, and just like the sleight of a magician's hand, a huge trove of coins fell from it like a stream. Remi stared in wonder as the coins continued to fall from her hand; everyone crowded around now to receive what she was offering.

The king smiled as he looked on. "Yes. She can give you anything you want! She can DO anything you want!"

As the people cheered and the king laughed, Alex looked up. A small object in the sky had caught his attention from all this "sentiment" going on here on the ground. A bird was rapidly flying towards Edhisu, and she noticed. She stopped giving the people coins and raised her hand up to the bird, which then transformed him into a teen boy. He fell from the sky, hit the ground hard and before he could speak, Edhisu cast a spell that bound his mouth together. The people gasped.

"It's okay, everyone. It's just a filthy Sile. Nothing more," she said with contempt. She motioned for the guards to take him away and the last they saw of him was the hurt expression in his big black eyes.

After the Sile was taken out of sight, the king left with Alex and the other prisoners in tow. The ones who were not picked stayed back as the guards dealt with them. He had to start immediately. The king had assigned him to be a runner. Alex would have to run and do chores for him as they fought in battle. Even outside the castle he would still have to do work for him.

Next, Alex would be partnered up with one of the other skittish prisoners. His name was Casimir and when Alex tried to introduce himself, he didn't get a word out of him. Instead he flashed him a small smile and paid attention to what the king was saying. He was assigning tasks to the others.

When he was done, he walked over to them to give their orders. "You two are going to run ahead of the others to the nearest villages and offer them to be spared. My original plan was to plow through as we head to Drakonia, but now that I think of it, they could be of great use to me. They can be my slaves as well."

Alex sent him a look of disgust and looked as if he were about to argue, but Casimir stopped him and nodded. The king gave them a map and let them be. Casimir grabbed Alex's wrist and pulled him in the direction of the nearest village on the map, Glemm Grove. They ran at a steady pace with Alex dragging behind. He had a choice to make. Run with Casimir and make everyone slaves, or abandon him, run, and try to beat the king to Drakonia. He would have to take the map with him and leave Casimir.

When he was about to make the decision, realizing he didn't know Casimir at all and would risk anybody to see his daughter again, Casimir turned towards him.

"I know what you are thinking. You are deciding whether or not to leave me dead here or come with me."

"Well… not exactly like that," Alex said, realizing what he was saying was somewhat true. Would he really leave Casimir to die?

He smiled. "You are free to do whatever, but I haven't told you about *my* plan yet."

Alex stopped. He had caught his attention.

"The king thinks we are going to either kill the people or enslave them. What I am going to do is recruit them. Your daughter will need all the extra help she can get, but we have to hurry."

Alex looked at him in fear. "How do you know about my daughter…?"

Casimir gave him a knowing look, like they shared a secret. "Let's say there is something much more to me than meets the eye. People see me as a shy, helpless man. What I actually am is a much more dangerous person. I know that you have two daughters, a best friend who is the Godfather of your children, and a late wife named after the goddess, Elena."

Alex could only stare at him in shock. He knew everything about him!

"Your eldest daughter, Scarlet, is a Dragon Master with her dragon named Drakon; named after your village, Drakonia. She has the Drakonian Blade in her possession that gives her endless magic at her fingertips. She has some serious trust issues as well.

"Then there's your other daughter, Edith," Casimir continued. "Now, she is a very interesting person. A beautiful young girl with a lot of power coursing through her veins; a lot more than you think. You don't know this about her, but she is the last sorceress on this Earth. I learned this from Scarlet, when she was a prisoner here. I didn't speak with her, but she did give me quite a lot of information." He then went on to explain the rest of Alex's family members and close friends to him. He was speechless. Casimir must be a mind reader to be able to know all this. More importantly, he had barely known Edith since the time she was two and he had been captured. It was so good to hear about her, and very surprising to learn she was a sorceress! He had a family of magicians.

Finally, Casimir finished listing off everyone Alex knew. "You can trust me, Alex. I use my ability for the good, not the bad. I am on the same level as you for wanting to kill the king. He captured me, tortured me, and forced me to use my ability against the people I love. There is no reason for us not to be working together."

Alex thought for a long time, then decided to stay with him. If they hurried, they could reach these villages, recruit the people, and reach Drakonia to help in the fighting. He would then see his daughters once again.

Casimir nodded in satisfaction and began running. Alex asked him what exactly his ability was. He didn't answer. Instead he only smiled sheepishly, lifted a finger up to his lips and continued.

Glemm Grove on their map was not that far off, but there was one major problem. A huge Sile camp blocked their paths and if they tried to go around it, it would take another day of travel time. They had no choice but to go through and hope for the best.

"We will have to be stealthy," Casimir said. "You know any fighting skills?"

Alex nodded and didn't say a word. He was kind of nervous entering a Sile's territory. They were known to be extremely dangerous creatures. It would be a whole different story if the king were with them.

As they entered the thick, green canopy of the woods, Alex glanced at him nervously and saw Casimir's eyes trained intently ahead of him. It looked as if he was trying hard to listen. Casimir heard his thoughts.

"Yes. If I can hear the Sile's thoughts I will be able to tell how far away they are, or if we have been compromised. The best we can do is to avoid the major sections of the camp if we are to get out of here alive."

"Hey, could you like not read my thoughts?" Alex said in discomfort. "I'd prefer to not have all my secrets be poured out into the world."

"My apologies, friend. Sometimes I cannot help myself. I am unable to stop the thoughts from entering my head, but if it will make you more comfortable, I will no longer respond to your thoughts and keep them secrets only for me."

Alex agreed. For some reason having Casimir read his mind really made him uncomfortable. There were secrets that Alex wished to keep to himself and just meeting him wasn't right at all.

As they quietly walked through the woods, Casimir would occasionally stop him and listen. He would then lead Alex to a certain spot, make him hide, and watch as six or more Siles just barely missed them. They were all in their human forms. They could overhear them speaking.

"Did ya hear what goin' on?" one of them said. "The li'l girl took control of the kin'dom. The king himself is plannin' an attack that will include us!"

"I did, Rusty. He also bringin' his dragon, Fryvis. That piece of-"

"Pfft. Who cares about that idiot! All he does is use us. Remember who you are, Dex. We are Siles. We take nothing from nobody."

"But what the hell are we doin' then! George thinks he can walk all over us, and we are lettin' him! Vixen, we *have* to do somethin' about this!"

All the Siles began to fight and shift. The one who was named Vixen remained calm but squinted down at them in anger. Dex shifted into a snake as Silico changed into a large, golden striped tiger and they fought. Alex was blown away at the sight of the different assortments of animals in the group.

Before things got out of hand, Casimir dragged him away.

"These creatures don't know much do they? They're the most feared beasts on Earth yet they can't seem to be in control of themselves. They have the power to rid themselves of the king but somehow, they are too afraid to do so. Heck, if I were a Sile I would do just that," Casimir told him once they were out of earshot of the creatures.

"I'm wondering the same thing. The types of Sile's they are they could easily fight back. I wonder what Vixen is though."

"Oh, that's easy. He is a dragon Sile. Reason why he didn't change form. We are in the woods, which makes it harder for him to shift. Plus, it would make all the other Siles jealous if they were to find out what he is."

"Okay, brainiac. Not everyone can know as much as you." Alex didn't know why, but each time Casimir used his special ability it just made him even more irritated.

Casimir sent him an apologetic glance and was about to say something, but then pushed Alex into the bushes. He looked up and saw him face to face with the creature. The thing didn't look happy as Casimir stared it down, remaining unfazed.

34
Scarlet

After Scarlet had given Jay the note with his best friend's name on it, she and Luke took off on Drakon at a rapid pace back home. She was still devastated about the letter from her dad and having to leave Edith behind. She couldn't believe that she didn't recognize him. He was her father for crying out loud! She admitted that he did look different from the last time she had seen him, but still. She would apologize one day to him, if she ever saw him again.

Luke could see Scarlet was quiet, well, aside from being mute, and he remembered he had something for her. He removed it from his side and handed it over. It was her Drakonian Blade. The jewel on the handle glowed brighter at her touch and she smiled. She had never been so grateful to have this sword in her possession. It had blessed her with amazing magic that never failed to help her out of tough situations. She placed it back in her sheath.

The three of them were off to a great start. Since Drakon was so much bigger than before he could easily travel across Ixaemithia. They just had to wait patiently, and by doing that they began to tell stories. Since Luke was the only one who could speak, he decided that he would tell Scarlet about his mysterious dagger. After Kagura had healed his snake bite, he didn't think much about this dagger, except for having those terrible dreams of death. Now he remembered and showed Scarlet. As he told her the story about it, she stared at the dagger in fear. What he was telling her was awful. She grew concerned for her friend.

Scarlet took the dagger from him and examined it. It had pretty rubies all over the handle with a short, sharp blade. When she touched the dagger, a cold sensation ran through her body and a headache spawned at the forefront of her head. She quickly handed it back. The dagger just gave her the creeps.

He chuckled, put back the dagger and they fell silent again. Scarlet wanted to tell him everything about her capture, but she couldn't. It really frustrated her. They plagued her with this disability, and it made her sad. Instead of trying to tell him, she gently rested her head on Drakon's scales and closed her eyes.

Scarlet stood over her baby sister's crib in pride. Eight years and she finally had a sister. Her parents never told her when she would have a sibling and would always stay secretive on the topic. Scarlet would see her best friend Luke with all his brothers. She just wondered why she didn't have any, and now she did. Her father picked her name. Edith for "The Blessed."

When she heard a noise from behind her, she spun around and saw her father smiling down at her. He had a clean-shaven face with bright eyes.

"Do you like your new baby sister?" he asked her.

She nodded furiously. "Can I play with her?"

He continued smiling, but he shook his head. "Not right now, darling. She needs to sleep before she can explore the world. She was just born this morning."

Scarlet remembered the birth. Her mother had to deliver the baby in their home and Scarlet wasn't allowed to see, but she heard her. Scarlet had cried in her Godfather's arms when she heard her mother's wails coming from the other room. She thought that she was being hurt, but Liam told her that it was normal, and she shouldn't have to worry.

Now she bowed her head in sadness and continued to stare at Edith. Alexander smirked and picked her up into his arms.

"How 'bout you and your buddy Luke play for a while. So that you can leave baby Edith alone and you won't be so bored. Alright?"

Scarlet nodded sadly and waited for him to get Luke over there. She decided to visit her mother and see how she was doing. She laid in bed with her eyes closed and her long, blonde hair flowing off the edge of the bed. Her stomach was still swollen from the pregnancy.

When she heard the door creak open, she opened her eyes and smiled weakly.

"Daughter, what are you up to?"

Scarlet looked down and shuffled her feet. "Daddy won't let me play with Edith."

She raised her eyebrows in surprise. "You are tattling on him?"

"What? No! He just won't let me play with her is all."

"Well, whatever your father says you will listen. Edith is not ready to play yet."

"Okay, Mommy." Scarlet apologized, then smiled mischievously and hopped onto her bed. She had so much energy and really wanted to play with someone. Her mother closed her eyes in exhaustion and sighed. She didn't have enough strength to stop her daughter.

Alex walked in to find Scarlet jumping up and down on the bed. The little boy holding his hand began laughing. Scarlet heard his laughter and screamed in excitement.

"Luke! Finally! Let's go play!" They both excitedly ran out of the house while Alex went to comfort Elena.

Scarlet and Luke ran to her backyard and played around for a bit. Liam came out and watched them play. What they didn't notice was someone knocking on their door. However, Scarlet did. She ran inside and opened the front door to find a bulking man wearing a uniform standing there. There was a dragon crest on his chest, and he had noticeably short black hair. Just when Scarlet was about to greet this man, she was pulled back by Liam and addressed him instead. He looked nervous.

After a few minutes of talking, Liam came back into the house in distress and hurried into the other room. A few seconds later he came out with her father who once had a bright smile on his face, and now wore a serious expression. Scarlet tried to go back outside, but her dad roughly grabbed her away from the door, set her in Liam's arms and walked out.

Scarlet struggled to release herself from him, and when she did, she ran up to the window. There she could see what was going on between her dad and the man. They seemed to be arguing about something and the man pulled out a large, green scale. When Alex looked down at it, his face dropped with worry. That's when the man attacked him. He punched her dad in the eye, making him fall to the ground and then kicked him in the side. Scarlet screamed as Liam rushed outside to try and stop the fighting. All she could see was her father laying there on the ground, motionless. She and Luke ran outside after them to find Liam tackling the man to the ground. She rushed to her dad's side as he was just coming around, and saw that he had a serious black eye with red stained on his lips. Scarlet screamed again, but her father wrapped her in his arms, took Luke by the hand, and ran back indoors. The last thing Scarlet saw was the once innocent scale lying on the ground.

Scarlet woke up from being on Drakon's back and a tear slipped down her cheek. She remembered it as clear as day and always searched for a meaning to that dream. She finally understood. Her dad had kept many secrets from her when she was growing up. She had always remembered that scale and how beautiful it was to look at, but she never knew what it meant. Till now. Judging by the first time she had met him as a prisoner, she finally made the connection that Alexander Shookram had a dragon.

After Scarlet made that sudden realization, Drakon roared and dove down to the ground. The village of Drakonia loomed ahead of them. People didn't run, but they weren't happy either. For some reason Scarlet had a bad feeling about this.

She hopped off Drakon, only to find herself being grabbed by the villagers and pulled towards the square. They didn't even bother with Luke and Drakon. Scarlet tried to force herself out of their arms, but it was no use. They held on too tight to her.

Once they reached the center of the village, they tied Scarlet up to a post and began slinging insults at her. A few decided to throw rocks. When Luke finally caught up, he pushed people aside.

"What on Earth are you doing, people? What has she ever done to you?"

"We know all 'bout the Shookrams," one woman said. "The moment y'all left we figured it out. Whenever one of ya disappears we always end up bein' the ones to pay the price."

"What do you mean?"

"And you," she continued, ignoring Luke's question. "You should be ashamed of yourself. Befriendin' a monster and leavin' with her. No wonder your family cut all ties with ya."

"What!" Luke looked around for his family and found them on the outskirts of the crowd. They didn't even make eye contact with him. Scarlet could only watch with tears in her eyes.

Instead of addressing the fact that he may have just lost his family, he silently stared at the woman. He held back tears, but his mouth formed into a sneer.

"Listen to all of you! Berating a person who is younger than you! Just for your information, we have experienced A LOT more pain than you idiots. You can give me trouble all you want, but it is just so, SO, not right to do that to someone who can't even defend themselves."

"Oh really? Miss Shookram here can't defend herself?" The woman stepped up to Scarlet and sneered into her face. Others began to glance around nervously.

"No, she cannot. King George took her voice away." His own voice grew louder as the anger spilled out of him. "He took an innocent girl's voice away! They carved that brand onto her face just so they could torture her! And you know what else? After all that she had the heart to leave her sister behind and come here! You are all in danger and yet Scarlet wanted to come back and save you all!"

"What do you mean?" another person asked.

"Drakonia is under attack. He is going to destroy most villages, including this one! Scarlet can save you!"

No one said a word. They all sat there in shock, even the woman. Luke was still seething and did not once glance at his family. Scarlet, after hearing all of this, really felt like giving up, but she couldn't. She glanced down at the ropes and came up with an idea. Her hands were free from the restraints, so she was able to grab the rope, burn it, and freely escape right in front of everyone's eyes. They all gasped.

Without even giving them a second look, she walked freely up to Luke and motioned towards the large tower. She made talking gestures, followed by her setting her shoulders and acting mean. She couldn't talk, couldn't write, or couldn't sign, so she hoped her acting would make Luke understand. At first, he didn't. When Scarlet continued to act out what she wanted to say, Luke would look on in confusion until she rolled her eyes and lifted her hand up to her head in a kind of salute only Drakonians knew about. Her hand rested at her head in a normal salute, and then her fingers fluttered down to her side. Then she squared her shoulders once more. Luke understood now.

"You want to speak to the Captain? Why?"

Scarlet shrugged and swept her hand towards the people. She pointed to herself, pretended to be stupid, and shrugged again. Everyone got that gesture and shifted uneasily, almost guiltily.

"Alright. I guess we can give it a try." They started walking towards the tower, but she stopped him. She told him to wait and ran over to his family. They were still looking at the ground. Baby Noah, Luke's little brother, was held in the arms of his mother. He was giggling; having no idea what was going on.

She smiled at the child, then glanced at the others. Byron, his older brother, had a sad look on his face and wasn't afraid to meet Scarlet's gaze. She pointed towards Luke, trailed her finger down her cheek, faking a tear, pointed to herself and shook her head. She continued to point to Luke, then to Byron, faked another tear, pointed to herself and shook her head again. She wanted to let Byron know that Luke was not bad. He was not a bad person. She was. That's when it hit her. She *was* a bad person. She had brought all her friends into danger, making them leave families and friends behind, and she had even left her own sister behind. The woman was right. She *was* a monster. She began to cry.

"Scar, no. Don't waste your time on them. They made their decision. I'd prefer to lose my family, who no longer cares, than to lose my best friend, who would sacrifice so much to only receive so little," Luke said, sending accusing glances at them. "You are worth so much more than them."

Scarlet wiped the tears away and nodded. They walked off. Byron took a step towards them but was stopped by a hand on his shoulder. His father gave him a stern look and shook his head. Byron looked back down in shame.

Luke and Scarlet didn't look back. With everyone behind them, they walked up to the tower entrance, where the Drakonian soldiers stood, and entered. They had never been in there before. They first walked into a nice looking, yet small, lobby; nowhere near as nice as the Ixaemithian castle Scarlet had been held captive in.

On the wall to their right was a map of the tower. There were many rooms that led up there, but the one they were looking for is the Captain's, just at the top of the tower.

"I have to warn you," a lady said from behind. They spun around to see a tall woman with curly, chocolate shoulder-length hair, sharp facial structure, and big round glasses. "Chief isn't too happy."

"We'll take our chances," Luke replied. "We have even worse news coming for him, Charlotte."

She only shrugged and walked away.

Scarlet tapped his shoulder, pointed at her and shrugged.

"That's Charlotte. I've been in here once before, with my family. She's just the Captain's secretary." Scarlet nodded and they silently climbed the stairs.

When they reached the top, they saw only one door and as they opened it, they came upon a very tall, stocky man with greying, blonde hair. His shoulders were set as he looked out a huge window overlooking the village.

"I see fighting going on down there," the man said in a deep, rich voice. "Something tells me that coming across you is very bad."

"What makes you say that?" Luke asked in defiance. "Everyone here seems so paranoid. What happened—"

"I wasn't talking to you." The man stopped looking out the window and stared directly at Scarlet. His sharp, blue eyes pierced hers as she struggled to understand what was happening.

"She can't spea—" He held up his hand to silence Luke once more. Scarlet could only stare at him in confusion.

"You're a Shookram. You can figure a way."

That made her even more confused. Just the way he said that kind of sounded as if he knew her somehow. Or someone from inside her family.

"Come, Scarlet. Don't you think I know everything that goes on in this village? Your history, your purchases, your activity. I know what you hold in your possession that can help you with your troubles."

Scarlet continued to stare, but Luke seemed to figure out what he was implying and grabbed the Drakonian Blade from her side. Too afraid to say anything again, Luke just held up the sword to the Captain and motioned for Scarlet to use it.

"I remember the first time you made this purchase. Didn't the Salesman tell you what the sword holds? What he said was true. Use your mind," the Captain said to her as he pointed to his own head with a small grin on his face. Scarlet looked down at her sword to see the jewel on the handle slightly glowing with her touch. She did remember what that man had told her. It held magic. She had thought that the sword's magic was what she had, but she kept forgetting that it was actually Drakon's magic, not the sword. She was a Dragon Master who could control the major elements of the Earth, but how far could she get just by using this blade? If what he said was what she thought he was implying, then...

"*I can use the sword to communicate?*" Scarlet blinked in surprise. She could hear her own voice in her head. The Captain seemed to hear her as well. Luke on the other hand could not and fidgeted with his foot.

"Smart girl. Yes, you can. If you do a little research on that sword then you can find out everything that it can do. Don't ask me how I know this.

"Now, we need to discuss the matter at hand. When you and your friend disappeared, a little mayhem ensued here. When that man was taken away and you vanished, everyone went a little nuts and they threw a riot. The same thing happened when a member of your family vanished as well. The people of this village believe you to be a family curse passed down by generations. Luckily, I was able to calm everyone down and made sure their lives weren't to be disrupted. They also believe that you are the reason why everyone is getting hurt so badly. Since you are back, it has unsettled the people. I assume that you have even worse news for us?"

Scarlet nodded vigorously, forgetting she could communicate again. She was a little hurt about what he had said, but it was the least of her concern right now. The king was approaching fast and right now the people needed to put their trust in her. She didn't care how much they hated her; she grew up with them, and now she was going to protect them no matter what.

"*An attack is imminent. Everyone here is in danger. All because of... me...*" Scarlet trailed off. What she said was true. This was all her fault; just like how that woman called her a monster. She pushed the thought away. She had to focus. "*I want to help out as much as I can. I want to make it up to everyone. I don't want to see them all die...*"

"I think I can arrange that. You know about this more than any of us, so I will put you in charge until we are safe once more." He trailed off, as if a new thought had just occurred to him. "It might not go so well with the others, but they will listen to me. You will have nothing to worry about."

"*There is also something that I don't wish to keep secret from you guys, but I can only assume you have found out. I ha-*"

The Captain held his hand up to silence her. "I know. You have a dragon. The last of its kind I presume. You must have had a strange adventure."

He had no idea. She had traveled with a Sile, a dragon, a sorceress, and her human friend Luke. She couldn't even consider herself "human" anymore since she could now perform magic. "*Thank you, Captain,*" she said about his help.

"Please, call me Mason."

They both shook hands and were ready to continue with the plan. Luke however had looked on in confusion; he had no clue what was being said between the two, only the Captain's words, and so he began to pace around the room. He occasionally peeked out of the large windows from time to time, but when the two were planning, Luke made one last look out the window and gasped.

"What the...? People are holding weapons down there!"

35
ALEXANDER

Alex, from his spot on the ground, looked up at Casimir with worry. His new friend stared back at the beast unfazed. The Sile snarled. It looked as if Casimir was thinking of a plan, and then he smiled.

"You know, Socrates, you gave me quite a scare just then," he said to the Sile. "Guess that's why you are only in your human form. Your other figure wouldn't have scared me at all. Is that why you haven't called for your buddies yet? Too afraid that you would lose me and blame you, a little bunny rabbit, for our escape? What would Roue think?"

Socrates glanced around uneasily and lowered his weapon.

"That's what I thought. Now, if you will excuse us, we will be heading on our way and out of your territory. We won't say a word to your pals if you turn back now and never see us again." Casimir began rubbing his hands together, as if he were enjoying this immensely. "If you don't, I will spill more of your secrets to them and they will kick you out of the pack. Or worse, just kill you. I really don't care.

"Oooh and what's this? You actually *fancy* one of the leaders. Bella is it? The Boukasian red wolf? No wonder you haven't told anyone. You would embarrass yourself in front of her. Maybe that's why Bella admires Roue a lot more than you. They are both wolves."

The Sile grew so angry that out of nowhere, he charged Casimir. He put his finger up and chastised him. "Remember." Socrates stopped, and begrudgingly turned around.

"That was amazing…" Alex said as he got up from the ground. Casimir didn't say anything but smiled and led him away. By now they had cleared most of the camp and ran into very few problems. They had only walked by, and hid, from a few more Siles that were out hunting in the woods. They then left the camp behind them altogether.

Alex looked at the map to see the location of the next place they had to go to. Glemm Grove was the closest, along with Vinmere, a rather small town, Renu, and the village where his late friend Ace had come from; Argonia. Between those two villages there were the Imperial Mountains. He swelled with dread. How were they supposed to cross the mountains?

Casimir took the map from his hands and examined it. "Those mountains could be a problem. Fortunately, there is a way to go around them. We will just have to travel near Blood Lake and to the other villages to pass the mountains."

Alex agreed and they made their way to Glemm Grove. At this point the trees were beginning to thin and they started to climb over huge meadow hills. Just at the bottom of one they saw the village, but with everything in ruins. All the buildings were collapsed to the ground with little smoke billowing from them. On the hill next to them sat a huge pile of rubble. Next to it was a lady softly crying into the dirt. Alex hurried over to her.

"Ma'am? Are you okay?"

She sniveled in her hands, wiped the tears away and smiled up at him. "Yeah… I'm fine. I should be done with mourning but… it's just so hard to accept a friend's death."

Alex crouched down next to her and put his hand on her shoulder. "Who died? If you don't mind me asking. And what happened here?"

"My friend was murdered a week ago. She was helping these travelers and asked to use my barn. A few days after they had arrived here, something bad happened. The whole village was flooded with Ixaemithian guards and they destroyed the whole place. They bombed my barn and when I found it like this, I had also found my friend dead among the rubble."

"The king screwed us all," Casimir said from behind. "Don't you worry, we will get our revenge."

"What are you guys doing then?"

"Well, my pal and I here were sent to persuade the villagers along our path to either join us or die. Stupid idiot. He left us by ourselves to do whatever without even a second thought."

"I presume he has eyes on us though," Alex added. "I mean the king *is* kinda stupid, but I know he wouldn't just leave us without having sight on us. He wouldn't know what we are planning; it would just look like what he thought he had first sent us out to do."

"Which is…? Whatever you guys are planning I would love to be a part of."

"Really?" Casimir said in surprise. "You'd help us recruit people to fight against the king?"

"Well, yeah. He took my best friend away. He has hurt many people. You know, my friend once told me that she remembers previous kings and queens of Ixaemithia, and they were all the same. Shared blood, motives and the same lust for power. Don't ask how she was able to meet all of them, but she hated him so much, and now she is gone. The least I can do is avenge her. She was so kind…" She continued to stare up at them for a second more, then her lips began to quiver, and her face crumpled as she cried once again; this time hiding her face from the men. Alex crouched down next to her and comforted her. He could relate. Liam had told him that he had lost his wife. Elena was his wife and his best friend. They had been through a lot together, and when his friend had confirmed her death, a part of his soul broke. The only reason he was still here and had not ended it all was because of his daughters. They still needed him, and he needed them. One day they would live together peacefully: without death and pain.

"I'm sorry to break this up but… we do need to hurry, and if there are no more people then we have to head to the next village on this map."

"Yes. Of course," she said in a hoarse voice. "I will get over her death soon." Alex helped her to her feet. "I haven't really introduced myself. I'm Alyssia."

"Nice to meet you, Alyssia. My name is Alexander, and my friend here is Casimir."

"Uh, Casimir Hughes, m'lady," he said as he took a dramatic bow. Alex just rolled his eyes at him, but Alyssia chuckled, making her tears disappear. He smiled brightly to the young woman and Alex, being uncomfortable, motioned for them to follow and led the charge to the other villages.

Later that night, they had reached the next village on the map. Vinmere. When the three first appeared, everyone immediately reacted and ran away. Others did the same but gave them the stink eye at the same time.

"Wait! Stop!" Casimir shouted. "We just want to talk! Listen!"

Alex and Alyssia glanced at each other before rushing over to grab Casimir. "Cas! Wait. We can't just barge in here and scare everyone," Alex said to him, using a nickname he had never used with him before. He didn't seem to pay attention, but he did calm down a bit and let them pull him back. When he calmed down enough, Alyssia let go, only to find herself facing a little boy with his sister at his side. He didn't seem afraid at all to come across these strange people.

"You them people who come to rescue us?" he said in a small, yet brave voice. "My sis 'n I are ready."

Alyssia crouched down in front of them to be eye level with the boy. "How did you know about this?"

"S'not important. I don' need no people callin' us freaks. We been livin' on our own n' are ready to leave. You wan' the king dead, yes?"

Alyssia was speechless, but Alex had let go of Casimir and he saw who she was talking to. "What up, fellow Augur?"

"A what?" she asked, confused, but he didn't answer. Instead he ruffled the child's black hair.

"Are you guys goin' to save Lyle n' I?" the little girl quietly said to Casimir.

"Well of course, Lily."

"Do they know each other?" Alyssia whispered to Alex. He shook his head and explained to her what Casimir can do.

"We just need your people here to have trust in us. You think you can convince 'em?"

Lily nodded and ran off with her brother to gather the other people.

"What just happened there?" she asked Casimir.

"Well, I just asked for help. What else happened?"

"I-" Alex stopped her. He knew Casimir would be stubborn and even though he explained to her his "special" ability, she was still confused.

They waited patiently for the little children to come back; they didn't have to wait long. They had led the people out into the open where most were sending them hate while others just looked hesitant, yet hopeful of the newcomers.

"I'll do the talking," Casimir said. He walked up to them with an air of confidence and smiled. "Greetings, friends. Please do not be alarmed by our presence. We are here to help and right now you will need it.

"Just the other day, we received word of an attack and everyone will be in danger. This came from the king himself and he sent us to come to your homes and do the opposite of what I have planned for you guys. He wanted for you all to lose your homes, and possibly your lives, but what I want from you is help. Your fellow village, Drakonia, is under siege and along the way your lives will be cut off short. I am not forcing you to do anything here, but if you want your life to continue normally then I suggest you come along with us and we can promise you safety and shelter. You will be able to avoid… well let us not get too caught up in that."

"But why do we have to go with you? You say something bad will happen to us if we stay, but why? Drakonia is far away from us. They should have nothing to do with us," a man said from the crowd.

"That is true, good sir, but that does not matter to the king. He does not care about people's lives and if you help us then we can guarantee you a perfect, normal life."

People started to agree with Casimir, but there were still a few skeptics that didn't believe what he was saying.

"If you don't then… I cannot help you there. I worry that if you do stay then you will not be safe. Please, come with us. After all this is over you can come back and be safe."

What Casimir was saying made sense for the ones who agreed, and the people came and joined them. The ones who didn't trust him remained in their spots.

"But…" Casimir looked at them in horror. He was no longer going to sugarcoat anything. "You could die if you stay here! Don't you get what I am saying?! The king will kill you!"

Just from saying that he gathered a few more people with him, but many remained where they stood. He continued to try and persuade them over to his side, but nothing was working. He grew sad.

"Cas, they won't come. What we need to do now is gather the people we could persuade and get out of here. It's their fault they can't understand," Alex said to him calmly. He too was sad that not everyone was listening to their warning, but there was nothing they could do. "We have to protect these people."

He nodded slightly and they left the village. The people were on their own now.

36
SCARLET

Mason and Scarlet ran over to the window at Luke's urging and saw every Drakonian surrounding the tower with many weapons at their disposal. A few of them carried torches and held it up to the woman they saw downstairs. Charlotte was freaking out as they backed her up against the wall. The Captain cursed under his breath and ran out the door with Scarlet and Luke following close behind.

"Hey!" Mason shouted once they reached the bottom. "Stand down! Now!" His deep, booming voice resonated throughout the crowd and made everyone quiver in fear. Scarlet was impressed. A crowd like this would have surely overthrew the Captain, but they were too afraid of him. It made her think if they would react the same way with the king.

"What is the meaning of this? Look, I know you are all scared, but we can do this! You have been tormented so much, and I understand that, but what is happening now is even more dangerous; you must put your trust in each other! No more attacking one another, no more distrust, from now on you will put all your faith into this young girl! I don't care what awful thing you have to say to her, or to this young man here, because if we are to actually beat this, then we cannot lose focus."

"But what if she is not telling the truth? She has hidden many secrets from people, and we are just supposed to trust her after disappearing for weeks? You, sir, are delusional and too old to understand real life now," a person said from the crowd. Multiple people gasped as those last words came out and watched the Captain to see how he would react. He looked angry, but like any other respectful human being he did not address the insult.

Instead he kept his voice calm. "No 'buts.' I want everyone to listen to her and that is an order. If anyone has a problem, then you come see *me*. Anyone else have anything to say to me before we start? No? Good." Then he turned towards Scarlet. "We start tomorrow." With that he gave everyone one last glare and strode back inside with Charlotte following close behind. Everyone grumbled, and even sent her hateful looks, before they turned around and walked away.

That evening, Scarlet and Luke hung out in the woods where they had felt at home all those weeks ago. Drakon was there with them and was giving comfort to his master. Scarlet thought she could only communicate to humans, but it turned out she could with Drakon as well. She told him everything that happened while she had been captured, what happened to her voice, and then told him how the people reacted the first time they got there. He was not happy to hear about that.

Ungrateful humans, he growled. *Can't they tell you are willing to sacrifice everything to protect them? You are showing a good heart and all they are doing is crushing it. If I were you, I would just let them all die.*

Scarlet silently chuckled. "*You say that because you are a dragon. If you were human like me then you'd act differently. It's in your blood to kill, big boy.*"

She was just playing with him and he knew it. He still growled and bumped his head against her.

Luke could only look on, not being able to hear the conversation, and fidgeted awkwardly. Scarlet knew this was bothering him, there just wasn't much she could do. She could probably try to make herself communicate with both at the same time, but right now just trying to talk with one person was taking her strength away. She wanted to fall asleep, but there was something she wanted to do first with Luke before she passed out.

Scarlet switched her concentration to Luke. "*Come with me, I want to talk to you.*" Luke brightened and hopped to his feet. Scarlet walked over to a large tree that they had usually hung their deer meat on and shoved her hand into the crack at its base. She pulled out another bow, considering that her sister had taken her bow with her and never returned it, and grabbed some arrows. Luke had his own bow and arrows. Scarlet motioned for Drakon to stay put and the two friends walked off into the woods.

There was something on her mind and it was about what Luke had said to her on the ride back home. He had said that the dagger he purchased in Renu gave him weird, bad nightmares. He had never specified what he dreamed about, but Scarlet had seen him the first time he had purchased it and he had looked so terribly awful. She just had to know what he saw.

After walking for a few minutes in silence, she finally brought the topic up. He seemed confused on where this came up from, but when she insisted, he gave in.

"I actually don't know what I had dreamed up then. They were actually just a jumbled mess of words in my head with a few visions that I suppose could be the… future?" His voice began to quiver. "But I'm sure that's not the case though."

"*What were the dreams?*"

He only shook his head. "I don't think I want to say…"

Scarlet stepped in front of him and put her hands on her hips. "*I can handle the truth.*"

Luke sighed and sat down on a rock with his head in his hands. "I know. I know. I just don't think I can ever think about it again. I tried so hard to keep it in the back of my mind, but now… it just hurts to think about it. If you really want to know then… I guess I will tell you."

He started off with the first vision he experienced with the dagger, which was when he was in the store where he had purchased it. The woman had warned him about the dagger, yet he still bought it and had a simple vision of a snowy landscape and a wolf that seemed to understand him. After that he would have dreams where it was either words being thrown around in his head, which he didn't quite understand what they were saying, or just having visions of what seemed to be the future.

"I can't say for sure if they were the future or just nightmares," he said. Scarlet looked at him more closely and saw that Luke was hiding something from her. He looked as if he was struggling to keep whatever he wanted to say in and instead walked ahead of Scarlet with his bow in hand. He avoided Scarlet after that, and they hunted in silence. When she tried prodding him more about his dreams, he did not address her, did not even look her in the eyes, he just hunted silently by her side, trying to keep the tears at bay.

When morning came, Scarlet woke up from lying next to Drakon and saw dawn just barely peeking over the horizon. The night before Luke and Scarlet had hunted for food, which had become awkward—they didn't do anything for the rest of the night. Now Scarlet was the only one awake and she saw Luke laying on the ground facing away from her. Drakon was sprawled out with his wings outstretched. For someone who was only a few weeks old, he sure was very big, and as she stared at him, he was still growing. She wondered just how big he could get.

Before Luke could wake up, she decided to just head back to the village on her own and deal with the people herself. She didn't want him to be her communicator and even though she could talk herself now, she wasn't going to say a word to anyone here after the way they treated her yesterday. She would just have to help the people be safe and teach them how to protect themselves.

She entered the village and found the Captain waiting for her. Next to him stood a woman who seemed a little familiar to her, but she couldn't remember.

"Greetings, Scarlet. Let me introduce you to Arantxa. She tells me you saved her husband from becoming a prisoner."

Scarlet raised her eyebrows in surprise. That's where she recognized her. She freed him when she ordered Drakon to catch that guard for her from a while ago. She didn't even know that he had come back here, and she certainly did not know that Arantxa knew it was her that had saved him.

"She would like to help you."

Scarlet nodded and smiled towards the woman. She smiled back. "No one understands," Arantxa said. "You are the most wonderful person here. Anythin' that has happened was not because of you. They should know that."

A tear ran down Scarlet's cheek at her kind words and she mouthed the words "thank you" to her. Arantxa smiled and they both got right down to business. First, they needed to make sure that the people understood what was really happening. Scarlet told Arantxa to tell every person they came across about what was coming and to ask whether they'd fight or hide. Scarlet didn't want people to fight if they didn't want to, but they couldn't just be left out here in the open where they wouldn't be safe. She would have to plan on a safe place, like a bunker, for people who didn't want to be involved.

As they were spreading the word, and Scarlet still receiving dirty looks, they met up with Luke, who had been trying to find her. He told her that Drakon had stayed back in the woods to guard the village. Scarlet told him of their plan.

"Me and..." Luke looked questioningly at Arantxa.

"Arantxa."

"Me and Arantxa will help people with fighting. You go and figure out how to keep the people safe."

Scarlet nodded and the three split off to do their own tasks. She decided to see Mason to confer with him on what to do. She found him just outside the tower, pacing.

"There you are," Mason said to her in a worried voice. "Something just happened, and it is not good. Come." With that he turned around and walked into the tower. Scarlet could only ponder, and try not to have a mini stroke, on what could have happened now.

Once inside the lobby, he led her in the opposite direction of the stairwell. In the ground just behind Charlotte's desk was a trapdoor and when he opened it up, Scarlet could barely see inside the dingy little area, but saw more stairs leading downwards.

As they climbed down them, Mason began telling her why he was so worried. "We found someone just outside the wall. He has short, black hair, stocky build, and… well I think you should see the rest for yourself…"

Mason opened a door at the bottom and a dim light peeked through. Chained to the opposite wall was the man he was talking about, his short hair disheveled, his uniform torn apart, and the left side of his face bleeding from an intricately carved brand; the same one she received just last week. His jet-black eyes pierced hers with an evil glint.

"*Ich will mit niemandem sprechen*," the man said in a strong accent. Mason had no clue what he said, but Scarlet, after using her sword's magic, could understand every word.

She wasn't sure how to speak his language, but just by ordering her sword to translate her language to his, she was able to communicate; he was not happy. "*I do not care that you do not want to talk. You work for the king. I want answers*," she said to him in the same language.

He didn't reply at first, he just stood there with a somewhat dazed look on his face and shuffled his feet on the floor. "Freak, you are the last person I want to talk to."

Scarlet felt something was off about the guy. She decided to explore more of her extended magic and found that she could read the guy's mind. She smiled cruelly and made sure to freak the guy out even more.

"*Axel, you speak English, do not try to hide anything from me.*"

Axel's evil black eyes creased in worry. "You know nothing about me, monster. I do not want anything to do with your sorcery."

"*Oh, Axel, I know everything about you. What did they call you? Schade? Were you a troublemaker working as the king's guard?*"

He growled and sneered. "Fine! What the hell do you want?"

Scarlet smiled in victory and turned towards Mason. "*I need you to find a place where the people can be safe from the attack. Leave me down here so I can keep drilling him. I can get the answers out of him. It'll just take time. Luke is out there preparing them to fight. It will be a lot faster if we all played our parts. I can get info, you can keep everyone safe, and Luke will teach people everything.*"

Mason nodded curtly. "Yes, ma'am." He left; leaving Scarlet to hammer Axel on everything he knew.

37

LUKE

Luke and Arantxa went around and told people what Scarlet wanted everyone to know. Most of the people didn't want anything to do with this, which made Luke angry, so instead of arguing with them he sent them away towards the tower. If no one was willing to fight, then Drakonia stood no chance of winning.

Arantxa seemed to have more luck with the people. She had gathered more than him and the place they met was just outside the village. Throughout the whole time of trying to get people to fight, Luke had managed to collect weapons that would help them in their training. Guards carried these types of weapons and Luke believed that there would be no magic involved in this fight, so he will just have to teach them how to use them.

The first thing on his agenda was to teach Arantxa so she could help him with the others. Since she was willing to learn, it didn't take her long to be able to handle the basics of sword fighting. When she learned how to hold a sword, how to wield it, and the stance she had to position herself in, he decided for her to now try and fight him. He had his trusty bow and arrows with him as his weapon, but he wouldn't actually use it. Luke told her to attack him by using what she learned, and she did. At first, she was a little slow and sometimes would fumble with her sword, but with practice she managed to knock his bow from his hands.

Luke praised her and they continued to practice. However, as time passed, Arantxa seemed less and less enthused about the training. Eventually she had to stop.

"What's wrong?" Luke asked.

"Nothin'… I just can't believe this is happenin'."

Luke could only shrug. "This will be the only time that it does happen. Hopefully. You know if we kill the king then nothing like this will ever happen again, but we can't just let people die for nothing. Now, let's go and teach the others."

Arantxa still seemed upset, but she brightened a little and they both headed to where they had left everyone. Luke passed out the weapons and began to teach them how to fight. They were not trying at all. It was frustrating for Luke because at this rate Drakonia was doomed.

However, there was this one little boy that seemed to be totally fascinated by everything. Since he was too young to hold a weapon, he pretended he was and copied every move Luke made. His short, fluffy brown hair flew all over the place as he pretended to fight invisible enemies and eventually knocked right into Luke.

He stumbled and fell but flashed a smile at him. "Hey there, little one. You havin' fun?"

The boy backed away sheepishly. "Sorry."

"Don't be. At least *you* have spirit, unlike everyone else here."

"Ma says people can be misunderstood. Everyone has a kind heart inside, but for most there is more evil than good. I've heard things about you, Luke. I don't think you're a bad person. There is more good in you than bad."

Luke was taken aback in surprise. He was such a sweet kid. "What's your name?"

He smiled. "The name is Jackson. Jackson Ashworth. Or just Jack."

"Nice to meet you, Jack. How would you like to help me?"

"Help you? Really? That would be great! What's the plan? Are we going to do some fighting?"

Luke smiled. "Well, no. First, we are going to help the people here stay secured. We don't want everyone to die. We want them to stay safe. So, I have to go see Scarlet. You want to come?"

"Yes!" Jackson was so excited. Luke couldn't help but laugh.

He told Arantxa what he was planning to do and left with the little boy in hand. He quickly made his way to the tower, assuming he would find her there, and found the Captain outside leading a bunch of workers who looked to be building a bunker.

Mason turned around and smiled tiredly. "Many people will not want to fight here. This bunker will keep the ones who don't want to get involved safe."

"That's good. I'm trying to train people but… they just don't want to help at all…"

"Yeah," Mason said sadly. "They are pretty stubborn, especially towards you guys, but in good time they will join in."

Luke nodded and looked down at Jack. He was tugging at his arm in impatience. It reminded Luke of why they were there. "Uh, hey, Chief? Have you seen Scarlet around?"

"Yes. She's down below talking with the prisoners. Charlotte will show you the way."

Luke thanked him and led Jack inside the tower. When Luke mentioned what he wanted to Charlotte, the young lady became distressed but didn't say anything. All she did was nod silently and walked them to the prison cells. She did not follow them down.

Jack squealed in fright and latched onto Luke as they walked down the stairs with the light of the torches flickering in and out of view. The first cell to appear was exactly the one they wanted to find. Inside they found Scarlet pacing and a prisoner chained to the wall. Luke looked closer at her and saw a crazed look in her eyes. The prisoner on the wall was no other but an Ixaemithian guard. He looked quite terrified.

They watched from outside the bars as Scarlet walked up to him, clutched her sword in her hand, and seemed to be speaking to him, which they both couldn't hear. The guard frowned.

"Why do you care?" he said to her. She stared intently at him and still had her hand on her sword. Now his eyes began to fill with fear. "No… Please no… You can't do this to me!"

Scarlet lifted her sword and before she could do what Luke assumed would happen, he quickly covered Jack's eyes as she let her sword fall onto the man's head; decapitating him.

Jack tried to uncover his eyes to see what was happening, so Luke turned him around and huddled against him. "Scarlet!" he yelled. "Seriously! Don't do that in front of a little kid!"

Scarlet perked up and turned around with a look of surprise. Then she relaxed. "*Oh. Sorry. Guess I got carried away.*" She let herself out of the cell and they climbed their way back up the stairwell. "*Who is this anyway?*"

"Just some kid that likes us. I wanted to bring him around and stuff because he is so interested in what we are doing, but I didn't know it'd be *that* bad."

She shrugged sheepishly. "*Well, he pissed me off. I couldn't stand the man any longer.*"

"What did you want from him?"

Scarlet looked down and didn't say anything. For once it seems as if she would not tell Luke anything. He could see a difference in her. From the once innocent, kind-hearted, playful girl he grew up with to a fierce, battle-scarred young lady. In only a matter of weeks everything had drastically changed.

When they left the tower, Scarlet wanted to go see Mason to learn of his progress. Luke followed, but Jack seemed a bit bored. He kept tugging at his arm, but Luke held his ground and joined in on their conversation. Scarlet was just telling Mason about the now dead prisoner. He looked horrified.

"How could you do that? Even for me that would be too brutal!"

She only shrugged. "*I did what I had to do.*"

He could only shake his head in wonder. "Well, good riddance then. We believe him to be one of the king's spies. You know he'd be here soon, right?"

"*Yes, but don't worry. I had a little chat with Axel. He gave me everything I needed.*"

That seemed to calm him down a bit. Luke on the other hand, having not heard the conversation, was distracted by the little guy. He motioned for Scarlet to see if he could go, which she nodded with approval, and the two left.

"You want to go practice sword fighting?" he asked Jack.

"Yes!"

Luke smiled and they walked their way back to Arantxa. Perhaps he could continue to try and have everyone involved in Drakonia.

Meanwhile in Vinmere, the remaining villagers continued with their lives. When they saw a shadow pass over their heads and people charge at them from nowhere, they began to panic. The king came into view and everyone burst into tears. Perhaps those travelers were right.

George looked among the cowardly people, saw that there were little left, and assumed that the job was done. The next task would be simple. If no one were to follow him then they would follow no one. Using the Magic of the Dragons, he obliterated everyone with fire, leaving scorched bodies on the ground.

He remained unfazed as all his subjects gasped. They had never seen their king use magic before. That made some suspicious of him. George didn't care. All he wanted to do was to focus on arriving to the other villages, burning them, and reaching Drakonia as soon as possible. That was exactly what he did. They all hopped back onto his dragon and flew off with incredible speed into the sky.

38

ALEXANDER

The next couple of days, the three led their newly found group to the next village on the map, Renu. It was a small village, like the last one, and hopefully they would be able to recruit everyone there and not have to leave anyone behind. Alex worried about those other people, but there was nothing they could do. They were strangers and people along the way would be harder to trust.

Casimir walked in front of the group in confidence with Alyssia next to him. He was telling jokes to her that made her laugh, but she seemed distracted and would occasionally glance behind her to look straight at Alex. There was something in her look, something he had seen before. He began to choke. He looked to the ground to escape her gaze as his face warmed into a blush.

"Well, ladies and gentlemen! Herrre we are!" Casimir shouted in a silly accent. He rolled his r's like he was some rich, fancy man. Alex rolled his eyes.

In the distance stood the small village, Renu. They had come through the wooded area and when they hit the meadow, Alex got a very strange feeling of dread. Something wasn't right. His heart picked up speed and he frantically searched his surroundings. He thought that maybe they were being followed after all, but there was no one in sight. There was just the never-ending landscape of weeds and flowers in front of them. It wasn't until they heard a piercing scream behind them that his suspicions were confirmed that something, or someone, was here with them.

"What's the problem?! What's happening?!" Casimir shouted in fear. The three of them rushed to the back of the crowd to find one of the men sprawled on the ground, shaking. Saliva built up and pooled around his mouth as he choked on it. Alex rushed to help him up and reared back at the sight of him. Two snakes were latched on to each of his legs. One on his calf and the other on his ankle. They tried to pull the snakes off but when they did, it was too late. He was already dead.

"W-what the hell?!" Casimir tried, but failed, to contain his fear.

Alex sent him a withering glare that told him to shut up. "We need to head back to the woods before any more of us get bitten. We are sitting ducks out here; we won't be able to see any predators come for us."

Everyone hurried back and grumbled as Alex figured out how to get them to the village. With the amount of people there they would have no chance of getting through the meadow without more deaths on their hands. They could go through in small groups, and it might take all day and night, but they had no other choice. Then there was the part of coming across a snake. They couldn't know what is ahead of them. That's when an idea struck him, and he looked down at his old wounds.

"I have an idea." With that he explained what was to happen. When he told them that he would go ahead of everyone and be the one to scout out any danger that could present itself in surprise, they were not enthusiastic about that.

"Are you crazy?" Casimir said as if he was a lunatic.

"You could get hurt!" Alyssia rushed up to him and hugged him tightly. Just like before he shut down and couldn't say anything. He couldn't even breathe. When she let go, Alex wheezed out the air he was holding and chuckled lightly.

“Trust me, I will be fine. I’ve survived a bullet wound and a sword stabbed in my stomach that should have killed me. If I can survive that then I can survive a little bit of venom.”

“But you just got lucky! You may be tough, but one day something like this will kill anyone! No matter how strong they are.”

Alex smiled. “Well, thank you Alyssia for your concern, but there will be more deaths if we are blind to what is in front of us. You guys shouldn’t have to worry about me.”

Before anyone else could protest, Alex strode back into the meadow and told everyone to stay put until he gave a signal. They had begun arranging themselves into small groups. Alex was careful of where he was stepping and swept from side to side; slowly stalking through the weeds to try and find the predators. If just by entering the meadow brought two snakes to prey on them, then Alex could only guess just how many there were altogether. His heart raced and he almost fled away from there, but just the thought that he had survived multiple fatal wounds, and his friend calling him the spirit of a dragon, was enough to settle his rattled nerves and force him to keep going.

When he was a far enough distance away and found nothing to harm them, he motioned for the first group to come. After a couple of hours of going slow and steady, five groups had managed to come out of hiding and Alex was still on edge. He was beginning to get tired and the blistering sun was of no help. He could feel his skin burning and his short hair clotting up with sweat, but he pushed on until something stopped him in his tracks. A huge snake laid curled on the ground, asleep. Alex had almost stepped on it. He stopped breathing and quickly, but quietly, moved back from it. He soon realized that was also a bad decision. Another snake slithered its way behind him and when he took that step backwards, he stepped on its body and the snake struck his leg. He doubled over in pain and fell to the ground. He must have walked right into a nest. He quickly motioned for the nearest group to stop and tried to pry the snake's jaws from his leg. It was fastened well to his leg. Its fangs were too deep in and the blood poured from his wound, but he didn't pass out. Not yet. He could feel the venom rush into his system as he continued to fight until the original snake he had come across woke and decided to strike his thigh. This time he screamed in agony.

The nearest group to him didn't think of being careful and trampled their way to Alex to help him. By the time they got to him everyone gasped in horror. He lay there in the weeds, unmoving.

Alexander woke up gasping as if he just awakened from a bad dream. He found himself lying on the forest floor back in his home village. Beside him stood an ominous hole underneath an upturned tree. In there he could hear a gentle rumbling that put his nerves at ease. By now it was dawn and he decided to get up for the day. He usually liked to spend his time in the forest, away from curious people, but he did miss staying with his best friend William. They did everything together and even though Alex always saw his friend as a poor soul for being cursed with anxiety and depression, Alex loved him as if he was his own brother. He would do anything for him.

Alex stood up and walked over to the hole. He spoke a strange language to it and then left the forest to go to class. Even though he was sixteen, he still had to attend like everyone else. He guessed that he lucked out. Only males ever got to go to school. Just one in every fifty females could go. That was why not everyone in the village had a basic education. To Alex they just talked weird and didn't seem to know much. Maybe that was why he liked to isolate himself.

When he arrived at the poor, sullen structure they called a well-working schoolhouse, he met up with his classmates in the one room of the entire building. Since Drakonia was known to be poor, they could not afford to rebuild anything in the village, so all students had to be in one room and learn the same subjects. There were only around thirty students in there, and all were male. Except one person who always made Alex blush. Elena Nouraura. He knew that he was non-existent to her; but every day he would only look forward to going to school just to see her. Which was probably why he always did badly in class. Sometimes he would see her in the village juts outside the tower, talking with her friends. The reason why she was in school was because of her father; he worked in the tower. Alex could just never stop thinking about her.

William, or Liam as he liked to call him, would just laugh every time he saw Alex salivating over her. He spoke to him in Boukasian saying he should just make a move instead of eyeing her all the time. Alex, even though no one else in the room could speak Boukasian, nudged him to shut up.

When the day went by and Alex, like usual, was not paying any attention, Liam did the one thing he always feared. He went up and talked to Elena and whispered into her ear. She blushed and smiled, but Alex, seeing his best friend speaking with her, made him jealous and he wanted to yell at him. He stopped when she came up to him with her huge pretty, blue eyes and her long, curly blonde hair flowing around her shoulders. He initially stopped breathing.

"I heard from your friend here that you would like to talk sometime," she said to him in the softest voice he had ever heard. He couldn't say a word and when he tried, he only stuttered. She laughed. "Come by the tower sometime, I would love to see you there."

With that she gave him the sweetest smile ever and walked out of class. Alex could only stand there, gaping, as Liam came up to him laughing and slapped him on the back. "Mission accomplished."

Alex woke up and looked around. His eyes were heavy and when he moved, the whole left side of his body was numb, but he managed to sit up. He found himself smiling at the dream he'd just had. It was the first time meeting his wife and even though she was gone now, that memory would always be with him.

Everyone else around him slept on the ground, except for Alyssia, who stood there watching over them, or at least him. "I didn't know anyone could speak Boukasian," she said out of nowhere, making him jump in surprise. "it is a very rare language here."

"H-how did you-"

"You talk in your sleep."

Alex couldn't help himself but smile sheepishly. "Of course. Yes, I speak Boukasian. I speak many sorts like Latin, Drakonian…"

Alyssia smiled. "You like to read, don't you? I assume that's where you got that from?"

Alex only shrugged. "I was isolated as a child. My only companion were books. Of course, the past seven years I couldn't do any of that, so I hope when I'm back home I can return to my normal life."

She smiled sadly. "I'm afraid nothing will ever be the same again. Not as long as the king lives."

"Well, I guess we'll just have to take care of that then, huh?" Alex felt no remorse for saying those words. Alyssia agreed and sat down next to him, which made him fidget in discomfort. Just having her close to him set his mind off and before he knew it, he pretended to hear something in the woods and walked off. He didn't know why, but for some reason he felt… guilty.

In the morning, everyone woke up and Alex, Casimir, and Alyssia led the people out towards "Blood Lake," which was next on the map. Casimir had told Alex that the venom he had endured the day before didn't seem to do much harm to him and when they had brought him to Renu he had been healed with healing herbs. Alex himself was surprised, yet he knew something like that would happen. He just didn't know why.

Casimir also went on to explain that after healing him, they did recruit even more people into their little group. Alex was excited to hear this. Sure, they might not be able to stand a chance against the king but maybe with the help of the Drakonians, then there was always hope of victory.

From the time they left the Ixaemithian kingdom, they still hadn't seen the king. They had thought he would have caught up to them by now. The prisoners, guards and the king were still all missing from the picture. Alex didn't care.

"Hold up!" Casimir exclaimed as he held out a hand to stop the crowd of people. Alex and Alyssia sent him questioning glances.

"I hear something…" He didn't explain any further and ran ahead of the group. Alyssia followed, but Alex hesitated. He knew better than to run into unknown territory with Casimir. If he heard something that would make him run off like that then Alex felt perfectly comfortable where he stood right now. The other people however felt inclined to follow anyway. Alex had no choice but to stamp out his fear and see what had spooked Casimir.

When they all reached the lake, Casimir just stood there staring into the water with a somewhat confused expression on his face.

"I don't get it… It should be right here…" he whispered.

"What are you trying to look for, Cas?" Alex asked him.

"They were supposed to be here… The voices in my head directed me to this lake, but there's nothing here. No creatures, no humans, nothing."

"Well, what about the animals, Cas? There are tons here and even hidden ones underneath the water. You know, like fish?" Alex was just playing with him, but somehow having Casimir like this made him feel uneasy.

"No, no," he said in a distracted voice. "Animal's thoughts are a jumbled mess. Creatures, however, speak the language of the humans, so I understand them." He paused. "What if there are creatures under the water…?"

Then he began to chant in a whisper. "*Stalkers of the night… they follow your blood. Don't let them in your sight, or you are gone for good…*"

"Why are we still pondering over this?" A man asked from amongst the crowd, not hearing Casimir's quiet chant. "We shouldn't take too long or else Drakonia will fall and your promise of food and shelter will all be for naught."

"Don't worry," Alyssia said to them. "We were just leaving. Right?" She cast Alex a sharp glare of impatience; the earlier awkwardness lost between them. He understood without her having to say anything: *Are we going to get this show on the road or what?*

However, Alex was frozen. He heard that chant, and it chilled him to his bones. He glanced uneasily at him and saw his eyes vacantly staring into the water. After a moment's pause, Alex approached Casimir hesitantly, as if disturbing him would break the peace between them. "Cas? We must go. Whatever you heard is not a threat. We can't waste any more time here."

He lifted him up to his feet and quietly led them away from the lake. Casimir had a dazed look on his face and would barely move. By now everyone began walking again, leaving the two behind.

"Alex," he said after a while. "You were wrong. They are a threat. They-" Casimir stopped and sent him an apologetic glance. He was having a hard time saying this. "Forgive me, friend."

Alex asked him what was to forgive, but he didn't tell him. "They were saying words to me. Words that even you could never understand. All I can see is fire and the taste of something metallic on my tongue. Blood. The same words are chanting through my head, even as we speak. 'Stalkers of the…'" Casimir drifted off into his own head.

"What are you talking about, Casimir? You are not making any sense." Alex tried to shake his friend out of his daze. Eventually he was able to, but Casimir couldn't remember what had happened.

"You were saying?" he asked him. Alex was stunned. Casimir was so graphic with his descriptions, but to then forget it that quickly?

“C’mon, we should catch up to the others.” Casimir ran up ahead, leaving Alex alone and confused.

As they made their way closer to Drakonia, multiple loud bangs rang out through the air. People began to panic and what really set them off happened to be right in front of them. They all came face to face with a huge red and blue dragon.

39

Scarlet

Back in Drakonia, Scarlet was just about to help a family stay secure in their home when she heard it. Just in the center of the village, a huge explosion took place and sent everyone reeling. People everywhere began screaming as a second blast shook the village. Luke ran up to Scarlet.

"What is going on?" he asked.

Scarlet could only assume that they were under attack, but how was a mystery to her. *We should have had more time to prepare.* It only seemed they were there for a couple of days; barely anytime to get ready. They soon found out why.

A shadow passed over their heads and when they looked up, their jaws dropped. A purple dragon touched down right in front of them carrying tons of people, including the king.

"You really think I'm that stupid?" he sneered. Guards that were riding the dragon jumped off and expertly wielded weapons on them. "Do you think I wouldn't know where you'd go after you escaped?" He shook his head smugly. "I shouldn't have let you live. You are a danger to everyone. Oh well, I won't make the same stupid mistake as before." He turned towards his subjects and motioned for them to attack. The family that Scarlet had been helping now fled from the area as the guards began a full-on assault. Scarlet immediately whipped into action. She drew her sword and charged at them. They were no match for her, and she easily slaughtered two at a time.

As more guards attacked, the king lifted from the ground on his dragon and disappeared into the sky.

Typical, she thought to herself. *Running like a coward.*

Luke charged at the guards with the mysterious dagger. The little ruby jewels on the handle looked as if they were glowing slightly. Perhaps it was just the light from the sun.

This group was easily taken care of, but when Scarlet and Luke turned around, they saw a man approaching them. He had fluffy blonde hair and sharp blue eyes. What made her uneasy was the tattoo on his face, letting her know that he was a prisoner like her, yet his gaze really set her off. She grabbed Luke by the hand and ran away. She didn't know what it was, but it made Scarlet afraid to fight him.

When she took off, they both heard shouting coming from behind them, but they didn't look back. She was just determined to get out of there. Eventually the yelling faded, and they stopped to catch their breath. They had ended up in the woods where all was quiet.

"Why were we running?" Luke asked in confusion.

Scarlet rolled her eyes. "*I don't know. Just because*." She was right. She didn't know why, but right now she didn't want to talk about it. "*Okay, so they are here already, which did not take long at all. Luke, you head back to the village and I'll find Drakon. Okay?*"

Luke nodded and ran off. Scarlet looked around and found herself in unfamiliar woods. However, with a couple of minutes of walking, she made her way back into the Forest of the Dragons. That's when she instinctively walked on the path that would take her to her little camp with her head lowered towards the ground, thinking. The Drakonians weren't ready for this. They won't even try! Scarlet and her friends can't just fight the king all by themselves. They need help! Scarlet thought that all would be lost, and they would just wind up getting captured again. She thought she could save innocent people from death; she was wrong.

As Scarlet was walking, she absentmindedly bumped right into someone. She snapped out of her troubled thoughts and instinctively drew her sword on them. Many people were crowded together and looking fearfully at her. This one woman however flashed her a look of distrust.

"Who are you?" she asked.

Scarlet didn't even bother wasting her magic on answering her. What she did use it for was to try out her new ability to read minds. She didn't know much about her sword's power, but when interrogating that guard, she could read his mind and change languages. So, she could read their minds too. When she did, she lowered her weapon. They were here to help Drakonia. Her father led them…

Her father… Scarlet desperately searched the group for him, but he wasn't anywhere in sight. *Where could he be?* She missed her family immensely.

The woman approached her slowly. "I said who are you? You have that brand on your face like those two prisoners who traveled with us. The thing is, are you good or bad?"

Scarlet still did not say anything. For some reason she despised the lady and obviously was pissing her off because she raised her fist in the air and readied herself to strike Scarlet. She countered her threat by raising her sword.

Before one of them struck, a little girl ran in between them. "Don'! Alyssia, this is Scarlet. She is Alex's daug'er."

"Now how do you know that?" she asked.

"I a Augur."

"Whatever that is." She turned towards Scarlet. "So, you're his daughter. Well? Where is he? He left on your dragon to your village."

Boy, was she irritating. She just made Scarlet want to grind her teeth together in frustration. How was she supposed to know where her father was? It was obvious that this woman and her dad had become friends on their journey here.

A little boy walked up next to the girl and smiled. "Li'le more than friends ay, Lily?" The two of them began snickering.

"What are you two talking about?" Alyssia said in confusion. Scarlet was also confused. The two smiled secretly to each other.

"Nothin'. We jus' know secrets is all."

"An' don' forget Lyle, they *both* feel the same way." More snickering.

Alyssia rolled her eyes. "So anyways, you know where he is?"

Scarlet looked at her as if she was stupid. Yes, she can be stubborn at times. "*Well how am I supposed to know? You guys stole my dragon and I wasn't here.*"

The woman looked at her in surprise as she saw Scarlet speak without moving her mouth. The two little children remained unfazed and the rest of the group shuffled their feet as they waited for whatever was happening.

"How did you…?"

Before she could answer, Scarlet felt the presence of Drakon and looked up above their heads. His mighty body blocked the view of the entire sky as he descended and landed gracefully onto the ground.

Master? Drakon growled. Scarlet walked over and patted the beast.

"*So, I'm assuming you came across my father. Where did you drop him off and who are these people?*"

He nodded. *He is near the tower. He says these people are here to help.*

"*Alright… Can you get these people out of here and into Drakonia?*"

Drakon dipped his head and nudged for the next few people to hop onto his back. Scarlet walked towards Alyssia. "*If you are friends with my dad, then show me a little more respect. I know you don't know me, and I don't know you, but I don't understand why there is hate. You become a part of his life and you become a part of mine. Got it?*"

Alyssia clenched her jaw and nodded, but what she said next made Scarlet's blood boil.

"Alright, but it will be kinda hard to do. You killed my friend. You killed Kagura."

"*What?! I didn't kill anybody! She was also my friend!*"

"Ever since you lot showed up everything went downhill. I found the wreckage of my barn with her body underneath all that rubble. I had seen you the day before and I knew you were on the run. With you just being here is a nightmare for us all."

A tear ran down her cheek as those awful words were said to her. Without even thinking she lashed out at Alyssia with her sword, cutting deep into her arm to reveal bone, and charged at the people that were just climbing onto her dragon. She knocked them to the ground.

"*I never wanted any of this to happen! If you can't trust me and can't respect me then you will not use my dragon! I don't care that you are here to help Drakonia. This is my village. Not yours. You disrespect me and this is how I will repay you. Goodbye!*" With that she took off with Drakon, leaving the recruits stranded a mile away from Drakonia.

Tears poured down her cheeks as the wind whipped in her face. Perhaps she had gone too far, but she couldn't take that mean woman any longer. They would have to do this on their own.

As they flew with Scarlet silently crying, Drakon began to worry for his master. He didn't know much of what happened, but he knew that she was in distress. Not wanting his master to be upset, he flew with incredible speed and landed in a throng of fighters. He didn't let them have the chance to react. He burned every single one to a crisp. As his master sat there in tears, he went on a rampage and didn't notice that when he was running around all over the place to try and kill them, he was actually lifting the Earth up into jagged shards. The Earth, as it rose from the ground, decapitated people, some good but most bad, and then the earthquakes began. At first, they were barely noticeable, then by the time Drakon realized what was going on, the rumbling grew so heavy, it split the ground into cavernous ravines that made people fall to their deaths. He was doing more harm than good.

When Scarlet's tears stopped, she acted. Using her magic, she ran alongside the cracks and sealed them up, making sure that nobody else could fall into them, and slowly they blended back in with the ground. Drakon growled furiously, realizing he just killed a lot of innocent people, but Scarlet waved him off. It was not his fault. He was still a baby.

As more guards approached them, Drakon took to the sky while Scarlet stayed on the ground and fought them. They were quite easy to fight. She had magic and they didn't, so she easily killed them and ran off to find the king; the one she knew was the real threat.

40
Alexander

Everyone ran in the opposite direction except for Alex. Even when the dragon roared in his face, he did not move. Instead he began to communicate with it. As he spoke the language of the dragons, the creature relaxed and told him his name.

"Nice to meet you, Drakon. I am no enemy to you. I personally know your master and I want to help."

How do I know to trust you?

"Please, I know your master's name, I know her sister, I know what she looks like, I know what she is planning, I know everything, and I need to see her right now."

Drakon growled.

Alex pleaded with him to take him to Scarlet quickly but before Drakon could agree, they heard another explosion off in the distance. The beast whipped his head around, growled furiously, and motioned for him to climb onto his back. He also made it clear that he would only take two people at a time.

Alex turned back towards the others. He would have to bring someone valuable first with him so they could fight without any trouble. His first thought went to Casimir. The guy was super valuable. He could fight *and* read minds. He would want him by his side any day.

Then Alex looked to Alyssia. He had not known her for that long, but he knew that she had fire in her heart. Just by losing someone it could fuel anybody with anger. He just was not sure of her fighting skills. With the rest of their group he knew no one. So, he just went with Casimir.

After letting him know of the plan, Alex told Drakon that the two of them would ride back to Drakonia on his back while the rest of the group walked there. There was not a split hesitation. They jumped onto his back and flew off into the sky.

Drakon was a magnificent beast. Alex could tell that he was only a hatchling. Even at his incredible size he was still only a baby. His own Sessyl was only at the age of twenty-six in human years when she passed, but in dragon years she was around the age of ten thousand years old. Drakon, judging by how big he was, would only be about a year old and around four hundred in dragon years. He was nevertheless an elegant creature.

The flight took but a matter of seconds, as his wings stretched across in enormous length, and they soon found themselves back where Alex had grown up. All the little structures were there, the village square, even the tower where he had spent so much time at as a teenager. His eyes welled up in tears as he remembered his childhood. Boy, did he miss this place.

The one difference were the explosions. What they had heard in the woods was what they were seeing now, and it was not a pretty sight. The square had huge gaping craters in the Earth and the top of the tower had crumbled to pieces. Just beside the tall building laid upturned Earth, looking as if it had been dug up, and people began running into the dirt filled area. Things certainly were different.

"This is your home?" Casimir asked.

Alex only nodded. His once beautiful home now resembled a dumping ground. They must have started their attacks already. Then again how did the king beat them there?

Drakon flew them to the ground and Alex thanked him. The humble creature bowed his head, then sensing an enemy presence, he whipped around to find five guards quickly approaching him, and fully let out a blast of fire on the men. That was the last time they would ever see the light of day.

Casimir decided to look around; seeming as if he was trying to hear a quiet conversation. Alex was beginning to panic. They had just landed themselves in the middle of a battle and they had no weapons.

"I think I can hear the king somewhere... If we can find and kill him then this'll be over sooner than it needs to be."

"Great," Alex replied distractedly. He picked up a large piece of metal from the ground and began swinging the sharp edge at the oncoming guards. The people around them were carrying swords, but most of them just dropped their weapons and ran for it. Very few were fighting. Alex, seeing this, picked up two swords from the ground and gave one to Casimir. "Hurry up and find him so we don't get slaughtered here."

Casimir flashed him a dirty look and didn't say a word as he continued to pinpoint the thought he was hearing. By now Alex was on a roll. He was rusty with a sword, but after a few swings here and there, he attacked with quick efficiency and killed all five of them. It still wasn't over. Guards just seemed to pour out of nowhere and attack.

Casimir's face finally lit with hope. "I know where he is! Follow me, Alex!"

They both ran off in the opposite direction with the enemy in tow. Everywhere they went there were still people running, a couple of them ramming right into the two of them. This one person managed to knock him clean off his feet, and when they offered to help him up, they quickly recoiled from him. Alex looked up to see a woman with sharp brown eyes stare back at him. She didn't look happy. Casimir stopped and ran back.

"What is going on here? Lady! We are on a mission here!"

She sent him a sharp glare but didn't say anything and spit on Alex. She then ran off. Her behavior took him by surprise, but Casimir just shook him out of it and yelled at him to run. They were still in danger.

Finally, after running across the village with more and more guards attacking, they came upon a house. A mother, father and a baby stood huddling against the wall as one attacker advanced on them. Alex didn't think and quickly ran him through with the sword.

"Thank you, sir," the mother said to him. Alex nodded and told them to run from here. When he rounded the house, his world stopped. Standing right there was the king on his dragon, but just as he was lifting off into the sky, he could see a girl fighting with a longsword that glowed slightly blue. She had wavy blonde hair and torn clothes. Beside her was a boy with ruffled brown hair. He knew exactly who they were.

Casimir, who was beside him, ran over to them. "Hey! You need any help?"

The girl looked over, then seeing his brand on his face, just like hers, her face grew in fear. She grabbed the boy by the hand and took off. Alex gave chase. "Wait! Stop! Scarlet!" Alex chased after his daughter, but she couldn't hear him. They soon disappeared out of sight.

"Oh…" Casimir said after catching up to him. "That was your daughter… My bad."

He shook his head slowly. "Doesn't matter. Long as I know she is safe, then everything is fine. Right now, we need to end this. Let's go." They walked back to find more enemies.

It was a never-ending stream of attackers. They soon found out just where the king had gone. He had picked up slaves from some unknown place and deposited them here in Drakonia. These ones did not seem friendly.

"Slaves," Casimir said. "They were the ones King George brought with him. Instill enough fear in them and they'll do just about anything for the one who is in charge."

"Well then, we will just have to find a friendly face." He knew one person that would be among them. He just had to find him.

Casimir nodded and went haywire on the slaves. He could be silly at times, but Alex was taken aback by his dark side. He wanted to see if he could try and reason with them. It was no use. They were just as dangerous as the guards themselves. Alex decided to fight alongside him.

It felt like an eternity as the slaves kept coming to fight them. By now Alex received multiple scratches left and right; nothing too serious. Casimir on the other hand wasn't doing so well. Ten enemies all at once jumped him and he could barely fight for himself. Alex had to leap in to help and when they both finished off the attackers, he got a good look at his friend. They managed to slice open his cheek and a deep cut just over his left eye. The hand that had been holding the sword bent at an odd angle. He was hurt. Badly.

Alex grumbled at his misfortune and dragged him off to the side. He would have to wait for treatment. Alex had to go. He continued through the village with all his might. The thought of never dying fueled his kicks and swings.

Amongst all the fighting, Alex finally found the one person he had been looking for. The man's shaggy hair was ruffled up and his eyes lit with excitement. When he spotted Alex, he rushed to him.

"My friend," Alex said to him. "*Venite hoc faciunt.* 'Let's do this.'"

41
Scarlet

Eventually, Scarlet found the king. Right on top of the tower. Fryvis' giant purple scales shone brightly down onto her from the sun. The disheveled bricks made by his claws rained down onto the people below. Scarlet wanted to encounter him and finish all this fighting, but first she had to figure out how to get up there.

An idea struck her and she decided to use the one magic element she had not exactly used. She put her hands flat out towards the ground and gently lifted herself off by using her air element. When she got the hang of it, she gradually lifted into the sky, but when someone grabbed her ankle and yanked her back down to the ground, she panicked.

Silently screaming, she blindly lashed out at the person who had grabbed her. When her concentration failed, her magic suddenly stopped, and she collapsed onto her attacker. She tried to run away but the man stopped her.

"Scarlet. Scarlet! Stop! It's me! Remember me?"

Scarlet stopped and turned around to look at him. He had short, rugged brown hair that was sticky with sweat and blood, he was wearing prison garments and had the same brand as Scarlet; one that every prisoner of the king had received. When she looked at his face, she could see him beginning to smirk.

"Miss m—" He was interrupted by Scarlet when she threw herself at him and hugged him tightly. She cried and repeatedly, and silently, mouthed his name. Well, his name for her.

Dad.

Alexander chuckled and hugged her back. "So, you *did* miss me."

Scarlet did not move. She just stayed in his embrace, trying to comprehend that she had her father back. Those times she spent in the castle; she had no idea who he was. And she was so stupid for not seeing it, but he did not even recognize her either until Scarlet had broken out of the castle. After so long being apart it was not a surprise that they couldn't recognize each other.

Alex held her for a little while longer, kissed her on the head… and then shoved her away. Scarlet staggered back in confusion until she saw that her dad pushed her out of the way of a guard who had tried to run them with a sword. Instead, he managed to lodge the sword into the side of the tower and struggled to pull it out.

"Looks like we can't have a proper family reunion. Let's change that." Alex was quick on his feet. He planted his foot on the guard's chest, knocking him back, and ripped the sword out of the brick wall with incredible strength. Scarlet could only watch in wonder as he wielded the sword and struck the guard. The life quickly faded from his eyes.

"Now then. Let's get out of here." Alex started to leave, but Scarlet did not move. She glanced up towards the top of the tower. Alex knew what she wanted but would not let her. "You can't confront him now. Not yet. Please, come with me. We will figure this out."

Scarlet hesitated, then agreed. He was right. What would she do when she came face to face with the king? She decided to go with him.

On their way to wherever Alex was taking her, they were continuously stopped by the enemy, but easily fended them off.

Once Scarlet and Alex fought off all the attackers, he led her out into the woods a little and into a small clearing with a house. She recognized that house. It was her old one. The one she had stayed at before her parents were gone.

"*What are we doing here?*" she asked him.

Alex turned around in surprise to hear his daughter's voice in his head, but he did not question it. "This is where we are staying. We all need to develop a plan to survive in this battle. I was expecting some people to be here by now but..." When Alex caught a glimpse of her face, which wore a little smirk, he could not help but laugh. "Okay, so obviously you ran into them. You know what happened?"

Her smirk disappeared. "*You wouldn't want to know. Let's just say they won't be here for a long time.*"

When he did not say anything Scarlet decided to ask him a question that was burning at her ever since she came across that group of people. "*Who is Alyssia?*"

Her father stopped just short of opening the door and looked back at her. There was something there in his expression that made Scarlet suspicious. Something like guilt.

"Uh, well, she's a, uh, friend... Yeah, a friend."

"*Nothing else?*"

"Nope. Just a friend."

"*Okay good.*" Then she added with a sly smile, "*because we don't exactly get along with each other.*"

"Oh yeah? Well that's not good."

"*Yup,*" she said while pushing past him and into the house. "*So, don't get any ideas.*" Scarlet may have been acting a little harsh towards her dad, but she knew what was going on. They were in love with each other. The look she saw on both of their faces and seeing that look before just confirmed her suspicions. She was not happy about it either. First off, she did not like Alyssia. Period. The way she treated her and accused her of killing a friend was enough to hate her for life. Secondly it would feel like her dad would be betraying her mom. Sure, she was dead, but it still hurt Scarlet to think about him being loyal to someone else. It just did not sit right with her.

After Scarlet had entered the house, Alex stayed back outside for a few minutes. When he walked in, he did not look at Scarlet directly and he was blushing profusely. Then she noticed a man with blonde hair, blue eyes, and had multiple bandages wrapped around his shirtless chest—the man she had ran away from. He was just staring at them.

"You and your ol' pa fightin'?" he asked Scarlet. "It's okay. The turmoil war going on in your head doesn't help."

"Knock it off, Cas," Alex said in irritation.

"What? I'm just trying to—"

"You know how I feel about it. It doesn't mean you can do that to my daughter."

"Yes, boss." Then he turned back to Scarlet and stood up. "I don't believe we did proper introductions. My name is-"

"*Casimir Hudges. You're an Augur.*"

He smirked. "Yes, I am *Drakonian, Princess.* While I've been checking you out you've been checking me out."

Scarlet raised an eyebrow when he called her a princess, but she could not help but smile. He was right. She was getting used to her sword's magic and could easily read minds now. Alex just stared at them in confusion; he had no idea what Scarlet was saying.

"Alright. Let's plan this thing out here," Alex said to interrupt them. "We need eyes on the whole village. We need to see just how many guards are here and attacking. Cas and I have an idea, but we don't know how he's getting them here. I've already sent Liam to scout around Drakonia. I just want eyes on the entire village. Scarlet, you have your dragon. Do you want to take him up into the sky and scout around?"

Scarlet did not say anything. What she really wanted to do was to find the king and kill him. She wanted to see the life bleed from his eyes and avenge the souls he had taken from this world, but Alex would never let her. So, she would have to do this on her own. Scarlet nodded and they continued planning. She was not listening. She was ready to take him down.

Over the next few hours, darkness had fallen, and Scarlet was on her last round of flying over the village. She could communicate with others, but they could not with her so all she did was focus on the person and just simply talk to them. She told her dad just how many were there on the ground. There actually were not that many. From what she observed a lot more people were fighting than she thought they would. Everyone was fighting well and doing great. Now it was time for her plan. She got done scoping out the place and memorized exactly where the king was. Just on the opposite side of the village there was a large bridge that had been placed between Ixaemithia and their neighboring land Boukasia. Underneath the bridge laid a huge ravine with chaotic waters that split the two lands.

As a child Alex had always forbade her to go there, even with supervision. She would never forget the day she went against his demands. She had been lucky that people who saw her heading in that direction immediately told her father, who then saved her from a quick death. She had never gone back there since.

Now however, she landed Drakon just on the outskirts of the clearing. The enormous stone bridge loomed ahead, empty. She could hear the quiet thundering of the river down below. Right on the other side stood the king with his dragon. He was looking out towards the woodlands of Boukasia.

"Oh Fryvis, you want to know the real reason why I wanted to come to Drakonia?" he asked his servant dragon. "I couldn't care less about the girl, although killing her would be fun and relieving. What I really want is across this bridge. Boukasia. They've resisted us many times in the past. Now that my plan is almost complete it'll be time to march right on over there and take control. That way I can have Kaggaegia all to myself."

"*Nice plan, George. There's just one problem with it,*" Scarlet said in his head.

The king sneered and slowly moved his hand to the sword at his side. "Oh yeah? And what's that?"

"*Me.*" With graceful speed, she threw her arms in the air and shards of lightning flew from her hands. She thought she had an advantage over him. She did not. Scarlet soon realized a big mistake and she cursed herself for being so dim-witted. A Dragon Master got their magic from their dragon. When killed they lose their magic. Since he had Fryvis then…

Scarlet watched in horror as he easily dodged her attack and raised his hand into a clenched fist. Suddenly she felt her right hand prickle in heat, and soon after in searing hot pain. She looked down to see her whole hand engulfed in flames. Scarlet panicked, but not losing rational thought, she quickly used her water magic and extinguished the flames before she received any major burns from it.

"What are you? Stupid? You think you can go up against me? I'm much stronger."

"*Yeah? Well, I am much more powerful.*" Scarlet indeed was, she just did not know the extent of her sword's magic. He did not need to know that.

As they stared at each other in silence, wondering who was going to make the first move, Scarlet could not stop thinking about what to do. She would soon find out the hard way.

Without hesitation he charged forward with sword in hand and struck the ground; causing the Earth from underneath Scarlet's feet to crumble away with the edge of the ravine splitting and careening towards her. King George just stood there and watched as Scarlet tried desperately to scramble out of the falling rubble. It was no use. She kept sliding further and further down towards the edge of the ravine. She could hear

Drakon roaring in the background and assumed he was going to save her. That was not the case.

When the ground just barely opened to reveal the river, she started to freak out inside her head, but was then lifted into the air and smashed right onto the ground. She was no longer on uneven terrain. What happened…

Scarlet scrambled to her feet and found the ground completely still. She quietly walked over to the edge to see someone dangling on the side.

"*Dad?!*"

Alex looked up and smiled. A dagger was stuck fast into the soil and he held onto it for dear life. "Hey, Scarlet. Didn't I warn you to never come here?"

"*What are you doing, Dad?*"

He grunted. He was having a hard time holding on. "Well, saving you. Duh."

"*How did you know I was here?*"

"What? You think I don't know my own kin? If anyone has my blood, then the first thing I would do is seek revenge. When I found out where he would be, I knew that you would be there as well."

Scarlet crouched down to help him. "*But Dad, why did you have to do that? You're going to die if you stay like this.*"

"Well, you have bigger problems right now than my death."

Scarlet looked up in confusion and quickly realizing what was happening, she threw up her hands to catch the blade that was about to enter her stomach. The king had snuck up on them and almost just killed her. Scarlet winced in pain as the sword sliced her palms, yet she did not let go of it.

As the king tried to hurt her, Scarlet looked around to see where Drakon was. He was not near them, but she could see him off in the distance fighting off Fryvis, who was way bigger and fiercer. Scarlet would just have to fend for herself.

George could see that she was distracted and quickly pulled the sword back; making her fall forward. He was fast. When

Scarlet hit the ground, he quickly lifted his sword back up and went to go strike her with it. She rolled away from range as he continued to swipe at her and never tiring out. He'd had loads of training; Scarlet had not. She began to stumble over her own feet as she tried to dodge his attacks. She was just getting scratched to hell by his blade.

What she did manage to do was mentally set the handle of his sword on fire. He yelped, dropped it and Scarlet took advantage with her own sword. She landed a few blows to his body, but he was still too quick for her. That was when he grabbed a dagger from his side and jabbed it at her stomach. Luckily, he missed, but not without a mark. Instead of having it enter her stomach, it sliced through her waist and sank deep into her muscle tissue. She screamed in silent agony and gasped for breath. She saw stars swim before her eyes and shook uncontrollably.

As Scarlet trembled on the ground, the king saw his chance and picked up his sword to drive it through her. At the same time, she was way too distracted by slowly, and painstakingly, pulling the object out of her skin. Tears sprang to her eyes as the pain took over her body, but she forced herself to continue.

When she looked up the sword was just about to strike her. She was not going to be fast enough. She was starting to lose focus of everything as the blood seeped down her side… And then something hard hit her from the right, making her crumple to the ground. When she looked up her father had taken her place, obviously successful in escaping the fall, and was now swaying on his feet. The king's longsword had struck his stomach.

"*Dad! Seriously? Again?*" Scarlet tried to get to her feet but the pain from her wound was too much and she could not move. "*No!*"

Alex continued to sway, but he did not fall. At first, he had a dazed look in his eyes as his blood leaked from the corners of his mouth. Then it cleared, and he began to laugh.

George looked on in horror as Alex, without hesitation, pulled the weapon from his stomach. Blood poured from his mouth and his wound quickly healed before their eyes.

"Looks like there is now someone more powerful than you!" he jeered. Scarlet could only lay there and watch her father act insane. She was so worried that he would just drop dead at any second. He did not. Alex, still grinning, slowly walked towards the king, who was now inching back in fear, and threw the sword at him. Scarlet had no idea how strong he is or how he got to be this way. That did not matter right now; it was helping them out immensely.

When he threw the sword, it landed a blow across George's face, slicing it from eye to mouth. It clattered to the ground and the king cupped his face into his hands. He looked enraged. As he dropped his hands from his face to reveal a ghastly huge scar with the skin sagging that showed bone underneath, he snarled and lunged for Alex. His fingers sparked with electricity as he passed it through Alex, and he doubled over in pain. He still did not fall.

As the two fought each other, Scarlet finally managed to remove the dagger from her side and stood up. The two dragons were still fighting off to the side. Drakon was not looking well. Many scales were ripped off his body and was covered in blood. Fryvis was not playing friendly with him.

"*Drakon, get out of here! Worry about you not me!*"

He hesitated. He did not wish to leave his master, but after more prodding from her, he eventually did fly off towards the village. Fryvis was not going to allow that. Scarlet could see that the dragon was going to take off after him as well, so using her magic, she created a trail of fire that engulfed the huge dragon in flames. His thick hide protected him from burning, but it was enough to anger him.

Fryvis roared and charged after her. Scarlet had forgotten about the two behind her and she completely froze in fear. She did not think this through. There was no way of getting out of this now.

As the huge beast lumbered towards her, Scarlet's mind raced. She was deciding what to do to defend herself when suddenly he skidded to a halt right before attacking her and completely changed directions. Scarlet just stood there in confusion when she felt a hand grab her shoulder. It was Alex.

"Run," he said, and before she could ask what happened he quickly dragged her away from the bridge. "King George fell."

42
Edhisu

After the king had left with his subjects on his personal dragon, Edhisu did not waste any time in taking control of the kingdom. People everywhere were distressed and confused, but she did not feel like addressing them, so instead she ordered one of the guards to deal with them. For a whole year now, she had surrounded herself with different scenery and a different culture. From being just a poor, innocent little girl to a rich queen, she learned a lot in her time. Being alive for ten years may seem small to people, but to her she had lived a whole lifetime and saw the good things, and the bad. The awful things were the ones to take control of her life. However, she disguised her feelings so the ones closest to her would not suspect. Not until she decided to make her presence known in just sixteen hours.

As Edhisu made her way through the castle, she felt her eye throb and swell even more. That boy had no idea what he had just done. He was playing with demons of death with horrifyingly strong power. And he messed with a creature like her. He was practically asking to die by her hands. She wanted that dagger.

When she made it to *her* throne room, two guards stood side by side, eyeing her. "So, wha' we s'posed to do wi't a li'l girl in charge? Ya know wha' ya doin' *your majesty*?" The two of them snickered, but Edhisu was not happy. It would take time for everyone to warm to her as their new queen, but for now she wanted the insubordinate guard to learn his lesson. She threw her mask over her face, leapt onto his suit of armor like a graceful cheetah, and expertly slipped her long sword against his neck.

"Why don't you have respect for me, Otis? Perhaps your *new* queen can teach you manners, and better language. My goodness!" Edhisu said in the deathly quietest, yet threateningly powerful voice. The guard quivered underneath her.

"H-how d-d-o ya k-know my name?"

Edhisu ignored his question. "Or I can just skip the trouble." With just a flick of her wrist she pierced the man's neck. It did not take much to do a lot of damage. She had nicked his trachea, the softest part in his neck. Now the blood flow would easily be released and in a matter of seconds Otis soon laid dead on the floor, surrounded by pools of blood. His friend who was smirking now stared at her in horror.

She lowered her mask once again. "This could be you too, but you are too valuable for me now. Just know this, however. You tell anyone and I will not hesitate to put you in the same fate as your friend here. Stay loyal and I will reward you. Got it?"

He nodded vigorously.

He bowed and then she exited the room. There she found a lynx curled up on her throne, asleep. She woke him up. "Get ready, Kioko. You're in charge while I join the battle of Drakonia. I have a Dragon Master to take care of."

The feline opened his eyes, revealing blue human-like pupils and nodded assertively to his master. She petted him on the head and dissipated into thin air.

43
Luke

Back in Drakonia, Luke was off in the woods and fighting the guards. After Scarlet had went off on her own, he could not find her anywhere. For some reason there was a group of people here with him and a leader that seemed very pissed. She would go on and on about a girl who took their ride and would curse her out. Luke could only assume that she was talking about Scarlet, but he did not say anything. He found it quite amusing.

Once he had found them, he promised to take them back to the village. However, they were now stuck here fighting just outside Drakonia. They were decent enough fighters. The leader, also known as Alyssia, made the most effect out of this battle. The others were just following her example. Luke had his trusty bow and arrows at his side and was spamming the arrows at the enemy. He was not injuring them much. They were very muscular men and even when the arrows hit them, they did not slow down. They were not even fazed.

When Luke ran out of arrows, the guards saw their chance and pulled out these black, metal objects that were small. At first, he did not recognize them. Then when they moved closer to him and raised it into the air he began to panic. They were pistols. Luke stopped what he was doing and took off in the opposite direction. He had never seen one of those in real life, but he knew they were terrifying and one shot from them, if aimed right, could instantly kill him. This thought sent his mind into a jumble and he did not think about the consequences of his actions. Turning his back and running away from them without changing direction made him an easy target. One of them fired off the pistol, hitting Luke square in the back.

Pain ripped through his entire body as the bullet shattered his spine. It was nothing like he'd ever felt before. He fell to the ground with his muscles twitching and the blood pooling quickly around him. Everyone there took down those guards without hesitation as Alyssia ran over to him and tried to stop the bleeding.

"I'm fine. I-I'm fine," Luke stammered. He struggled to get up. "I c-can walk. I'm f-fine."

"You don't sound it. From what it looks like that bullet shattered your spine. I'm surprised you can still even move."

He grunted and stood up. By now all emotion was wiped from his body, including pain, and his whole left arm went completely numb. He could not move his neck either. "I'm fine. We j-just need to get out of h-here. They n-need us in D-Drakonia."

"Alright fine, but you need to let one of us know if you are having a hard time. I don't want anyone to drop dead here."

"Yes, boss..." he whispered and slowly walked back to the village. The others trailed close behind while Alyssia stayed right there next to Luke in case he decided to drop then and there. Even though she despised the people that killed her friend she could not stand to see anyone hurt, especially with Luke's case so serious. Blood was just pouring down his back from the bottom of his neck. His left arm shook badly, and his feet were all over the place. She was surprised he was still alive and walking.

They were not far from the village and they did not come across many enemies along the way. They were slowly dwindling away to a small number. Luke, through the grogginess of his mind, wondered why that was. Were the people of Drakonia finally taking part in this thing? If so, then the Ixaemithian army was extremely easy to beat.

Once in the village, they all gasped at what they saw. Every building was either beyond recognition or just barely standing. The tower was still going strong. Nobody was in sight except for a few stragglers trying to find cover. They were bruised badly. Some of the people from the group went over to go help them.

"We n-need to find Scarlet," Luke said to them. His speech was beginning to slur. When he said her name Alyssia cringed. Luke obviously could tell she hated Scarlet but right now he did not worry about that. He saw her and a man running at them at full speed. Scarlet was limping badly.

"*Luke?!*" Scarlet noticed him and took off towards them. He wore a lazy smile with droopy eyes. She immediately knew that something was wrong. "*What is it? What is wrong?*"

He did not reply. He seemed a bit out of it and swayed a little on his feet. Then she noticed Alyssia and all emotion was wiped from her face. Same could be said for Alyssia. They stood there, face to face, causing tension between them. Luke, through blurred vision, saw the man that Scarlet was with walk towards them.

"Please, we don't need this right now. Alyssia, my daughter and her friend here did not kill your friend. If you were in our position, you would know what happened. Scarlet, if you lost a friend then you would be as angry as her right now, but that does not mean either of you can act like this. Especially at this time since we are in the middle of a battle." Then he turned to Luke with a look of concern. He placed his hand over his wound; making him flinch. "Hello, Luke, my name is Alex. We are going to help you. What on your body hurts?"

Luke was still having a hard time responding. He could not move his neck and his eyes just could not focus. What he was able to do was move his right arm.

"Neck… pain," he said while using that arm to point out the areas that were most painful to him. "Back in… pain. Arm…

shoulder… fingers… numb…. Legs… twitchy. Throat… h-hard to breath….” Suddenly he collapsed into Alex's arms. Scarlet began to freak out, but her dad calmed her down and looked over Luke's injuries. The blood stopped but the skin started to peel away to reveal the bullet itself.

“He was shot,” Alex said. “This isn't good. We will have to get this bullet out before it becomes infected. Let's take him to our home and fix him up. It won't do him any good if he stays out here in the open.”

By now Luke had lost consciousness and was slightly shaking. Alyssia stepped forward with a look of determination. “Let me carry him home. He was with me at the time that he was injured. He is my resp— Hey!” She was interrupted by Scarlet, who pushed her to the ground and practically ripped Luke from her dad's arms. He was a little bit heavy for her, yet she was very stubborn. She was not going to have her do anything. Luke was *her* best friend.

Alex could only shake his head and sigh while Alyssia stood up roughly with dirt falling from her clothes. Scarlet was obviously having a hard time with him and was not going to give up.

“Alright. Scarlet!” Alex shouted to her. “You made your point, but if you continue like that you will hurt yourself.” He rushed over to help her. She was right underneath the tower and just above them they heard a huge crash. Near the top they saw Fryvis with the king and pieces of the structure flew at them. Then the giant beast opened his mouth and a bright blue light shot from it. The light, which looked to be lightning, struck the tower. He continued to do that until the base cracked and began to tip.

“Scarlet… Scarlet!” Alex realized that she could be crushed in an instant if she did not move out of the way on time. She looked up in horror as she struggled to carry herself and Luke out of harm's way. She was not going to make it. When that sudden realization hit her, she stopped struggling and just stood there looking at Alex.

"Scarlet! Drop him! Get out of there!" Alex was now panicking. He thought about losing her just like losing her mother and that was just enough to drive him over the edge. "NOW!"

When she refused to drop Luke Alex went ballistic. "God dammit!" Without thinking he charged forward just as the tower was about to hit the ground. He smashed into Scarlet, who dropped Luke and went flying out of the way. Then it crashed to the ground and everything went dark. There was so much dirt and smoke that it blocked everything from view. She did see Luke near her, but half his body was underneath the rubble of the tower.

As the dirt and smoke cleared, Scarlet scrambled to her feet and rushed towards the ruins. Alex was in there.

"*Dad!!*" She tried to communicate with him to see if he was still alive. There was no reply.

"No, oh no! Alex!" Alyssia also rushed forward to help. They dug through piles of bricks just to find him. Everyone choked on the air, making it even more difficult to carry out the task at hand.

After ten minutes of everyone scraping their hands raw someone shouted to get their attention. Scarlet rushed over to find that they had uncovered a limp hand. Hope fluttered into her chest as she rapidly dug him out. First the whole arm came, then the neck and face. He was not dead. His eyes were open, he was just staring at Scarlet, and his mouth showed to have multiple teeth knocked out, so there was blood all over him. He groaned and wheezed loudly.

"Scarlet… why are you always getting into trouble…?"

She silently laughed with tears running down her cheeks and continued to uncover him. Alyssia just sat there in astonishment.

"Alex, how the hell are you still alive?"

He chuckled and winced in pain. "Maybe I have a lot of faith?"

"In what? First the snake bites and now this? If this happened to anybody then they would be dead!"

"Well actually… Never mind, but I am not just anybody. Maybe there *is* a reason why I am not dead." As he finished speaking, he screamed in pain as they got done uncovering his body and had begun to lift him up. It was now obvious that he had multiple broken bones in his body. "Don't… move me…. My legs and spine will heal on their own. Scarlet, why don't you and the others bring Luke back to the house while I heal and Alyssia watches out for me."

"*But-*"

"Do you prefer to switch places and have her bring Luke instead? And not to mention that she has no idea where to even bring him. Perhaps you would like them to wander around the village while Luke dies from infection? Or-"

"*Okay, okay fine!*"

"That's what I thought. Now, I believe Luke is not out of the clear yet. Isn't he also under here? He'll have broken bones as well so just go bring him home and fix him up."

Scarlet nodded and reluctantly walked away from her father with Luke in her arms.

Later that day, Scarlet remained outside with her dragon while Luke was being treated inside. It did not take long for Alex to return home in perfect shape; even his teeth had grown back. He was now in there as well helping.

Scarlet was outside to help Drakon with his own wounds. He was so scratched up that most of his scales had been ripped off and covered in blood. He had a crazy limp and was continuously whimpering in pain.

"*You're just a baby, Drakon. You shouldn't put yourself into that much trouble.*"

He growled. *When my master is in trouble, I will do what I must to protect her.*

"That's sweet, but I wouldn't be a master if I lose my dragon, now would I?"

He did not reply. She had a point. Instead of arguing, he just let her treat his wounds. Her mind was preoccupied at the moment; she worried about Luke. When she had gotten a good look at his wound the fear of him dying just took hold of her and would not go away. The way he acted as well scared her. She was so afraid of losing him that she did not even realize that as she was washing Drakon's scales she accidentally ripped some off and made him growl even louder.

"*Sorry.*" Scarlet continued to mindlessly wash Drakon.

When she was almost finished with her task, her father came out of the house and walked up to her.

"Luke is awake and wants to talk to you," he said quietly to her. She did not answer him. She was on the verge of tears. Alex saw this and crouched down to comfort her. "Scarlet, Luke is completely fine. In fact, he's in there making jokes for everyone. The only injuries he has are a shattered spine and a sprained ankle."

"What, you think having a shattered spine isn't bad?"

"In his case he is fighting it really well. The only serious thing it did to him was disable the use of his arm and set off the nerves in his muscles. Nothing more. He can move fine on his own, but he is a little sore and exhausted."

"Yeah, then eventually his whole body will deteriorate, and he will die."

Alex sighed. "Scarlet, please just go in there. He really wants to talk to you. After all of this is over, we can then get him properly treated for his wounds."

Scarlet hesitated at first, then stood up and walked into the house.

When morning came everyone was fully awake, even Luke, and they were planning on what to do next. After having a stressful night with Scarlet's tears and frustrations, Luke was not feeling well. His whole body hurt, especially his back, his ankle throbbed in pain, he could not feel his right arm, and he could barely move his neck, but he told everyone that he was fine. He did not want to worry anyone and tried to make them happy during this dark time.

He had been told to stay on the couch as they planned on how to end this battle. There were many people in there and they would use them to kill the rest of the guards. Alex, who Luke now knew was Scarlet's captured father, had no clue why there were so few guards. He said that all of them were trained very well in fighting and the fact that they were dwindling to such a low number amazed him. Luke could not care less; it just meant that the fighting was almost over, and everyone could go back to their normal lives. What they are really focused on was killing the king.

As Luke sat on the couch, he tried to eavesdrop on them from the other room. He wanted to be a part of this as well.

"You know the king is planning something else, Al. If there are so few guards, then what else is happening?" a man Luke had never met said.

"If that is true then we have to find him and kill him before anything else happens. If they don't have a leader then they will crumble and we win," another person said.

"One thing you guys don't know is that my daughter and I already tried that. We almost died."

"But what if all of us joined together in killing him? We would have a much bigger chance in defeating-"

"No," Alex interrupted. "If we couldn't do it then we have to think of something else. He and Scarlet both have dragons and magic. If we were to kill him then it would have to be her. Half of you will assist her and the other half will come with me to figure out the rest of his plan."

"And how would we do that?" Alyssia asked. "Drakonia is surrounded by thick foliage and we aren't exactly friendly with his subjects. It would be nearly impossible to find out."

"And that's where the rest of my plan comes in. Liam here knows a little bit about what is going on…"

Luke, from his couch, strained to hear what else he was trying to say, but now it sounded as if they had gone outside and he went back to feeling useless. He wanted to help so badly, he would just have a hard time walking and would not exactly be of much use. He would have to let them do all the work.

Or he could sneak out of there and help secretly. Sure, he was crippled, but he couldn't just stay in there when everyone out there would be risking their lives. If he was near death already, then why not?

When he was sure that everyone was gone, he slowly stood up and gingerly put weight on his sprained ankle. It was stiff and painful, but he fought through it. The pain level in his ankle did not even compare to that of his spine. When he stood up his spine moved and sent him into agony. When he walked, every step sent new jolts of pain all along his spine. He still could not move or feel his arm.

With each movement he tried not to scream in pain and eventually made it out the door. This was torture to him. Perhaps he should not do this after all, but he was already outside. He was not going to go back in. No one was in sight. He left the property alone.

It took him ages to reach the village, but at least he did not come across any guards to attack. It was completely silent. What was there yesterday was no longer there today. He could no longer see the tower. It was a strange sight and he felt like Drakonia was nothing without the tower. He wondered if it fell when he was unconscious. When he drew closer to it, he found that the actual tower was just lying there on the ground in ruins.

As he turned away from the fallen tower, he felt something hit his chest. He thought nothing of it, considering that he could not even look down, but when he began coughing with a lot of spittle, he raised his hand up to his mouth. It came away with blood. Beginning to panic, he reached out towards his chest and found a small object stuck there. Inside his head he heard screaming and realized that it was Scarlet. He turned around to find her standing there in horror and when he tried to speak, blackness consumed his mind. For once he would never wake up again.

44

Scarlet

Scarlet could feel the world crumbling around her. Time slowed as she saw the golden dagger soar through the air straight to Luke and strike him hard in his chest. When his body hit the ground, time sped back up and her best friend did not move again.

"*LUKE!!!*" Scarlet tried to communicate with him, but there was nothing. She threw all her weapons to the ground and ran right to him. She threw herself at him, found his eyes lifeless, and a silent, choking sob shook her body. She mouthed the word "no" repeatedly and hugged his body, crying.

They had left Luke at the house earlier that morning and Alex had sent everyone to do their duties. He kept Scarlet behind to talk to her more about the plan when they saw Luke out and about. Then she saw what happened and could do nothing to stop it.

It seemed like forever, but when there were no more tears to shed, she looked up to see her father standing to the side, looking uncomfortable and sad to see his daughter in so much anguish. He did not want to interrupt anything.

When Scarlet looked in the direction the dagger had been thrown, she gasped. The wolf she had seen before was looming menacingly on the hill. Alex also noticed.

"What are you doing here, Edhisu?!" he shouted. "The king made you stay at the castle!"

The wolf turned towards him, growled, and dimmed before their eyes. It was like a blur and Scarlet thought her eyes were going out of focus from crying a lot, but seconds later everything cleared. Her heart shattered completely. Alex remained unfazed and angrily walked up to the little girl.

"You've done enough damage in this world, Edhisu. Why don't you just go away?"

"*Dad...*" Scarlet did not know what to say. The little girl standing before them wore such an evil smile on her face that she was surprised to even see it there. Alex had no clue who he was talking to.

"No, I haven't done enough damage, *Father.* This world is a mistake that needs correcting."

Alex stared at her in confusion and astonishment as Edhisu walked up to Scarlet, who was seething with rage. "Why so mad, sister?"

"*You know why, Edith. How could you do this? Why? You were such a sweet, innocent little girl. You don't need to do this.*"

"But I do. I've been hiding my true identity for a long time. I've experienced things that you can't even imagine. And the power. So much power... You have no clue what it does to your head."

"*Yeah, well I think I've an idea about that.*"

Edith squinted at Scarlet's sarcastic reply. Her poor dad just stood to the side, still looking confused and quite distraught over the events that were taking place.

"*Sukaretto*, when I am done here, I can finally set my plan into motion."

"*Don't call me that. And what plan?*"

Edith did not say anything. Her brown eyes began to slightly glow, and her hands lit with power. Seconds later they all looked up to see a dragon flying overhead. It was not Drakon. The purple creature known as Fryvis landed next to them. The king was on his back.

"Why did you summon me, Edhisu? And why are you here?"

She still did not say a word. When the king grew mad of her silence, he jumped off his dragon and briskly strode towards her. What happened next shocked everyone there, including the dragon. Edith gave him a smug smile and without hesitation she lifted her chin at him. And then he collapsed. He did not move again.

Edith sighed. "A silent heart attack never hurts. No suffering, no pain. Now that he is out of the way and most of his guards dead, I think I can go further into my plan." Then she smiled. "And you wanted to know what it was." Without a moment's hesitation she lifted her hands up towards Scarlet and shot her with a multitude of lightning bolts. Scarlet fell back and hit the ground hard. Her body convulsed uncontrollably as the electricity passed through her. Her father rushed to her side and stayed with her as Edith slowly walked up to them.

"My plan is simple. I want to take over everything. I killed your king and now I'm going to kill you."

"How about no," Alex said furiously. "How about you leave us be and do whatever the hell you want."

"But Daddy, you know I can't do that. I can't have anyone standing in my way." She sent more lightning towards them, but Alex was quick on his feet and scooped up Scarlet, who was just recovering from the shock, and dodged the attack. Her eyes lit with fire and continued to attack. Alex still maneuvered around every one of them with great skill. Scarlet just came around and eventually helped her dad in attacking Edith. She was not holding back. Scarlet was incredibly angry at her sister. She killed Luke, her best friend in the whole world, and caused a lot of pain to them. Then she realized something else.

"Wait. Where is Jay?!"

Edith looked confused, then remembered and her face cleared into an evil smile again. "Oh him? Well he was a disgusting creature, what did you think I did?"

That did it for Scarlet. She attacked her with everything she had, which included every element she could control. She smacked Edith with a multitude of jagged lightning, blasts of searing-hot fire, and once she was able to shield herself from her attacks, Scarlet used her air and sent her flying through the sky. Hopelessly stuck in the air, Edith sent her palm straight at her and shot off more lightning to disarm Scarlet. She dodged them, but not before she threw her hand down, slamming Edith onto the ground. She finally did not get back up. Scarlet lifted her sword and gently placed it at her neck.

"*I will kill you right now*," Scarlet said in so much anger that she began to shake.

Instead of fearing for her life, Edith smirked. "Go ahead, sister, but I've been in your head before. You don't have the strength to. You may be mad now, but you won't kill me. I am your loving sister. You really want to see me dead?"

Scarlet froze. She was right. She could only see her as innocent. Alex saw that she was struggling.

"Don't, Scarlet. You don't have to kill." Then to Edith, "I hope you're happy."

"Quite." She easily moved the blade from her neck and stood up. "Let's make a deal then. Since you aren't strong enough to kill me, I will let you stay here in Drakonia. You're not really much of a threat to me. However, if you leave this village, I will hunt you down and kill you. Deal?"

Scarlet looked as if she wanted to argue, but Alex cut her off. "Yes, yes, fine. Deal."

Edith looked satisfied and hopped onto Fryvis. The dragon was not too keen on her riding him, since she killed his master, but with a little magic she was able to make the beast switch allegiance and they soon flew off into the sky.

Scarlet fell to her knees and just let everything out into tears. She was physically and emotionally out of strength. She had lost so much in just a few weeks, yet she also gained from all this. She had her father and Godfather back, and Drakonia was safe, but she'd lost her friends, Luke and Jay, and now she lost her sister. She did not know how much she could take of this. Alex crouched down and hugged her for a while till her tears dried. She relaxed against him, taking in that she had her father back, and she just let her mind go blank.

When people trickled out of hiding, Scarlet and Alex stood up, found that everyone was unharmed, and decided to help them out. The village lay in ruins. There were bodies littered all over the ground. Scarlet had walked back to Luke, closed his lifeless eyes, and picked him up. She felt bad for him. In the last few hours before his death Luke had suffered. He never deserved this and now Scarlet hoped that he was in a better place and would never feel pain again.

She walked with her father, who held another body, and they began digging a cemetery for everyone who had lost their lives. Even though the Drakonians did not trust the Shookrams, they now worked alongside them and began the restoration of Drakonia. They came across a few guards here and there, but they were quickly detained. As for the prisoners that had to help in the attack on Drakonia, many people were arguing about either punishing them or setting them free. Alex, alongside Liam and Casimir, approached the battered chief to silently converse with him. The man had a look of recognition on his face when he saw Alex but did not say anything as they quickly decided what to do with them. They had been prisoners themselves and they did not think it fair to keep them that way. Mason agreed and instead of punishing them, he granted them citizenship of Drakonia. They all stood there surprised while a few of them wept at the prospect of being free once again. A few native Drakonians grumbled.

For the next few days everyone rebuilt and settled down again, but Scarlet was not happy. She would never be happy again. This battle happened so quickly, yet the damage was incredible. She did not help in rebuilding her village, she did not help them with the new Drakonians, and she did not help them with their loved ones. The last day of the battle she helped, but after realizing that no one in this village cared about her still just made her really upset and made her not want to be involved. All she did was spend her time at the cemetery next to Luke's grave. She could not forgive herself for what had happened to him. She should have watched after him. Should not have let him out of her sight. All she could do was thank whoever is up there that they took him away from a cruel, messed up world. She would still miss him.

Alex would see his daughter there every day, but he would not interrupt her mourning. He knew what grief felt like. He just hoped that it would not consume her life.

Everyone could finally relax. Alex, Casimir and Alyssia stayed together while their group made the decision to return to their own homes. The mind reading twins from Vinmere, Lily and Lyle, wished them farewell, especially to Casimir, which made him terribly upset, and walked away with the adults.

Everyone's troubles were far from over. New threats came into their lives that could affect everyone here in Kaggaegia. Scarlet and the others feared that the future would hold even more heartbreak.

CPSIA information can be obtained
at www.ICGtesting.com
Printed in the USA
LVHW020010280423
745413LV00009B/183

9 781639 372386